Here's to Friends

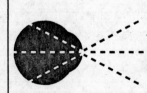

This Large Print Book carries the
Seal of Approval of N.A.V.H.

THE FOUR LINDAS, BOOK 4

HERE'S TO FRIENDS

MELODY CARLSON

THORNDIKE PRESS

A part of Gale, Cengage Learning

GALE
CENGAGE Learning®

Detroit • New York • San Francisco • New Haven, Conn • Waterville, Maine • London

GALE
CENGAGE Learning·

LIBRARY OF CONGRESS CATALOGING-IN-PUBLICATION DATA

Carlson, Melody.
   Here's to friends / by Melody Carlson.
      p. cm. — (Thorndike Press large print Christian fiction)
   (The four Lindas ; bk. 4)
   ISBN 978-1-4104-4288-8 (hardcover) — ISBN 1-4104-4288-8 (hardcover)
   1. Female friendship—Fiction. 2. Middle-aged women—Fiction. 3. Large type books. I. Title. II. Title: Here is to friends.
   PS3553.A73257H47 2012
   813'.54—dc23   2012001828

Published in 2012 by arrangement with David C. Cook.

Printed in Mexico
1 2 3 4 5 6 7 16 15 14 13 12

HERE'S TO FRIENDS

CHAPTER 1
ABBY

Trying to catch her breath, Abby shuffled her way into the women's locker room, barely able to put one heavy foot in front of the other. Feeling twice her actual age, she eased herself down onto the only unoccupied bench and gazed around the steamy room. Women with firm, sleek, healthy bodies paraded themselves around in various stages of undress as if trying to rub it in.

Lowering her eyes in defeat, she stared down at her pudgy white thighs and found herself craving cottage cheese. Without a doubt, she had lost her ever-loving mind. Why else would she have allowed Janie and Caroline to talk her into this? And why would she have bragged to Paul about her grandiose plan to join the fitness club?

"I'm starting tomorrow," she'd boasted to her husband last night. "After I become a member, I'll start off by taking . . . what's it called? A circuit-something class. I think that's what Caroline said."

"You're starting with a circuit-training class?" Paul frowned at her. "You sure you want to do that?"

"Janie and Caroline said it's really fun — a bunch of women working out together with upbeat music. It's probably like aerobic dance. I loved doing that back when the girls were little."

His mouth twisted to one side. "Yeah, but circuit training is hard work, Abby."

"Are you saying I can't do it?"

He shook his head. "I'm saying you should start with something easier. When I joined the club, I started with a trainer and a special —"

"Yeah, well, you were recovering from a heart attack, Paul. I'm in a lot better shape than you were."

He looked skeptical.

"I've been walking three or four times a week." Abby put her hands on her hips. "I've even lost a little weight this fall."

"Yeah, but starting out with circuit train-ing —"

"Why do you always have to rain on my parade?"

"Because I *know* you, Abby."

"Meaning?"

"Meaning if you start out with something

8

too tough, you'll give up."

"I will not!"

"I'll bet you don't last a week."

"I will!" she insisted. "You'll see. I'm going to join the club and take that class. And maybe I'll go in five days a week at first, to jumpstart things. I could swim on Tuesdays and Thursdays and —"

"Why don't you just use that a free one-week coupon I gave you?" he suggested. "Make sure you know what you're getting into before you plunk down all that dough."

"I *know* what I'm getting into. Janie and Caroline swear by that class. They go three times a week and love it."

He looked like he wanted to say something but stopped himself. "All I'm saying is that the club is pretty expensive, Abby, and I think —"

"You think I'm not worth it?" She shook her fist at him. "Sure, it's fine for you to belong to the club, but poor old Abby doesn't deserve —"

"That's not what I'm saying." His brow creased. "You're worth it. I just don't want to see you pay all that money up front and then change your mind." Of course, he took the opportunity to list all the activities Abby had started but never finished. But instead of falling for that old bait and getting into a

9

ridiculous fight, Abby took their counselor's advice *and* the high road.

"If you love me," she calmly informed him, "you will support me in this. I'm making a healthy decision for my life, and you should respect that, Paul."

He held up his hands in surrender. "Fine. Just take it easy, okay? Don't kill yourself on the first day. Remember, slow and steady wins the race. Pace yourself."

"That's exactly what I plan to do."

But Abby's plan, like the best-laid schemes of mice and men, had fallen by the wayside after she joined the club and paid her membership fees in the morning. It wasn't that she was trying to impress anyone in the circuit-training class. She knew better than that. But as she went from station to station, attempting to figure out the confusing machines and determine the realistic weights and master the forms, she understood she'd bought more than she'd bargained for. Trying to stay one step ahead of the perky, energetic woman who followed Abby in the circuit was no picnic either. The petite blonde kept nipping at Abby's heels. "You know there's a *special* class for people who don't know how to properly use the equipment," she sniped as Abby untangled herself from one of the machines.

As she tried to hurry along, Abby decided to call this snippy woman Trixie, after an ill-tempered Chihuahua Abby's daughters had begged her to get for them long ago. Fortunately Paul got fed up and found the feisty dog another home.

"Maybe you should try out the pool aerobics," Trixie said in a snarky tone. "I hear the *older* ladies really enjoy the *slower* pace." She folded her toned arms across her flat abdomen, leaning against a pole and scowling as she waited for Abby to move to the next machine.

The last straw came about midway through the class. Abby knew it was midway because she'd kept one eye on the lethargic clock the entire time. She'd never seen a minute hand move so slowly. Trixie laughed loudly upon discovering that Abby had been using the biceps machine without weights attached.

"You gotta be kidding," Trixie said. "You'll *never* get into shape doing that."

Fed up and worn out, Abby had released the handle and let the bar slam back into the machine, which she knew was a no-no. Glaring at Trixie, she'd turned on the heel of her frumpy walking shoes and stormed out. No doubt Trixie was hugely relieved. Right now, she was probably telling everyone how hopeless and out-of-shape Abby was, and how fat old women like her should be banned from circuit training and maybe even the entire fitness club. So humiliating.

At least Caroline and Janie, who were stuck in a bank appointment regarding Caroline's mother's estate, hadn't been there to witness her embarrassment. That was something Abby could be thankful for. What had made her think she could pull off something like this? She felt like crying. Paul was right. She had wasted their money. She really was a failure.

As she slowly stood, searching the room for some sort of a stall or private area where she could discretely disrobe, she wondered how hard it would be to convince the club to refund her membership fee. Maybe there was some sort of twenty-four-hour cancellation clause. She would have to find out. But first she needed to find a place to change.

"Excuse me," she asked one of the only women with clothes on. "Where are the changing rooms?"

The woman laughed, waving her hand around the open area. "This is it."

"Oh." Abby nodded stiffly. "Yes . . . okay . . . I'm new here." Wondering why she hadn't noticed the insane lack of privacy during the tour of the club, Abby picked up a white towel from the neat stack and sniffed it. At least it smelled clean. And it was actually rather soft and thick. Nice. As were many of the other amenities that had distracted Abby from noticing the absence of dressing stalls.

It figured that she'd been too busy checking out things like attractive tile designs and chic light fixtures and rain-shower heads, too distracted by fluff to be concerned with function. She reminded herself that she'd arrived in her workout clothing (which, like her, was out of style and out of shape) and had no need for a changing room then. Really, she should just get over herself and strip down and not worry about what anyone else thought. That's probably what Caroline and Janie did when they were here — why couldn't Abby?

"Janie and I have so much fun at the club," Caroline had said when the Four Lindas club met last week at the Clifden Coffee Company. Abby, Janie, Caroline, and Marley — who as schoolgirls had all shared the first name of Linda — were discussing their upcoming cruise to Mexico. They talked about spray-on tans, waist-trimming swimsuits, and how they had only six weeks to get into shape. Motivation was high, especially with the holidays upon them. But for Abby, the initial thrill of winning her Mexican cruise for four was quickly turning into high anxiety. She hadn't purchased a new swimsuit since her three daughters were kids, and the sorry, threadbare thing she wore in the hot tub at home was not fit for public viewing. Neither was her body!

"You and Marley really should come try out the club," Caroline urged Abby. "We can get you free passes."

"I know," Abby said. "Paul's always telling me that."

"But if you guys joined, we could do classes together," Janie said. "We could encourage each other to get fit."

"The club's running a special until the end of the year," Caroline told them. "If two people sign up, the second membership is half off. You and Marley could split the difference."

"I don't know." Marley shook her head with a doubtful expression. "I've never really been a fitness-club sort of girl. I think I'd rather do yoga or Pilates."

"They have those classes too," Janie told her.

"Yeah, but I like working out on the beach. I take my iPod filled with my own music and just do my thing. I guess I'm still just a free-spirited hippie at heart. Kind of a

14

lone wolf. Well, except for my Lindas." Marley smiled. "Count me out."

"I wish I had that kind of discipline," Abby admitted. "Even walking regularly is a challenge for me, unless I have someone to go with me."

"That's why you need to join the club," Janie insisted. "It's more fun to work out with your friends by your side."

"That's right," Caroline agreed. "You can do this, Abby."

So Abby had decided to trust her friends and, like the Nike ad said, just do it. But now that she'd "done it," she was sorry. She should've listened to Marley. Even to Paul. Abby should've known she wasn't a "fitness-club sort of girl" either.

Finally Abby decided that a shower stall could function as a dressing room *and* shower. Safely behind the translucent curtain, she peeled off her sweat-soaked clothes and dumped them on the floor, where they got drenched while she showered. Relieved to be away from the curious stares of onlookers, she had to admit she was a complete misfit here. That was ironic, because she remembered a time when she was the kind of girl who thought others were misfits, including old friends like Janie (who'd turned into a geek in high school).

Not that Abby picked on anyone. But she had been one of the "cool" kids, a cheerleader even. She'd been the kind of girl who never got teased in any locker room.

Now Janie was fit and beautiful. Someone like Trixie wouldn't think of picking on Janie. Or Caroline either. As Abby shampooed her hair, she realized that in this club, she wasn't only a misfit — she was a sideshow freak. She could probably charge admission. Maybe that would help to recoup her wasted membership fee. Because she knew she was never coming back here. Never.

That's how Abby comforted herself as she took a very long shower, utilizing endless hot water and generous handfuls of the club's luxurious soaps and shampoos. At least she'd get some of her money's worth! By the time she finished, she felt marginally better and squeaky clean. As she dried off, feeling a bit more like her old self, she was almost rethinking her previous resolution to become a fitness-club dropout on the very first day.

But as she attempted to wrap the fluffy white towel around her fluffy white body, she was reminded of reality. The towel was too small! Staring at the six-inch gap where the ends of the towel refused to come together, she wanted to scream. *What is wrong with this place? Can't they afford bigger towels?* Or perhaps this was the club's subtle message. They didn't want any overweight, out-of-shape, fitness-challenged people to join their ranks. Of course, that was why it was called a "fitness" club. You had to be *fit* to join. Perhaps what Abby needed was an *unfit* club — a place with queen-sized towels, easy-to-use machines, no skinny naked bodies, and donuts! A place where someone like Abby would fit in.

Finally, struggling to hold the loose ends of the towel as well as her soggy workout clothes, Abby emerged from the shower stall and made her way back toward the locker area. The room was a bit less crowded now. At the lockers, she dropped her wet clothes on the tile floor, still trying to cover her backside with the mini-towel as she extracted her clothes from her locker. Then she went to a relatively quiet corner. Just a few feet away, two partially dressed young women chatted amicably over the pros and cons of — *give me a break* — colon cleansers. Huffing and puffing, Abby bent over, hurriedly tugging her clothes onto her still-damp body, trying not to listen to the sordid details of these women's bathroom habits.

17

As Abby sat down to put on her shoes, she also tried not to stare at the young brunette who had just stepped up to the sink area. Wearing nothing but a contented smile and some very skimpy panties (or maybe just dental floss), this woman positioned herself in front of the brightly lit mirror. Happily blow-drying her short hair, she seemed oblivious to the fact that she was only two feet from the door, and that anyone in the hallway on the other side would see her standing there, topless, if it swung open. Was the girl nuts, or simply an exhibitionist, or maybe a porn star?

Maybe Abby was a prude or old-fashioned or just plain uncomfortable in her own flabby skin, but she just did not understand this sort of thing. She had raised her three daughters on the principles of modesty and propriety and sensibility, and she hoped they knew better than to run around buck naked in public.

The door flew open, and Caroline and Janie burst into the locker room. "There she is!" exclaimed Caroline. They didn't even give the nearly naked brunette a second glance as they came over to join Abby.

"So how was it?" Janie asked Abby. "Are you sore yet?"

Abby shrugged. "A little."

"Wow, you're fast," Caroline observed. "The class only got out a few minutes ago. How'd you even have time for a shower?"

"Because she *skipped out* on class," someone announced from behind them.

Abby turned to see Trixie swinging a sweat towel in one hand and looking smug.

"Hey, Serena," Janie said in a friendly tone. "How's it going?"

Trixie, aka Serena, smiled at Janie. "Pretty good. I had a nice little workout." She wrinkled her nose. "Unlike *some* people."

Caroline frowned at Abby. "Did you really skip out on the circuit class?"

"I did half of it," Abby assured her. "A full thirty minutes. Besides, Paul warned me to take it easy today."

"You can take it easy and still do the full hour," Janie explained. "Just go slower and —"

"Go slower?" Abby growled. "When you've got a Chihuahua nipping at your heels?"

Janie frowned. "There were dogs in the class?"

"Just the female kind," Abby retorted.

"Huh?" Caroline looked confused.

"Never mind." Abby picked up her wet

19

workout clothes, wondering what to do with them.

"What happened?" Caroline pointed at the soggy mess.

"Did someone hose you down?" Janie asked wryly.

"No." Abby held her head high. "I was multitasking."

"What?" Janie studied Abby curiously.

"Changing, showering, and doing my laundry," Abby proclaimed. "All at the same time."

Caroline laughed. "Hey, I saw that on *Seinfeld* once. Kramer was —"

"Never mind." Janie chuckled like she'd seen that episode. "Back to the circuit training," she said to Abby. "It's better to do the full hour and just go slower and use lighter weights and —"

"*Lighter* weights?" Trixie snickered. "Like that would even be possible." She'd already stripped down to her underwear, revealing a set of abs that would make a six-pack jealous. "She wasn't using *any* weights."

"Really?" Janie looked disappointed.

"Oh, don't pick on her," Caroline said. "At least she showed up. That's the first step."

"That's true," Janie conceded. "Getting started is always rough, Abby. At least your first day is behind you now."

Abby made a weak smile as she dumped her wet clothes into her gym bag, right on top of her shoes. She'd sort that mess out later. Mostly she just wanted out of this place.

"Good job!" Caroline slapped Abby on the back. "Just wait until we're in class with you. We'll bolster up your spirits."

"And by January, you'll be in the best shape ever," Janie said optimistically.

"You really think so?" Abby tried not to sound too negative as she picked up her heavy bag, but she could not imagine working out with her energetic, trim friends urging her to try harder. No, today had opened her eyes. It was hopeless.

"You'll see. Next time will be better," Caroline said kindly.

Abby wanted to tell them there was not going to be a next time, but she had no intention of confessing her failure in front of all these women, especially Trixie. More than that, she wondered how she would break the news to Paul. Even if he didn't say, "I told you so," he would be thinking it. She would see it in his eyes. He would add today's failure to his already long list of her shortcomings. Then he'd stick it in his pocket and save it for the next time he wanted to give her a reality check.

CHAPTER 2
JANIE

After their workout, Janie and Caroline usually treated themselves to a smoothie at the juice bar. While they were waiting for their order, Janie checked her phone messages. It wasn't as if her law practice was really taking off, but she did have a couple of pro bono clients whom she tried to be available to, and after years of the fast pace in Manhattan, she still found it difficult to disconnect completely.

The first message was from Victor, inviting her to dinner as well as a Christmas concert on Friday. Naturally, she would accept. But it was the second message that made her look for a chair — she needed to sit down to hear this one.

"Hi, Mom," said a flat-sounding voice. "This is Lisa. Remember me?" Lisa's laugh was hollow. "Well, anyway, Matthew keeps telling me to call you. So guess what? I'm calling you. But as usual, you're not there.

You never really were there, were you? Don't bother checking your caller ID to call me back. This is a pay phone, and I'll be gone by the time you listen to this. Same old, same old. I'm gone, and you're not there. Bye, Mom."

Janie felt her heart sinking. Despite Lisa saying not to call back, she checked the caller ID. It did look like a pay phone. Also, the call had been placed more than an hour ago. Lisa probably was gone by now.

"Are you okay?" Caroline asked as she set their smoothies on the table. "You look like you just saw a ghost or something."

Janie swallowed hard and then shook her head. "Just a voice mail . . . from my daughter."

Caroline blinked. "Lisa?"

Janie nodded, surprised that Caroline could even remember Lisa's name. She had only mentioned her daughter a few times to her friends. Lisa wasn't exactly a happy subject in Janie's life. "I wish I hadn't missed her call."

"Call her back." Caroline stuck her straw in her drink.

Janie explained why that wasn't possible.

"Oh. You mean she doesn't even have a cell phone?"

Janie shrugged. "She might. But if she

does, she doesn't want me to know that number. She's very secretive."

Caroline leaned forward a bit. "Do you think she's still doing drugs?" she asked quietly.

"It's hard to say. She's told Matthew that she's not, but that might just be to get money from him. She knows that I won't give her money anymore. I've promised her help and airline tickets and a place to live, but I just can't dole out any more cash to her. It's like handing her a loaded gun."

"Yeah, that's wise on your part."

"It's just so hard." Janie felt like tears were close.

Caroline reached over and put a hand over Janie's. "But, hey, she called you, Janie. Think about that. I mean how long has it been, anyway?"

Janie did think about that. "A while."

"So maybe she's coming around, you know?"

"I just wish I'd been there for her. That's what she always used to say . . . that I was never there for her. Maybe I shouldn't have gone back to work when I did." Janie sighed. "But the kids were in their teens. They seemed so grown up. And the way I was raised — you know how my parents were so checked out and distant — I suppose it taught me to be fairly independent. I guess I thought if it worked for me, it should work for them."

"Seems like it's working with Matthew. He's doing pretty good, isn't he?"

"Yes," Janie agreed. "He is."

"Everyone knows that when drugs come into the picture, everything changes. You can't blame yourself for that, Janie. It's not like you introduced Lisa to drugs."

"No, of course not. While Phil was sick . . . well, it was hard on all of us. I was so distracted with caring for him and figuring everything out. Matthew used school and friends as his escape. Lisa . . . well, you know what she did."

"But she called you," Caroline said hopefully. "Don't you think that means something? Maybe she wants to come visit you for Christmas."

"Maybe." Or maybe, and more likely, she just wanted money.

"Is Matthew going to come out here for Christmas?"

"I'm not sure. I invited him, but he's got that new girlfriend, and I'm afraid he's going to decide to go to her place instead."

"For all of winter break?" Caroline frowned. "Seems like he could come out here for just a little visit. He hasn't even

26

seen how you fixed up your parents' old house."

"Speaking of parents' old houses, now that everything's all settled with your mom's estate and the insurance and everything, what do you plan to do with your house?"

"You mean besides hire a bulldozer to flatten it?"

"You wouldn't do that."

Caroline shrugged. "I don't know. Mostly I just want to move on — to be rid of it once and for all, and all the memories that go with it."

"I remember feeling like that too. Overwhelmed." Janie took a sip of her smoothie. It was hard to believe how much she'd changed in the past four or five months. More than ever she wished that Lisa would call her back and have a real conversation. Better yet, she wished Lisa would come to visit and see how much her mother had changed. "I wanted to be rid of my folks' place too," she admitted. "But now I'm glad to have it."

"I honestly don't think I'll ever feel that way, Janie. Really, I should just sell it."

"As is?" Janie doubted that Caroline could even find a buyer for a partially burnt house. Certainly no mortgage company would finance a property like that.

"Maybe. It's such a wreck."

"But if you fixed it up, we'd be neighbors again. I loved it when you were only a couple of blocks away."

Caroline seemed to consider this. "It'd be so much work, so much money."

"You have the insurance money. And the work could be good therapy. I was surprised at how much I enjoyed fixing up my parents' old house."

"Yeah, but you had Abby to help you. Now she's got the bed-and-breakfast to keep her busy. Did you know she's got real guests coming next weekend, staying for a whole week?"

"Good for her." Despite her partnership in Abby's business venture, Janie usually tried not to think too much about Abby's bed-and-breakfast. Mostly she wanted to remain a silent partner, but sometimes it was tricky, because she knew Abby had to get the inn up and running in order to keep up with her loan payments. "But back to you, Caroline. I really think it would be good for you to renovate your mom's house. You know, watch something that seems worthless and hopeless come back to life, better than it's ever been. You could think of your work as a job, because you'd be investing in your future."

"Except that I don't know anything about that stuff. I've always lived in apartments or condos with other people to take care of maintenance and things. I don't even know how to paint."

"I was the same way," Janie reminded her, "but it's not that hard to figure things out. Maybe I could help you. I learned a lot doing my house."

Caroline looked slightly interested. "Do you think there's any way my house could look as good as yours? Or even close?"

"I don't see why not. Don't forget that, right now, your backyard looks a lot better than mine."

Caroline smiled. "Thanks to my friends."

"Remember when you thought that was impossible? Yet we managed to do it, and without you even knowing it."

"I still go out there and sit sometimes when the weather's good. I think Chuck likes it better than the backyard at the bed-and-breakfast. More room to chase a ball. It's a nice yard."

"See, already there's something there worth saving. You should at least think it over. Because even if you decide to sell it, you'd probably have to do some fixing up anyway. Why not just go for it?"

"Maybe I will." Caroline nodded. "Maybe so."

For the rest of the day and all day Tuesday, Janie kept her phone charged and on and close by. If Lisa called, she planned to be there — Johnny-on-the-spot. But Lisa didn't call. Even when Janie went to the fitness club Wednesday morning, she planned to zip her phone into her workout-pants pocket. "Where's Abby?" she asked Caroline as they were getting ready to go to their circuit-training class.

"Not coming," Caroline glumly informed her.

"Why not?"

"She said it's too hard."

Janie reached for her phone, punched the speed dial, and as soon as Abby answered, Janie let her have it. "Abby, you need to get yourself over here right now. You made a commitment, and even if Caroline and I have to drag you through the paces, you're going to do it."

"When did you become an army sergeant?" Abby asked drolly.

"Where are you right now?" Janie barked.

"The B and B."

"Good. It'll take you two minutes to get here. Now get going *or else!*"

"Or else what?"

"Do you really want me to tell you?" Janie thought hard. "Don't forget we are business partners, Abigail Franklin. Running a bed-and-breakfast is hard work, and your health is almost as important to me as it should be to you. Now get yourself over here immediately!" She hung up.

"Do you think that'll work?" Caroline looked skeptical.

Janie shrugged as she pocketed her phone. "It was worth a try."

"It would've worked on me," Caroline told her as they did some stretches.

Janie laughed. "Abby thought I sounded like an army sergeant."

Caroline nodded with wide blue eyes. "You did. Remind me to stay on your good side."

"Well, Abby needs friends like us. Sometimes she does give up too easily. I know she wants to get in shape. She's always talking about it."

"Except you know what they say. Talk is cheap."

But just as they were heading down the hall to the class, Janie saw Abby entering the building. She looked partly angry and partly scared.

"Come on," Janie told her as they met her

at the registration desk. "Just bring your bag with you so we're not late." Then she and Caroline escorted Abby to class, where they corralled her between the two of them and coached and cajoled and encouraged and threatened and bribed her to complete a full hour of circuit training. Sure, she didn't always have any weights on the machines and sometimes her feet were moving pretty slowly, but at least she made it to the end.

"Congratulations," Janie told her.

"Thanks a lot," Abby said a bit breathlessly.

"You did it." Caroline patted her on the back as they exited the room.

Abby sighed as she picked up her gym bag from where they'd left it by the door. "Now if you'll excuse me, I have decided to do my showering at home today."

"Why?" Janie asked.

Abby glared at her. "Because I want to."

Caroline frowned. "But we always get smoothies afterward and you —"

"Look," Abby shot at her, "you two may have bullied me into coming here, but I will not be bullied into parading my flabby, saggy body around a locker room filled with a bunch of fitness freaks, thank you very much!" And with that she turned from them and marched toward the front door and left.

"Well." Janie just shook her head. "You'd think she didn't even appreciate us working out with her."

"The thanks we get!" Caroline laughed.

They were almost to the dressing room when Janie felt the vibrating buzzer of her phone. She'd turned the sound off because she knew she wouldn't hear it above the noise anyway. "You go ahead, I want to get this," she told Caroline as she unzipped her pocket and pulled out her phone. "Hello?"

There was no sound on the other end.

"Hello?" Janie said again, moving over by the foyer in case she was having a bad connection. "This is Janie Sorenson." She wanted to check her caller ID but didn't want to move the phone from her ear.

"Mom?"

"Lisa!" Janie said happily. "Is that you, sweetheart?"

"Mom?"

"Yes! It's me."

"Mom —" Lisa's voice broke, and she was crying.

"Lisa, are you okay? What's the matter?"

"I . . . I want to come home."

Janie felt tears filling her eyes. "Yes, sweetheart, I want you to come home too."

"But where is that?"

"Where is what?"

"Where is *home?*"

"Oh." Janie knew what Lisa meant. Her daughter was remembering where she'd grown up, thinking of their apartment in Manhattan. "Well, Lisa, they say home is where the heart is. My heart is here in Clifden, Oregon. I really hope that you'll think of it as your home too."

"Oregon?" Lisa sounded disgusted. "You mean where your parents lived? You've really moved there for good?"

"Yes." Janie knew that Lisa knew this already. But she also knew that Lisa's mind wasn't always working the way it was meant to work. "I think you'll like it here," Janie said calmly. "The ocean is beautiful."

"The ocean?" Lisa's tone grew slightly wistful.

"Tell me where you are," Janie said gently. "I'll come and get you."

Lisa told her she was in Phoenix, staying with friends, but that she couldn't stay with them much longer. "You could just send me money for a plane ticket," Lisa suggested.

"I'd rather come out there," Janie told her. "I'd like to see Phoenix. Then we could fly back together."

"I don't know." Lisa was getting cold feet.

"Just wire me some money, Mom. It'll be a lot cheaper that way."

"I want to come get you," Janie insisted. "I want to use my frequent-flyer miles. And that means I have to fly with you." That was actually a lie, but after years of being lied to by Lisa, Janie thought it was an acceptable lie — anything to get her daughter back with her, to help her.

"I don't know, Mom. I need to think about this."

Then as Janie was explaining why this was the best plan, she got that sense that she was talking into the airwaves. "Lisa?" she said. No answer. "Are you there?" She looked at her phone and saw that they were no longer connected. Lisa had hung up. She checked the caller ID, and, seeing it was a pay phone, she tried it. Of course, that didn't work. The pay phone wasn't set up to receive calls. Janie blinked back tears as she slowly walked to the women's locker room.

Why did it always have to be so hard with Lisa? Couldn't she see how badly she was hurting herself? How badly she was hurting the ones who loved her? She didn't trust her own mother — and Janie would gladly die for her daughter. Instead, Lisa would trust her so-called friends. Lisa would put her life in the hands of thugs and addicts and pushers. But she wouldn't even let her own mother pick her up at an airport and bring her home. What would it take to get through to her?

CHAPTER 3
MARLEY

Marley was incredibly fulfilled in her reinvented life. Painting to her heart's content in her compact beach bungalow on the Oregon coast was beyond anything she'd ever dreamed of. Even the hermit factor didn't bother her too much. Plus, having her three Linda friends nearby, not to mention Abby's mother right next door, was more than enough to keep her social calendar full. But the icing on her happy cake was her blooming romance with gallery owner Jack Holland. She was glad neither of them felt any urgency to move things along. They had set a perfect pace at this stage of the game. Really, life was good! And having recently entered into a very real relationship with God — what more could she want?

Yet something felt slightly amiss today. She couldn't put her finger on it exactly — just this feeling of uneasiness. Perhaps it was how animals felt before an earthquake or a tsunami. She looked out over the ocean, but all looked normal, peaceful, soothing. She finished off the last of her coffee and told herself it was probably just midweek madness. It was an old malady that she should've put far behind her by now, but sometimes old habits died hard. Back in her early thirties, about the same time her marriage hit the skids, Wednesdays had always depressed her. Her son, Ashton, had been getting old enough not to need her so much, and her husband's workweek started on Wednesdays and ran through the weekend. Marley would pack his little black wheeled bag with freshly laundered and ironed clothes, and he would happily head off, piloting commercial airplanes to some interesting-sounding connection (including some connections with a few flight attendants). She'd be stuck at home, playing the perfect housewife. Although a part of her was relieved to have John out of her hair on Wednesdays, another part of her would become depressed over her sad little life. Thus she called it her midweek madness.

To be fair, she hadn't experienced it for several years. And since moving on, she rarely thought about John. Mostly she was thankful that she'd escaped a bad situation before she was too old to rebuild a life. So maybe it wasn't midweek madness at all. She rinsed her coffee cup and set it in the sink. What was wrong with her? Why did she feel out of kilter? She'd taken her usual morning "commute" (her beach walk when she communicated with God). She'd even read her Bible (something Abby's mom had been encouraging her to do). Even so, she felt like something was wrong or missing or out of balance, like she hadn't turned off the stove or had forgotten a dentist appointment, which she knew was ridiculous. She looked at her calendar. The only thing there was her regular Wednesday date with Jack's granddaughter, Hunter, but that wasn't until this afternoon.

Still, as Marley got out her palette and paints and moved her easel into a better light, she wondered if she'd missed something. Someone's birthday? She stared blankly over the foggy seascape outside her house and wondered, *What's wrong?* Abby often complained about hormone meltdowns and mood swings, some of the fringe benefits of menopause. But so far, other than a random or ill-timed hot flash, Marley hadn't been too troubled. Plus she'd been doing an herb routine each morning, and she thought it was working. Whatever was troubling her, it wouldn't help to obsess over it. So she just committed it to God. He was big enough to handle it.

Feeling somewhat better, Marley squirted a glob of cobalt-blue paint onto the palette. Right now her friends were probably sweating over a grueling workout at the fitness club. She didn't feel the least bit sorry about not being with them. She was glad she hadn't succumbed to their pressure and joined their ranks. Even Abby's enticement of 50 percent off hadn't tempted her. Marley chuckled to remember Abby's complaints. It sounded like the club was a torture chamber filled with overactive, underweight, and seriously witchy women. Marley could so do without that.

She was just locking her creative attention onto the large blank canvas in front of her, envisioning a bright colored seascape in her head and starting to sketch, when her cell phone rang. With brush in midstroke, she was reluctant to stop, but then she remembered that Ashton hadn't called her in a couple of days. He was still recovering from a broken heart and sometimes needed to process the emotions. So, setting down her paint-filled brush, she hurried to answer.

"Marley?" It was Jack, and she could tell

he was worried.

"Yes," she said quickly. "What's up?"

"Uh, well, there's a problem."

"What's wrong?" she asked with concern. Probably because of her earlier premonition, she braced herself and imagined the worst. Someone was dead, a terrorist attack was coming her way, or perhaps Jack had just been diagnosed with an untreatable brain tumor. She held her breath and waited.

"It's Jasmine." His voice was full of sadness.

"Is she okay?" Marley felt a bit of relief. Not that she didn't care about Jack's daughter, but Jasmine always seemed to be getting into some kind of trouble.

"I'm sure Jasmine is fine," he said with an edge of exasperation. "But she's taken off with Floyd somewhere."

Marley knew that Floyd was Jasmine's most recent love interest. The attractive young man was charming enough upon first encounter, but it was plain he was a drifter at best, and who knew what else at worst. The first time she'd met Floyd, at a dinner party hosted by Jack a week or so ago, Floyd had proudly confessed to her that he was a rolling stone and planned to keep it that way. Marley had wanted to suggest to him

41

that it might be best for him to just keep on rolling, because Jasmine really didn't need someone that unsteady in her life right now. Nor did Hunter. But Marley knew she hadn't earned the right to speak so bluntly. "What about Hunter?" Marley asked Jack. "Did Jasmine take Hunter, too?"

"That's the problem."

Marley felt confused. "You mean she *took* Hunter?"

"No."

"She left her behind?" Marley wanted clarification, and she wanted it fast.

"Yes, sorry. That's right."

Marley felt a huge wave of relief. "But you think *that's* a problem?"

"I don't mean that, not how it sounds. Hunter is definitely not the problem, Marley. And I'm glad Jasmine didn't take her . . . to wherever she and Floyd have gone."

"I'm glad we agree on that."

"I'm sorry, Marley. I don't mean to sound like such an old curmudgeon. It's just that, as usual, I'm caught in a lurch. There's Hunter, of course, but with Jasmine gone, I'm shorthanded here at the gallery. It's not as if business is booming right now, but I can't exactly afford to just close up shop."

"No, of course not. Do you want me to come down there and give you a hand?"

"Not exactly. Mostly I just wanted to make sure you still planned to pick Hunter up from school today. You still do Wednesdays with her, right?"

"Absolutely."

"Oh, good."

"So does Hunter know what's going on? With her mom, I mean?"

"I don't know for sure."

"How did you find out?"

"Email."

"Really?" Marley was curious. "So what did she say? Is she just going AWOL for a day or two?" That was Jasmine's usual routine. She'd meet someone on a Friday night and take off for the weekend, which could be rather challenging since Jack's gallery was busier on weekends than during the week. Hunter was used to hanging at the gallery, but it was a lot to expect of a seven-year-old.

"It's hard to say. Her note was pretty vague, but I have to admit that something about it feels different this time. I could be wrong, but it almost sounds like she took off for good."

"No. She couldn't mean that."

"I don't know, Marley. I got a bad feeling this time. I mean worse than usual."

She could hear the pain in his voice. "I'm

43

so sorry, Jack. Don't worry, I'm here for you. You know how much I love Hunter. I'll be happy to have her as long as you need —"

"Don't get me wrong, Marley. I'm not dumping her on you."

"That's not what I meant. I'm just saying I'm glad to have her around. I really like Hunter."

"Yes, that's a comfort, Marley." He sighed. "I just feel like I'm getting too old for this nonsense. I wish Jasmine would just grow up."

"I know. I think it takes kids longer these days."

"I guess so."

"So, really, don't worry about Hunter. And we have something very special to do today. She's looking forward to it." Marley almost spilled the beans about her plan to take Hunter to the Pottery Shed but then remembered that Hunter had made her promise to keep it "secret." Their plan was to glaze pottery pieces for Christmas presents, and Hunter wanted it to be a surprise. Marley didn't want to spoil it.

"I should've known you'd have things under control." He made a wry-sounding chuckle. "Too bad you're not Jasmine's mother — maybe some of your sensibilities would've been passed on to her."

Marley laughed. "Sensibility doesn't happen overnight."

"I suppose that's true."

So she promised to bring Hunter by the gallery before five as usual, assuring him that everything would be okay. "You're not alone in this, Jack."

"Thanks, Marley. You have no idea how much that means to me. I know how much Hunter loves you, and at a time like this, well, I just really appreciate it."

As she set her phone down, Marley wondered if her sense of uneasiness and apprehension had been related to this. Perhaps something in her spirit had been trying to warn her that a challenge was coming her way. She wondered about Jack's concerns — what if Jasmine really was gone for good? What would become of Hunter? Most likely Jack would get custody. Though Marley would be more than willing to help him, she wondered how realistic that would be. Playing grandma was one thing, but she felt too old to be a full-time parent of a young child. Not that Jack was asking her to do anything like that. She knew their relationship hadn't reached that level, but what did this really mean? She cared deeply about Hunter and Jack, and she was willing to do what she could to help out, but how would they manage it? Would they shuffle the seven-year-old back and forth between them like a library book? Even if they could manage Hunter's care, how would it ultimately affect the girl?

Marley looked around her tiny bungalow. As much as she liked having Hunter here, this place really wasn't big enough for an active child on a full-time basis. Plus, Marley didn't even have a second bedroom. Hunter would have to sleep on the couch if she stayed here. Besides that, there were no kids living this far out of town. Hunter would be isolated. Marley briefly considered the possibility of setting up camp in Jasmine's apartment. That would be the selfless thing to do — allow Hunter to live in her own room, ride the school bus, be around a familiar place.

Except that the mere thought of living in those low-income, cardboard-quality apartments was so depressing that Marley couldn't bear it. That place would drive her nuts in no time. Plus, how would she keep up with her painting in such an uninspiring place? Painting was not a hobby; it was her livelihood.

Instead of obsessing over all these nit-picking details and possible pitfalls, Marley decided again to hand the whole bit over to God. He could lead her. He would see her through. Certainly God cared about cast-off little girls like Hunter Holland. Marley was sure of it. Between Jack and Marley and the God of the universe, Hunter would be just fine.

It wasn't until Marley was picking up Hunter at the grade school that she realized Hunter might not be aware of her mother's departure yet. Or, if she did know, she might be feeling a little bummed or confused or abandoned. Whatever the case, Marley decided the best way to handle the situation was to be as honest and open as possible. Besides, it wasn't as if this was something entirely new to Hunter.

Trying to act natural, Marley met Hunter by the office and hugged her. It wasn't until after Hunter had filled Marley in on the latest developments between friends and activities at school that Marley decided to dive in. "So, your grandpa told me that your mom has gone somewhere with Floyd," she began.

"Yeah." Hunter was digging through her backpack for something.

"You know about that already?"

"Sure." Hunter was actually sounding unconcerned and fairly normal.

"So did your mom tell you she was going?"

"Uh-huh."

"When did she tell you that?"

"I don't know. A while ago. I think she's in love with Floyd."

"Oh." Marley tried to wrap her head around this child's nonchalance. Sometimes it was difficult to believe that Hunter was only seven. Marley remembered Ashton at seven (more than twenty years ago). He'd been very needy and insecure, but that probably had as much to do with Marley as anything. She'd sheltered and protected him a lot. "So what did you think when your mom told you that, Hunter?"

"I dunno." There was a rustling of papers. "Here it is," Hunter said triumphantly. "I thought I'd never find it."

"What's that?"

"The permission slip for our field trip. We're going to do our Christmas program at the place where the old people live."

"Oh." Marley nodded. "That's nice."

"But my mom has to sign this." Suddenly there was an anxious tone in Hunter's voice. "Or else I can't go. And afterward we get to have a party and Santa will be there. I *have* to get permission or I can't go."

"We'll get you permission," Marley assured her.

"But Mrs. Hanford said *our parents* have to sign this."

As she slid in the car and glanced in the rearview mirror, Marley saw Hunter holding the rumpled paper up, waving it frantically.

"Your grandpa will sign it for you, Hunter."

"But Grandpa's not my mom or my dad!" Hunter was starting to cry.

Marley pulled into the Walgreen's lot and parked. She got out of the car, hurried to the back, and slid in next to Hunter in the backseat. Slipping an arm around the sobbing girl, she pushed some curly strands of red hair out of Hunter's face. "It's okay," she said soothingly. "Your teacher will understand. Really, your grandpa is like a parent. He helps take care of you. I'm sure it's okay for him to sign the release form too. Because he does help parent you. You know that, don't you?"

Hunter nodded. "I guess so."

"Your teacher knows that too. Don't worry. You'll get to go on the field trip. I'm sure of it."

Hunter looked up at Marley with scared brown eyes. "Is Mommy coming back this time?"

Marley didn't know what to say. "Oh, you know, she *always* comes back, Hunter."

"But that was *before*. Before she met Floyd." Hunter wiped her nose on the sleeve of her jacket. "She loves Floyd. She said so. What if she doesn't come back?"

"She'll come back."

"How do you know? Did she *tell* you she was coming back? I want to know the truth, Marley. I want to know!"

Marley pulled Hunter close to her again. "I don't honestly know for sure, sweetie. But I do know this — you have people right here who love you very much, people who will take care of you. You have your grandpa and me. And we won't let anything bad happen to you. Now, you know that's true, don't you?"

Hunter sniffed and nodded. "Yeah."

"So let's just make the most of it, okay?"

"Okay." Hunter handed the permission slip to Marley.

She smoothed it and folded it in half, slipping it into her purse. "So do you still want to go to the Pottery Shed today?"

"Yeah." Hunter brightened. "Can we still do that?"

"Absolutely!"

Marley tried to keep their conversation lighthearted. Focusing on school and

Christmas and today's activity, she was careful not to mention Jasmine or Floyd or anything that would bring them back to the topic. As they picked out their first green-ware pieces and Marley gave Hunter some tips on applying light-colored glazes first, she felt fairly certain that Hunter had temporarily forgotten about her missing mother. Then after Hunter finished a brightly striped popcorn bowl for her grandpa, she started in on her second piece, an oversized coffee mug. She carefully painted a purple and yellow butterfly on one side. Then, turning it around and in her best second-grade lettering, Hunter painted the word *Mommy* across the other side.

"See?" She proudly held it up for Marley to see.

Marley nodded. It was such a sweet and resilient and forgiving gesture that it took all of Marley's self-control not to cry. "That is lovely, Hunter. Your mother is going to love it."

"I know."

Marley thought of her own mom. Some-times, while growing up, Marley had felt her mother was distracted by her own interests and her own pleasures. Pulled by her husband and her circle of friends, she'd let Marley live her own life as she liked. Just

51

the same, her mom had always been there when Marley needed her, and she had never walked out on Marley. Never. It probably would have been just as unimaginable to Marley's mom as it was to Marley that any mother could do something like that.

CHAPTER 4
CAROLINE

If these walls really could talk, Caroline felt fairly certain she'd place both hands over her ears and make a mad dash out of this derelict house and never come back. So much anger, disappointment, and dysfunction had been contained in these rooms since the time her father had purchased the house nearly sixty years ago. Oh, her mother put some effort into making it a pleasant home. When Caroline was little, she recalled her mom planting some trees and shrubs, and she'd even tucked some flower bulbs in the beds alongside the walk. For years the tulips and daffodils would pop up in the early spring . . . until weeds and neglect won out.

Caroline remembered the summer Aunt Fanny came out to visit. Her mother had been so excited to see her favorite aunt. The house still looked pretty good back then. It was less than ten years old, and the laminate countertops weren't cracked and pitted and stained yet. The vinyl floors still shone, and the avocado-green carpet was still fashionable. Other than a couple of holes in the walls, which her mother had attempted to patch or cover, the place was presentable. Caroline's mom even made a new slipcover for the couch out of a green and gold floral pattern, and she'd purchased new sheets and a sky-blue bedspread for Caroline's bedroom, so Aunt Fanny could use the small space as her guest room while Caroline camped in a sleeping bag on the living-room floor.

Thanks to Caroline's dad's short-fused temper, Aunt Fanny's visit was cut short, and no relatives ever came to stay with them after that. Caroline suspected that word had spread: Something was wrong with the Mc-Canns in Clifden.

Even so, Caroline had to give her mom a little credit. The downtrodden woman had tried to improve their lot in life, at first anyway. While cleaning and sorting through old things, a box of faded snapshots had jogged Caroline's memory. At first Caroline hadn't been able to believe her eyes: photos of Caroline and her older brother dressed for church and smiling. Shots of them in new pajamas in front of a Christmas tree.

One with Caroline and her brother and father on the only camping trip they'd ever taken together. It had to have been the first day, because they still looked clean and happy. That trip had also ended earlier than planned, and she remembered the miserable, silent ride back home.

Sure, her mother had tried to make their lives better, back when the kids were still small, but time and troubles wore her down. Eventually, she gave up. She gave in to her husband's tyranny, and the gradual deterioration of their home seemed to be evidence of her defeat. It was a sad house.

Despite Janie's optimism, it was impossible to imagine that this sorry sight could ever be transformed into a happy place, a home that anyone (particularly Caroline) would willingly chose to reside in. Still, Caroline had always liked a challenge. Janie was right. If Caroline wanted to sell the place (and she was certain she did) she'd have to address some of these issues anyway. Plus there was the insurance money to help. And until Caroline's California condo sold, she wasn't exactly in a position to be choosy about where she lived. Also, she couldn't take advantage of Abby's hospitality in the bed-and-breakfast forever.

For that reason, Caroline, dressed in old

jeans and a sweatshirt, purchased a sturdy pair of work boots and some work gloves, as well as a few tools, including a shovel and a wheelbarrow. She called the city garbage service and requested one of those big green Dumpsters, which had been delivered that morning, and now she was attempting to single-handedly empty the house of decades' worth of hoarding. By noon she was overwhelmed.

"I can't do this," she told Janie on the phone. "It's useless." Caroline looked around at the mess that seemed to be growing instead of shrinking. "If I had a book of matches I'd —"

"Don't even say that," Janie exclaimed. "I'm your attorney, and we barely got you cleared of blame in the other fire."

"Too bad the whole place didn't burn, then." Caroline sighed. "Well, not with Mom in it. I wouldn't have wished that."

"Any plans for lunch?"

Caroline looked down at her grimy clothes and laughed. "Yeah, you should see me right now. I doubt that I'd even be welcome at Burger Boy."

"No, I meant I could bring you something. And maybe I could help —"

"No way. I mean lunch sounds good, but you can't help me, Janie. I wouldn't ask anyone I like to help with this. I don't even like having Chuck in here. You wouldn't believe the piles of rat droppings I've —"

"Okay, spare me the details. But I'll bring lunch and some phone numbers."

"Phone numbers?"

"Remember the guys who helped on your backyard, and Mario?"

"Huh?"

"Mario was the guy who helped with my tile projects. We hired some of his friends to landscape your yard. Remember?"

"Not really." Caroline frowned at the mess in the living room. "Maybe I'm like Mom, getting early Alzheimer's. They say it's hereditary."

"Well, we did try to keep the whole thing under wraps," Janie said in a gentle tone. "And you were rather distracted at the time. Caring for your mom took a toll."

"That's true."

"Anyway, I'm in my office but wanted to run out to get something for lunch. So I'll grab you something too, and then I'll come over there and you and I will brainstorm. Okay?"

"Okay." Caroline felt doubtful. "You're sure you want to come over here? I mean, it's pretty bad."

"It'll be a *working* lunch." Janie said goodbye, and Caroline looked around the filthy kitchen, where she'd been emptying cupboards, and wondered where they'd even have a clean spot to eat. Then she remembered the backyard, the one happy spot in this miserable place. The temperatures had been in the sixties, so it wouldn't be too cold for a winter picnic if they kept their coats on.

She was just finishing wiping off the chairs and table when she heard Janie's voice calling through the open windows of the house.

"Out here," Caroline yelled back.

"There you are," Janie said as she and Abby emerged from the house. "You weren't kidding about how bad it is in there."

Caroline nodded. "I thought we'd eat out here."

"I insisted on coming too," Abby told her. "Seeing your house makes me feel so much better about the progress I've made on the B and B."

Caroline wrinkled her nose at her. "Thanks. It's nice to be the poster child for *Disgusting Homes and Gardens*."

Abby held up a notebook. "We're going to help you get organized, Caroline. We know that's not exactly your gift."

Caroline sighed. "You got that right."

So, as they ate, Janie and Abby helped

58

Caroline to come up with a plan of sorts, writing down lists and phone numbers in Abby's notebook.

"I don't know why I thought I could do this all by myself," Caroline admitted as they were finishing up. "My mother was such a hoarder. Even though I'd cleaned out a lot of stuff right after she died, I barely scratched the surface. Then my brother came in here and created even more chaos." She shook her head. "I swear, the harder I work, the worse it seems to get. It just feels hopeless, not to mention depressing."

"Trust me," Abby assured her. "This is the easy part."

"You're kidding." Caroline stared at her.

Abby gave her a knowing look. "I'm serious. Cleaning the junk out and demolition goes quickly. It's putting the place back together — getting it right — that takes time."

Caroline groaned. "Maybe I should give up."

"No," Janie insisted. "You can do this."

"That's right." Abby handed her the notebook. "This is your brain."

"Flat little brain, isn't it?" Caroline said wryly.

"You know what I mean," Abby scolded. "Follow these guidelines, and you could

59

have this place nearly habitable by Christmas."

Caroline laughed.

"The first thing you need to do is call Mario," Janie commanded as she pointed at the phone number. "Don't hesitate. Because I'm guessing that since it's December, he and his buddies won't be too busy. Those guys are amazing. They'll get this place cleared out in no time. Seriously, your head will be spinning."

"But what if they throw away something important?" Suddenly Caroline was worried. "What if there's something valuable or there are mementos or —"

"Caroline," Janie said kindly but firmly, "you don't want to turn into your mother now, do you?"

"Well . . . no, not exactly."

"You can oversee things," Abby suggested, "to make sure nothing important is lost."

"Just let it go," Janie said with some impatience. "Honestly, what you don't know won't probably hurt you."

Abby laughed. "Yes. Ignorance most likely is bliss."

"Besides," Janie added, "from what I could see, there was nothing but garbage in there."

Caroline nodded. "You're right. I'll call

those guys and let them shovel it all out. The sooner the better."

"Wise woman."

She smiled at Janie and Abby. "What would I do without my friends?"

As it turned out, her friends were right. Within the next three days, Mario and his guys had not only removed all the trash from the house, but they'd taken out all the cabinets and fixtures and flooring as well. A few things had been recycled, but most of it was just plain rubbish. By Thursday night, when Caroline walked through the strangely empty house, only the walls, some of the doors, most of the windows, and the sub-flooring remained.

"You were right," Caroline told Abby on Friday. "Getting the place cleaned out went fairly fast."

"Now things will slow down." Abby wiped her forehead with a sweat towel as they headed for the locker room. They'd just finished circuit-training class — Abby's third time this week!

"Do you think there's even a slight chance Paul would consider acting as contractor for me?" Caroline asked hopefully.

"I doubt it. Paul really hates remodels." Abby pursed her lips as if she was thinking, or else she was in pain from the workout.

"Although he was just complaining that things are pretty slow. He always seems to be obsessing over finances. Who knows?"

"Will you ask him for me?"

"Sure." Abby nodded. "Why not?"

"Thanks! I appreciate it."

It wasn't that Caroline was overly fond of Paul Franklin. Oh, he was a fairly nice guy, but sometimes he could be a bit of a chauvinist, especially when it came to his wife. Caroline wasn't even sure how Abby put up with it most of the time, although he did seem to be changing some since his heart attack two months ago. Mostly Caroline wanted his help because he was a good contractor. He knew how to get things done. Whether it was realistic or not, Caroline wanted the house to be habitable by the New Year. Then she would list it to sell and hope that real estate up here in Oregon was moving faster than it was down in LA. Something had to sell, and soon. Otherwise, she would need to go get a job.

Caroline wasn't afraid of work. Good grief, she'd worked most of her life — and in some pretty menial sorts of jobs, too. Waiting tables wasn't exactly glamorous, although in a good restaurant the tips could be worthwhile. But caring for her mother had consumed several months, and Caroline was ready for a break. She hoped to avoid employment until after the cruise to Mexico.

"What's Mitch up to these days?" Janie asked Caroline as they enjoyed their reward of smoothies after their showers. Abby had excused herself to get back to the B and B, where she was expecting her guests to arrive sometime today.

"He's in Chile until mid-December," Caroline explained. "Then he doesn't have any traveling to do until after the New Year."

"So what's going on with you guys?" Janie pressed. "I know your relationship was kind of on hold while you were caring for your mom. But what now?"

Caroline shrugged. "I'm not sure. I mean, Mitch keeps asking me to travel with him, but I don't know."

"Has he ever talked of marriage?"

"Not specifically." Caroline thought about this. "I guess I'm kind of relieved that he hasn't. I honestly don't think I'm ready for it yet."

Janie just nodded.

"I haven't told him this." Caroline paused.

"What?" Janie looked curious.

"Well, I'm not sure he'd understand, but I just don't think I'd want to travel with him if we weren't married."

63

"Why wouldn't he understand?"

"Well, I think he might assume that I'm the same girl I used to be back in LA during the early eighties."

"What kind of girl was that?"

"Oh, you know" — Caroline waved her hand — "fast and easy."

Janie kind of laughed. "Yes, I can just imagine you with your big hair and glitzy clothes, clubbing and living the life. Meanwhile, my nose was to the grindstone, working long hours seven days a week, hoping to establish myself as a New York attorney."

"Yeah, you always were the smart one, Janie."

Janie just shook her head.

"Anyway, I guess it's about time I tell Mitch that I'm not that kind of girl anymore."

"Don't you think he knows that, Caroline?"

"Maybe. But I think I'll lay my cards on the table, and before Christmas."

"What if he thinks you're looking for some kind of a commitment from him? Fishing for a ring for Christmas?"

"Hmm. I hadn't thought of that." Caroline considered this. "I don't want to give him the wrong idea. I'm serious, Janie — I'm not ready for that. I realize I'm not getting any younger, but marriage is, well, so permanent."

"Not always."

"No, not always. But you know what I mean. If I get married at this stage of the game, I want the commitment to last until the end of our lifetimes. That's pretty permanent. I've always dreamed of being married to the right guy — I mean, a guy I really love, someone I can laugh with, grow old with, sit by the fire and walk on the beach with."

"You mean someone besides Chuck," Janie teased.

Caroline laughed. "Someone *along with* Chuck. You know what they say — love me, love my dog."

"Do you think Mitch is that guy?"

"I think I'd like it to be Mitch. But I'm not sure he's ready for that. He's pretty committed to his business. It's going strong and growing — and that means a lot of travel. I wouldn't expect him to give that up for me." Caroline pointed to Janie. "Enough about my stalled love life. How about you and Victor? Any word from his ex? Donna's not planning any more surprise appearances, is she? Christmas?"

Janie frowned. "I don't think so. Victor told me that she's been back to her therapist, and she actually emailed him a short apology." She chuckled. "Kind of a narcissistic apology, but at least she made the effort."

"So?" Caroline studied Janie.

Janie shrugged. "We're still together if that's what you mean. But I'm not particularly interested in hearing wedding bells either. Not just yet anyway."

"But sometime?"

Janie smiled. "Maybe. But, really, I'm kind of enjoying being single. It feels like I've barely gotten my feet under me — I mean after leaving New York, getting settled in Clifden — and I've only just started my own practice. I like this feeling of independence. I'm not ready to give that up yet. I think Victor understands."

"Any word from Lisa since that last call?"

With a sad expression, Janie shook her head.

"Don't worry," Caroline assured her. "She'll call."

"What makes you so sure?"

"Even in the most dysfunctional relationships — and you know I speak from experience — I truly believe a girl wants to connect with her mother. Don't you?"

Janie nodded. "Yes, I think so."

Caroline folded the paper napkin into a

triangle. "As messed up as my poor mom was — you saw her, she was almost completely out of her head — I still miss her sometimes. I'm really glad I was able to spend the last few months of her life with her even though it was hard. I wouldn't trade that for anything."

As Caroline walked through the freshly gutted house that afternoon with her notebook in hand, trying to decide what kinds of things she wanted done with the place, she decided that she would complete this renovation in honor of her mother's memory. Maybe it was silly or sentimental, but that's what she planned to do. She would get the house back to its former self — and better. She would see that it became a place her mother would've been proud of. Perhaps someday her mom would take a sneak peek down from heaven and give the house — as well as Caroline — a nod of approval.

Chapter 5
Abby

It was the day Abby had been waiting for. *Real* guests — not her friend Caroline or Victor's crazy ex-wife — *real* paying customers were coming to her bed-and-breakfast today. Sure, they'd been referrals from Jackie Day's B and B down by the waterfront, but even so, they were honest-to-goodness guests. Even though the inn wasn't 100 percent complete, it was good enough, and this week's visitors would prove that. The question was, where were they?

At five o'clock, she called Jackie. "What time do guests usually check in?" she asked, although she already knew the answer.

"You never know," Jackie said. "That's one reason I find it easier to live at the inn."

"Right." Abby had considered this, but she knew Paul would throw a fit.

"You can always make a policy," Jackie advised her. "No checking in past a certain hour — say nine o'clock."

"Nine o'clock?"

"Well, for your guests' sake, you have to be reasonable. You don't want to limit yourself so much that your B and B goes empty most of the time."

"It's just that nine is so late. We sometimes go to bed around then."

"Seriously?"

Abby chuckled. "Yes. Paul and I are turning into regular old-timers, Jackie. We go to bed with the chickens."

"Not me. I'm a night owl."

"Then maybe we should have all the night owls stay at your inn and the early birds can stay at mine."

Of course, Jackie didn't like that idea much, but she told Abby to be patient and said that she'd actually directed some other guests Abby's way during the holidays.

"But I won't be open during the holidays," Abby told her.

"Is this a business or a hobby?" Jackie demanded.

"Well, it's a business, of course. But I'm still trying to figure things out. I'm starting out slowly until I get all the kinks out. I'm still in the experimental stage."

"So you're experimenting on the guests I sent your way?" Jackie said in a scolding tone. "You'd better treat these people right, or you won't have much repeat traffic."

"I am treating them right," Abby defended. "You should see this place. I've pulled out all the stops. Fresh flowers in every room, great toiletries, the best linens, soothing classical music, and I've got a killer breakfast menu lined up for the next week."

"Oh." Jackie sounded concerned. "What's the deal? Are you trying to run me out of business?"

"No, not at all, Jackie. I'm just trying to follow your fine example." Abby glanced over to where she'd placed a china plate of freshly made snickerdoodle cookies by the sign-in book. Should she feel guilty for doing a little extra something to make her guests feel welcome? She wouldn't tell Jackie about the special handmade chocolate mints she'd bought to put on the beds at night, or the elegant crystal goldfish bowls with live fish swimming happily about that she had placed in the bathrooms. Jackie didn't have to know everything about this place. Hopefully the word would spread quickly enough.

Abby went into the laundry room, where she'd stashed a couple of crates of Christmas decorations, some extra things she'd borrowed from her own collection at home. Her plan had been to get them placed about the inn to give it a festive holiday atmosphere. Seeing she had time to spare, she decided to go ahead and get started.

She was midway through stringing a faux pine garland around the stairway banister when she heard someone coming in the front door. Excited that her guests had finally arrived, she turned toward the door with a big smile. "Welcome!"

"Yeah, right," Paul growled as he came into the foyer, shaking rain off his parka and stomping his feet on the pretty welcome rug. "Do you have any idea what time it is, Abby?"

She peered over at the clock above the mantle in the front room. "Seven forty-five," she told him as she came down the stairs.

"And you're still here" — he frowned around the space — "decorating for Christmas?"

"I was waiting for the guests to arrive and —"

"And meanwhile your husband is home alone, waiting for you to arrive." He reached over and took several of the snickerdoodle cookies. "When was the last time you made these for me?"

"You're not supposed to have white sugar and flour," she reminded him.

"Or dinner either, so it seems."

"Oh Paul." She came over and just shook her head. "You don't have to be jealous of the B and B."

"I'm not jealous, Abby, I'm mad."

The door was opening again, and, worried it would be her real guests, Abby wanted to shoo her rude husband into the kitchen. But before she could, in walked Caroline. As usual of late, Caroline had on her work clothes and a ball cap.

"Greetings," Caroline said cheerfully. "Hey, this place looks great, Abby." She turned to Paul as she peeled off her wet jacket. "And how are you doing, Paul?" She smiled warmly at him. "Did your wife ask you my big question yet?"

He frowned. "What big question?"

"Don't ask him now," Abby warned her. "Paul's in a snit."

"I'm not in a snit," he retorted. "I'm just hungry and tired of waiting for my wife to come home."

"And I'm waiting for my guests to arrive." Abby glanced nervously to the door. "I'd hate for them to walk in while you're throwing a fit."

"I know!" Caroline said. "Why don't I take Paul to dinner?" She pointed to his work clothes. "Someplace casual, since we didn't dress up. After your guests arrive, you can meet us." She smiled at Abby. "My treat!"

Abby nodded eagerly. "Yes, great idea. Now hurry along before the guests get here."

"What if I don't want to —"

"Come on, Paul," Caroline urged him, tugging on his arm. "Let's get out of her hair. How do you expect your wife to run a successful business if you're hounding her all the time?"

"But I —"

"No arguing." Caroline was pushing him out the door, looking back at Abby. She winked. "We'll see you later." Then she held up her thumb and forefinger like a phone. "Call me."

Abby nodded with relief as she blew Caroline a thank-you kiss. No sooner were they gone than another couple came in. "Welcome," Abby said again. Smiling warmly at the neatly dressed thirtysomething pair, she moved to her position behind the registration table that she'd set up in the foyer. "You must be the Hawleys," she said as they closed the door.

"Is this the Coastal Cottage?" the man asked.

"That's right," she said pleasantly. "Welcome to Coastal Cottage."

"But I thought there was a water view," he told her in a slightly disgruntled tone.

"Besides the *rain,* that is," the woman added as she removed and shook off her scarf. "Does it *always* rain like this on the Oregon coast? It felt like we drove through a flood to get here."

"Western Oregon is known for its rain." Abby's smile stiffened. "It's what keeps the place green and pretty. But don't worry — we get sunshine, too. In fact, the forecast gets better in a few days."

"But you're still not on the ocean," the man pointed out again.

"No, we're not. But we are conveniently located near a lot of nice —"

"I was certain this place had a water view," he persisted. "The river or the bay or some sort of water?"

"Besides the rain," the woman said again.

"You might be thinking of the other bed-and-breakfast in town," Abby told him. "It has a bay view, but it's also —"

"Yes, that's it," the man said. "I think we're at the wrong place." He reached for his wife's hand. "Come on, Tara, let's go."

"But your reservation *is* here," Abby said quickly. "And you will be charged for your first night whether or not you stay."

"But this is the wrong place," he insisted.

"You were referred here from the other B and B," Abby explained in a tight voice, "because they are full."

"Oh." He pressed his lips together with an irritated expression. "So we might as well stay here." He turned back to his wife. "But they can't make us stay more than one night."

"Maybe we'll like it," she said hopefully. "It's kind of cute."

He rolled his eyes. "But it's not by the water."

As she ran his credit card for one night only, Abby tried to pretend that this hadn't started all wrong. She smiled and spoke in an amicable tone as she gave them the tour, explaining when and where breakfast was served.

"Are we the only guests here?" the man demanded.

"Well, I've only just started this place up and —"

"Hopefully you won't be shutting it down soon." He laughed in a rather snide way.

"Oh, Glen," the woman said, checking him.

"Hey, you can't promise a water view then not deliver. That's like a bait and switch, and unless I'm mistaken, it's against the law."

"But I didn't promise a water view," Abby explained. "That's the other B and B."

"It was misleading," he told her as he took a couple of the cookies.

She just nodded with a frozen half smile. "I'm sorry you felt misled, Mr. Hawley. I do hope you enjoy your stay. Would you like me to show you to your room?"

"If it's not too much trouble."

Keeping her smile in place, Abby showed them to the master suite, and Mrs. Hawley commented on how nice it was. That was something. But Mr. Hawley's attitude made Abby feel slightly sick inside. What if every guest reacted like that?

Abby went into the kitchen and then kept on going to the laundry room, where she closed the door and turned on the faucet of the laundry sink, and while the water gushed down the drain, she just cut loose and cried. What had made her think she could do this? Or that running an inn would be fun? Really, Abby should have her head examined. As usual, Paul was right! Not that she planned to let him know about this. At least not yet. If she was going to go down, she would go down fighting.

Abby held her head high as she walked into the diner. She smiled and waved at Paul and

Caroline, who were seated by the salad bar. No way was she going to reveal what a disaster her first guests had turned out to be.

"You're just in time," Caroline told Abby as she sat down. "I think your husband just agreed to be my contractor."

Paul shrugged. "It's no big deal."

"It is to me," Caroline insisted. She stuck out her hand. "Do we have a deal, Paul Franklin?"

He gave her a lopsided grin, then stuck out his hand. "Yeah, I guess we do."

Caroline nodded to Abby as she shook Paul's hand. "You're our witness."

"So did you get your guests all tucked into bed?" Paul teased. "Read 'em a bedtime story and give 'em some milk to go with their cookies?"

"Yes," she retorted, "then I kissed them good night."

They all laughed.

"So really," Caroline asked, "how did it go? Were they totally wowed by how great the place is?"

"Oh, yes." Abby tried to sound convincing. "*Wowed* is the word."

"You're going to be so busy," Caroline said as she picked up a roll. "I'll really need to get into my own place before long. But don't worry, I'm on it."

Abby planned to set Caroline straight later — just not in front of Paul.

"Sorry I was so grumpy earlier," Paul told Abby. "You know how I get when I'm starving to death."

She nodded. "And I'm sorry I didn't get home earlier. I know how low blood sugar brings out the beast in you. I can see that I still have a few bumps to iron out in this whole B and B business."

"Speaking of food, you want me to flag down the waitress?" Caroline offered. "Their fish and chips are pretty good."

"No, thanks. I think I'll just graze tonight." Abby stood and made her way over to the salad bar, relieved to escape any more talk about her bed-and-breakfast. She really didn't like telling lies, not to anyone, and especially not to her husband or friends. It tied her stomach in knots. She wasn't even very good at it. As she loaded her plate with greens and other supposedly healthy things, wishing she was having fish and chips instead, she wondered how long she could keep up this charade. How long until everyone figured her out and she was forced to throw in the towel? Which would be, of course, a fine-Egyptian-cotton-luxurious-bath-sheet sort of towel.

CHAPTER 6
JANIE

Janie didn't want to make a habit of going into her office on Saturdays, but she'd scheduled an appointment with a woman who worked full time during the week and had sounded desperate for a legal consultation. After ninety minutes of patiently listening to complaints about a disconnected marriage and a discontented woman, Janie decided that Sheryl Bowers needed more than just legal counsel. On the bright side, Sheryl and her husband, Jeff, had married late in life and had no children together. That was something.

"Have you been to a marriage counselor?" Janie asked carefully.

"Jeff would refuse to go. He thinks everything is just peachy."

"Does Jeff know that you're seeing me today, inquiring about divorce?"

"No. And I don't want him to know either."

"What would he do if he did know?"

"Probably start hiding money and assets to make sure I don't get much in the settlement. For all I know, he's doing that now anyway."

Janie looked at her notes again. "And you've been married for almost eleven years?"

"Yes. As I said, it's a second marriage for both of us."

"You keep your finances separate, but you never signed a prenuptial agreement."

"He wanted to sign one, but I refused."

"Jeff has no idea that you're considering a divorce?"

Sheryl ran her fingers through her short drab hair and frowned. "I don't think so."

"And you have no idea how he'd act if he knew? He doesn't exhibit any anger or control issues?"

"No, not really."

Janie pressed her lips together, tapping her pen against the side of her laptop and thinking. "You really need to discuss this situation with your husband, Sheryl. It's not really fair to start filing for a divorce while he's completely in the dark. If he feels blindsided, it'll make the divorce process more difficult for both of you."

Sheryl nodded. "Yes, that's probably true."

"It's possible that with some good marriage counseling you could —"

"I don't *want* counseling," she declared.

"So you're finished with this marriage? Is that what you're really saying? Even if it could be saved, you're done?"

Sheryl looked down at Janie's desk, then nodded.

"May I ask if there's someone else in the picture? Another man, perhaps?" Janie might be a couple years younger than Sheryl, but she hadn't been born yesterday.

Sheryl continued looking down at the desk. She was not going to answer, but it seemed fairly obvious that something or someone had turned her head. Why else was she going to this much effort?

Janie sighed. This was just the kind of legal case she had absolutely no interest in working on. An unhappy woman, probably already immersed in an affair, even if only an emotional one, trying to get the most she could from her husband before ditching him. Corporate law would be preferable to this.

"May I ask something else?" Janie said a bit hesitantly.

"Sure, why not?"

"When you married Jeff, when you made that commitment to him, did you think your

81

marriage would last? Did you *want* it to last?"

Sheryl looked up. "Of course!"

"Then what changed your mind?"

Sheryl started to talk about her husband more specifically, citing how he wanted to go hunting and fishing and traveling to crazy remote places like Montana, plus a bunch of other "irritating" things. But nothing on the Jeff list seemed too serious — no fighting, no cheating, no abuse, no addictions. The man didn't even sound stingy — just a bit clueless and unwilling to "grow old gracefully," as Sheryl put it. As Janie listened to the complaints, it seemed that nothing was really a deal breaker, not in Janie's mind anyway.

"It's not really a marriage," Sheryl finally told Janie. "We share the same roof and sometimes the same bed, but we mostly live our separate lives. We even took separate vacations last year. He went to Alaska, and I went to Palm Springs with a friend. We had a very restful time. Meanwhile Jeff was up there tramping around in the wilderness with a bunch of moose and grizzly bears. Anyway, I'm just tired of this nonsense. I want out."

"I recommend you speak openly to your husband, Sheryl. Tell him how you feel. If he's as apathetic about your marriage as you seem to be, perhaps you can agree on a no-fault divorce and save yourselves a lot of time and money and trouble." Janie suspected this would be unlikely, because the husband appeared to have more to lose financially than the wife. Even so, Janie didn't want to end up in the middle of what could easily become a hostile dispute.

"Are you saying you don't want to represent me?" Sheryl sat up straight in the chair, glaring at Janie.

"I'm simply saying that I would first recommend you make some effort to get quality marriage counseling and see if it's possible to reconcile your differences. Out of respect of marriage commitments, I'd never tell an unhappy couple to run out and hire attorneys. If your marriage truly can't be saved, I would still encourage you to be forthcoming with your husband and try to resolve your differences outside of divorce court. If that's not going to happen, I'd be happy to recommend some experienced divorce attorneys who could be of more help."

"But I heard you're doing some pro bono work," she said in a slightly pleading tone. "That's why I called you. Like I said, my husband is the one with the money."

Janie got it. Sheryl was here in the hopes that she would get free legal representation. "Then you should be very thankful you live in Oregon, Sheryl, because it's not a community-property state."

"What's that mean?"

"Oregon is an equal-distribution state. So if you choose to divorce, you'll probably get a fifty-fifty split anyway."

"Really?" Sheryl's eyes lit up, and Janie could almost see the dollar signs there. "So I really do have a retirement plan after all?"

Janie didn't know how to respond.

Sheryl waved her hand. "Sorry. It's just that Jeff keeps saying we don't need a retirement plan. He acts like he thinks he'll never get old. But let me tell you, it comes a lot faster than you think."

"Oh." Janie just nodded.

"I'm not originally from this state. I didn't know that there was a fifty-fifty split here. That's a huge relief. You're sure about that?"

"It's the law." Janie closed her notebook and laid down her pen. There was more she could tell this obnoxious woman about the law and the divisions of property in the dissolutions of marriage and how it usually didn't go smoothly, but she just didn't want to go there right now.

Sheryl stood and smiled. "Well, thanks for

your time."

Janie smiled stiffly. "Good luck."

Sheryl had been gone less than two minutes when someone else knocked on the door to Janie's office.

"Come in," Janie called as she closed her laptop.

"Hey," Caroline said as she entered the office, closing the door behind her. "I hope I'm not disturbing you, Janie, but I saw your client leave, and I thought you might not be too —"

"No problem." Janie pointed to the recently vacated chair across from her desk. "Have a seat." At least Caroline wouldn't be here to discuss the upside of divorce and how to make the most of it.

"I need some advice," Caroline began. "Not legal advice, but friend to friend."

"Go for it."

"Well, Paul has agreed to be my contractor on my house renovations and —"

"You're kidding. How'd you get him to do that?" Feeling slightly indignant, Janie remembered how Paul had flatly turned her down on her remodel. As juvenile as it seemed, Janie felt jealous and actually wondered if it was because Caroline and Paul had been some of the "cool" kids in high school, while Janie had been stuck hanging with the nerds. No, she decided, that was not only ridiculous, it was childish.

"I know," Caroline said, "I was surprised too. But I guess things really are a little slow for him this time of year."

"Anyway, that's great news, Caroline." Janie smiled, thankful that her friend hadn't been able to read her thoughts. "I'm sure Paul will do a great job for you."

"Yes, but there's a little snag. Paul has strongly encouraged me to hire Bonnie Boxwell to help."

"Oh." Janie nodded. "That could be a problem."

"Yeah. I mean it was one thing when you hired Bonnie to help with your house, but you didn't know that she was the other woman and —"

"To be fair, we never established that Bonnie and Paul actually had an affair. As far as I could tell, it was more of a business friendship that got a little too friendly, at least too friendly for Abby's comfort."

"I know. But Abby still has some hangups about Bonnie." Caroline glanced over her shoulder as if she expected Abby to pop into Janie's law office.

"What did Abby say about Paul's suggestion?" Janie asked.

"Abby doesn't know yet." Caroline

frowned. "I hate to rock her boat. She seems a little stressed."

"I thought she was all happy about her guests and all."

"I thought so too, but I was just in the kitchen and she seemed a little glum. Oh, yeah, that reminds me, she told me to invite you to come up and eat breakfast leftovers. She made enough to feed a small army and, as far as I can see, her guests barely touched it. Not only that, but it sounds like they're checking out today."

"Checking out?" Janie felt concerned. "Why?"

"I'm not sure. I just overheard the guy telling his wife that he wanted to go look for another place to stay."

"Oh, dear." Janie shook her head. "That will probably upset Abby. She was so looking forward to having them here for a whole week."

"Yeah. She seemed pretty bummed. And that's just one more reason I don't want to mention the Bonnie situation to her."

"I can understand that."

"So what do I do?" Caroline held up her hands. "Paul said he'll start work on Monday if I can get my ducks in a row. And he said the only one he knew who could help me to do that was Bonnie Boxwell."

"Well, other than Abby." Janie sighed. "She's pretty good at that sort of thing too, but she's got her hands full with this inn. I have to admit that Bonnie takes décor and design to a whole new level. I really don't think you'll be disappointed if you hire her."

"Unless it ruins my friendship with Abby."

"Oh, your friendship is sturdier than that." Janie smiled. "Remember, Abby forgave me for my Bonnie transgressions."

"I know. Maybe I could just forget to mention it to Abby. For a while anyway, until she's feeling better about the B-and-B situation."

Janie stood. "Breakfast leftovers are sounding good to me. I haven't eaten yet. If the guests are gone, maybe we should go foraging before Abby puts it all away."

As it turned out, Abby had really outdone herself. The crepes and blintzes and sausage and bacon and eggs were impressive.

"I know, I know," she told them as she waved her hand over the feast still spread in the dining room. "It was temporary insanity on my part. Maybe I was thinking of that old Costner movie *Field of Dreams* — if I cook it, they will come."

"Well, we came," Janie told her as she took a second crepe. "And it's delicious."

"Yeah, if this B-and-B thing doesn't work

out for you, you might want to consider a restaurant," Caroline suggested.

Abby groaned. "Do you know how much work that would be to run a restaurant? I'm sure Paul would leave me."

"But you could promise him three solid meals a day," Caroline said.

"So your guests are really checking out today?" Janie spooned some raspberries onto her crepe.

"How'd you hear that?" Abby asked.

"I mentioned it to her," Caroline admitted. "I overheard them talking in the foyer this morning."

Abby let out a long, sad-sounding sigh. "It seems I'm a failure as an innkeeper."

"No, you're not," Caroline told her.

"I am." Abby nodded in a dismal way. "The guy practically accused me of a bait and switch when he discovered that the inn isn't on the ocean."

"Did you advertise it as that?" Janie asked.

"No, but my website does have some scenic photos that might be misleading."

"I've seen your website," Janie said. "There's a lighthouse picture and a dunes shot, and some ocean photos as well as some other local spots of interest. Those are the sights you're encouraging people to come see here on the coast. Surely they don't think they'll see all those things while staying right here in the B and B. They expect to look out the window and see all of that?"

"I don't know." Abby shook her head. "The Hawleys seemed to."

"Hawley?" Janie asked. "Is that the guy applying for the city manager job?"

"I don't know." Abby shrugged. "He didn't mention anything — well, other than my 'false advertising.' "

"I heard someone at the fitness club talking about a guy named Hawley. You know the city has finally decided to hire a replacement for Cathy."

"Well, I sure hope they don't hire that sourpuss." Abby scowled. "The sooner he leaves my inn and Clifden, the happier I'll be."

"So he didn't check out yet?" Janie asked, confused.

"Not officially. They went out to look around the town. I'm sure if they find a better place to stay, they will check out. Although Jackie's B and B is booked."

"Then they'll probably stay here," Caroline assured Abby.

"Great." Abby scowled.

"So you really don't want their business?" Janie asked.

"Oh, I suppose I do." Abby stood and picked up the big platter of blintzes. "It's just that it's not turning out to be quite how I hoped it would be." Her eyes filled with tears. "I think . . . I'm afraid I've made a big mistake. I . . . I'm just not cut out to be a businesswoman." Then she let out a sob and turned and ran.

Caroline and Janie exchanged glances then both simultaneously stood and followed Abby into the kitchen, where she was standing in front of the sink, crying.

"You have done a beautiful job putting this place together." Janie put a hand on Abby's shoulder. "Anyone with any sense would be grateful to stay here. Everything is so lovely and elegant and tasteful and clean. Even without an ocean view, it's got a lot of the same amenities as a five-star hotel."

"And your food is killer," Caroline assured her.

"The Hawleys are vegetarians." Abby blew her nose on a paper towel.

"Well, that's their problem," Janie said.

"You just need to give it some time." Caroline put her arm around Abby from the other side. "You've barely opened your doors. Christmas is coming, and then there's winter, and well, maybe it won't be too busy at first."

"But I need to make the mortgage payments." Abby turned to Janie. "Believe me, I will make payments. I promise you, Janie, I will keep up my end of this deal."

"I'm not worried, Abby. And I love having my office in your basement."

"And I love having you here. But I need to bring in some income — my savings won't last forever. Eventually I have to make some money on this place."

"You will," Janie said with confidence. "But Caroline is right. Starting an inn in the winter is probably a challenge."

"Hey, maybe you need to do something to lure people in here," Caroline said. "Give them something they can't resist."

"You mean like a bait and switch," Abby said bitterly.

"No, I mean like a winter special, or a coupon, or a free night if someone stays for like, say, three. Something to get some attention. Everyone likes to feel they're getting a deal or a special offer."

Abby's eyes brightened. "You know, Caroline, that's not a bad idea."

"Go online," Janie suggested. "See what other B and Bs do to get business. Learn from them."

"I'll do that," Abby said eagerly.

"And don't worry about the silly old Hawleys," Caroline told her.

"Maybe they were just your initiation," Janie joked. "Now you're officially in the club and it'll go better from here on out."

Abby smiled at both of them. "What would I do without my friends?"

"Have way too much food left over." Caroline plucked a blintz off of the tray on the counter.

They helped Abby clean up the breakfast things, and then Janie returned to her office to lock up. She checked her appointment calendar for the rest of the month, which was shockingly open, and wondered if she'd made a mistake in turning down Sheryl as a client. Really, could she afford to be that choosy? Here she was, partnered with Abby, but what if Abby's inn didn't make it? What if it continued to flounder and fail? And what if Janie's fledgling law practice went bottom-up as well? Were they crazy, at this age and stage in life, to take these kinds of risks, reinventing themselves at a time when they'd probably be wiser to plan for retirement? Good grief, in five years Janie and her friends would all be in their sixties! Janie remembered when her parents were that age — in her mind, it was as if they'd both had a foot in the grave.

Yet Janie didn't feel that old. Oh, sure, she

had a few new aches and pains occasionally and she couldn't do everything she used to do. Plus there was this whole business of hot flashes and bouts of irritability and an inability to focus at times. But for the most part, Janie still felt fairly young and vital. She wasn't ready to start thinking about retirement. Why should she? Well, except when she had "clients" like Sheryl Bowers. That alone gave her cause to question her long-term career plans.

Janie caught a glimpse of herself in the bronze-framed mirror by the door. Her auburn waves hadn't started to gray yet, but there was no denying that the color had faded some, and gray was probably right around the corner. Still, it wouldn't be anything a good hairdresser couldn't fix with more highlights. Even the crow's-feet by her eyes weren't too distressing. Plus there was always Botox, although she was determined not to go that route if she could control herself. All in all, things could be worse.

She picked up the yellow legal pad from her desk and tore off the pages of Sheryl notes. She wadded the paper into a tight ball and lobbed it into the trash basket. Growing old might be fine for some people, but why rush things? Wrinkles, gray hair,

94

and sore joints would arrive in their own due time. There was no stopping them. But she was not going to obsess over things like retirement plans, elderly health care, and AARP issues today.

Today she was going to remind herself that she would never be younger than she was right this minute. She was going to count her blessings — and thank God for them! Tonight, she planned to dress up like a much younger woman and go out with Victor and kick up her heels. Let those who wanted to sit back in their rockers and be old have at it. Janie was going to live like age really was just a number!

CHAPTER 7
MARLEY

By Saturday, Marley was feeling a little weary. It wasn't that she didn't love Hunter, or Jack for that matter, but she just didn't know how long she could keep up this pace of playing substitute mom and substitute sales clerk at the gallery while trying to paint. Still, she didn't want to be selfish, and she knew that people were more important than things. She also knew that Hunter, though a pretty resilient girl, wasn't ready to be dumped at the babysitter's.

"Any word?" Marley asked Jack as she and Hunter came into the gallery. It was the changing of the guard, as she called it in her mind. She'd been picking up Hunter after school and keeping her for the afternoon, then dropping her off with Jack and remaining in the gallery until closing. This let Jack take Hunter home and have something of a normal evening — fixing dinner, doing homework, that sort of thing. But since today was Saturday, Marley had kept Hunter for the entire day.

"Nothing," he told her with his usual sober smile.

"So how's it going?" she asked, changing the focus from Hunter's missing mom to the gallery.

"A little slow, thanks to the weather, I think. But I'm hoping it'll pick up this weekend. I ran that ad in the paper this week."

She nodded. "The holiday shopping coupon."

"So how was your day?" he asked Hunter. As usual, she filled him in on the details of what they'd been doing, actually making it sound much more exciting than it had really been. But today it had been housework, after Marley had realized that her little beach bungalow was in dire need of a good scrubbing, and she wasn't sure how Hunter could possibly glamorize that.

"I got to wash windows," Hunter told him proudly. "But first Marley let me paint them with the soap. Then we took pictures of them. It was really cool."

"Hmm." He rubbed his chin. "Maybe you should do that at my place too."

"No way, Grandpa." Hunter shook her head. "Your house is *all* windows."

Marley shrugged. "See the price you pay for that gorgeous view, Jack?"

"Thanks for doing this," he told her as he reached for his coat. "You know tonight we stay open until seven."

"No problem," she assured him. "I brought a book to read if it's slow."

"I'll make it up to you," he promised.

"Don't worry about it."

"And I've placed an ad for a new employee," he said quietly. "I've been asking around."

"You're going to give someone else Mommy's job?" Hunter asked with concerned eyes.

Jack looked stumped.

"I think your grandpa is just looking ahead to the holiday season," Marley said quickly. "A lot of shops hire extra help at Christmastime. Right, Jack?"

"Exactly." He nodded with a grateful expression.

"I can work when school gets out for Christmas," Hunter offered. "Mrs. Hanford said we have a vacation."

Marley and Jack exchanged glances — Marley knew they were both wondering how they'd keep Hunter occupied during her two-week winter break.

"You guys have a good evening," Marley

said as she put Hunter's hood back over her head and ushered her toward the door. She leaned down and kissed the girl's cheek. "I will see you tomorrow."

"And I'll call you later tonight," Jack called out as they left.

Marley liked being alone in the gallery. It was so quiet and calm, and Jack's selection of jazz music was always soothing. And the smell in here — that gallery smell, a mixture of paints and wood scents and the spiced tea that Jack often brewed in the back room — was always familiar and comforting. Really, there were worse ways to spend a Saturday night, and she'd seen plenty of them in her lifetime.

Still, as she walked around, looking at the familiar pieces of art, including her own — which she wished would sell — she felt worried. Yes, this was a slow season, but her paintings were her livelihood. If she wasn't creating them, increasing her stockpile, she wouldn't have inventory to sell when things finally did pick up with the warmer weather and the tourists. But she was determined not to worry about that.

Just go with the moment, she'd been telling herself. *Enjoy playing grandma. Help Hunter to feel loved and at home and not abandoned.*

Even so, it was hard not to be seriously

miffed with Jasmine at times. What kind of mother did this? Marley stared at one of Jasmine's pieces — an intricate pen and ink drawing of the waterfront. "Make it marketable," Jack had encouraged his daughter after Jasmine had complained that her other pieces weren't selling. Of course, Marley understood why their typical clients were hesitant to hang pictures of dragons and demons and scary subjects on their walls, but, as with all things, Jasmine was determined to be her own free spirit. Marley could relate to that on some levels, but when one had a child to support, not all rules could be broken.

"Jasmine is like her mother," Jack had told Marley last night when they'd talked on the phone after Hunter had gone to bed.

"How so?"

"Well, Diane was a free spirit too. We met in the late sixties, and she didn't want to get married. She said marriage was too institutional and traditional," he'd explained. "Even when she was pregnant with Jasmine, Diane was sure our love was enough to keep us together and make us a family. But I'm more old-fashioned, so I put my foot down and insisted that a baby needed a married set of parents." He sighed. "I guess I just didn't understand."

"Understand what?"

"That she *really* didn't want to be married. Diane left me when Jasmine was a little younger than Hunter."

"Did she take Jasmine with her?"

"Not the first time. But after about a year, Diane decided she wanted Jasmine after all. Of course, that led to some pretty rough years and custody battles. Finally, the judge convinced Diane that if she really cared about her child, she'd continue to live in the Bay Area and share custody. And for a few years she did."

"And then?"

"About the time Jasmine was hitting her turbulent teens, Diane decided to leave again."

"With or without Jasmine?"

"This time we let Jasmine decide. She was only fifteen, and I know it was hard on her, but she finally decided to stay with me and finish school with her friends." His laugh suggested he wasn't amused. "I wasn't sure whether I had won or lost that battle because, take it from me, parenting a rebellious teenage girl was no walk in the park."

Marley wanted to point out that the situation with his daughter hadn't improved a whole lot since then but controlled herself. No sense in rubbing it in. "Kids," she said, as if that said it all.

"Yeah."

"Even so, you gotta love 'em."

"Agreed. And I shouldn't be too surprised that Jasmine turned out like this. I do take some responsibility for it, but I think genetics has a bit to do with it as well. Like mother, like daughter."

A long pause had followed, and Marley wanted to ask him if he had any kind of long-term plan for Hunter — in the event that Jasmine had bailed permanently — but it was late, and she was tired. She suspected that Jack was too. So they'd simply said good night and hung up.

Still, as Marley wandered aimlessly around the gallery, she wondered. What would Jack do if Jasmine really was done with her short stint of "motherhood"? Of course, she knew the answer to that — Jack, despite being sixty-four, would raise Hunter himself. And he would do an excellent job of it. Perhaps the real question was where Marley would fit into this new equation. Where would she want to fit in? The truth was, she wasn't even sure.

The jingle of the bell on the door brought her back to reality and the present.

"Hello," she called out in a friendly tone, making her way toward the front of the store. As usual, she tried to be congenial without being pushy, always keeping a comfortable distance between herself and a potential customer.

"Attractive gallery," the man told her as he started to browse a wall of watercolors.

"Thank you."

"I've heard good things about this place."

"You're not from around here?"

"No. I'm from Santa Barbara."

"I'll bet they're having better weather down there."

"You can say that again. I came up for my favorite niece's wedding — it was Friday night — and I've never seen a soggier bunch of guests. Everyone got drenched getting from their cars to the reception. But like I told my niece, rain on your wedding day is good luck."

"Good luck?" Marley wasn't so sure.

"It's true. Well, at least it used to be in some cultures. Rain meant good crops, as well as plenty of children."

"I guess that makes sense." She considered this as she tried to appear busy by wiping down the glass countertop by the cash register. Come to think of it, her wedding day, despite a forecast for rain, had been surprisingly sunny. That figured.

"Aha," the man said with what sounded

like appreciation. "Now these are really nice."

She looked up, realizing that he was in the area where her pieces were displayed. Well, her paintings as well as several others. But, out of curiosity, she decided to wander on over. To her pleased surprise, he was staring at one of her works.

"I really like this." He nodded with appreciation. "Is this a local artist?"

Marley felt her heart skipping a beat or two. "Uh, yes, as a matter of fact."

"The use of color and composition is so fresh and lively. It makes me think of Gauguin and Tahiti, warm beaches, tropical places." He chuckled. "I'm sure that would be appreciated around here — especially this time of year. But I'm guessing the artist has spent a considerable amount of time in the islands."

Marley cleared her throat. "No, not actually."

"Really?" He turned and looked curiously at her. "Are you sure about that?"

She smiled. "Actually, I'm positive." She pointed to the placard with her name on it. "I'm Marley Jacobs."

He looked surprised.

"Actually my legal name is still Marley

Phelps, but I use my maiden name to paint with."

"Really?" He studied her. "*You* painted these?"

"I did."

"And you've never lived in the tropics?"

She shook her head. "Not because I never wanted to."

"Then why don't you?"

"What?"

"Go live somewhere tropical." He smiled. "I'm sure a talented and successful artist like you could afford to live wherever she liked."

She thought about this. "Well, the truth is, I've only just restarted my, uh, my art career. And I recently relocated to Clifden, which I have to say isn't always this rainy and gloomy. In fact, I heard the sun will be out again tomorrow. Then you'll see it's actually quite beautiful here."

"I'll have to take your word for that." He turned back to her paintings, folding his arms across his front and leaning onto his back leg. "My flight home is in the morning."

Marley was unsure of what to do. Normally, if someone showed interest in a piece of art, she would be quick to talk about it, explaining a bit about the artist and the work. But in the case of her own art, she was suddenly tongue-tied. She had never been good at selling herself or her own work. Explaining the pieces felt awkward. Besides, it seemed obvious that the man already had a good understanding of art in general.

"I really like this," he said quietly, almost as if talking to himself.

"Thank you," she murmured.

He turned to look at her again, almost as if he still wasn't convinced this was indeed her work. "And you say you just recently restarted your art career?"

She nodded. "I'd been somewhat shut down, if you know what I mean, a bad marriage . . . and things. But then I got out, and once I really started painting, it's like I couldn't stop. I do my pieces extremely quickly — it's like they're in my head and I can hardly get the paint onto the canvas fast enough." Just saying this gave her the urge to grab a paintbrush and get back to work. But because of helping with Hunter, she'd barely painted these past few days.

"Is this the only place your work is shown?"

"Yes. Well, other than the pieces that have already sold." Feeling a bit more confidence, she continued. "A designer in town is quite fond of my work. So are some friends. So my art is making it onto some local walls." She smiled uncomfortably.

"I'm not surprised."

"Thank you."

"I'm going to tell you something that might surprise you."

"What's that?"

"I think I could get you about five times as much for these paintings down in Santa Barbara."

"Seriously?" She looked skeptically at him.

He just nodded. "I have a gallery — a rather nice little gallery in a great location." He pointed to her largest painting. "In fact, I think I could almost add another zero to that price and many of my customers wouldn't blink an eyelash."

Marley blinked both eyes. "Really?"

He smiled at her. "In fact, case in point, I'll buy this one from you tonight. I assume you can ship?"

"Yes — sure — no problem."

He turned to look at the others. "In fact, I'll buy them all."

Marley felt slightly faint. "You will?"

He laughed. "Yes. And, mark my word, I won't be sorry either."

As she wrote up the large purchase, she felt lightheaded. For a moment, as she was running his credit card, she felt certain that this was a hoax. Either someone was secretly filming her for one of those "got you" reality shows or his card was stolen. But the transaction seemed to go through. Besides, she told herself, as she wrote down the shipping information, nothing could be sent until Monday. If Thomas Hatfield was a crook, they would know by then.

As she was finishing up, Thomas handed her a second business card. "You keep this one for yourself, Marley," he told her. "And feel free to contact me if you'd like to do more business." He glanced around Jack's gallery. "If you like, we can cut out the middle man too."

"Well, I . . . uh, thank you."

He put his wallet back in his pocket. "And if you'd ever be interested in doing a special show, just give me a call, and we'll see if we can set something up. Perhaps in the spring." He reached out and shook her hand. "It's been a pleasure to meet you, Marley Jacobs. I think you're off to a brilliant start in your art career."

"Thank you!" she exclaimed. "Thank you so much!"

"Thank *you*," he told her. "I'll have to thank my niece for tipping me off about this gallery. Well worth my time." Then, just like that, he left.

Marley felt like the slightest breeze could blow her over as she leaned onto the counter by the register for support. Had that really just happened? Was this for real? She actually opened the register again, just to pull out the receipt and stare at all those numbers, that total. She couldn't believe it — but it was not a dream.

She looked at the clock and saw it wasn't even seven yet, but she was tempted to close the gallery anyway. She wanted to call her friends and invite them to meet her in town to celebrate! No, she decided, she would be sensible and reliable. She would finish up her shift first and celebrate later. She'd tell Jack about this stroke of good fortune when they talked later tonight, after he'd had time to feed Hunter, spend some quality time with her, and get her tucked into bed. She wouldn't interrupt him. In the meantime, Marley felt she'd burst if she didn't tell someone *right now.*

She pulled out her phone and thought about her friends. Janie was probably out with Victor, and Abby and Paul sometimes took in a flick on Saturday evenings. So she decided to call Caroline first, quickly spilling her good news. Then, after Caroline let out an ear-splitting shriek, she insisted on meeting Marley in town for a celebratory dinner. "I needed an excuse to do something fun tonight."

"It'll be my treat," Marley told her.

"And I'll spring for the champagne," Caroline promised.

It wasn't until Marley was locking up the gallery that she began to wonder about that "extra zero" Thomas had mentioned earlier. Had he been serious? If he was serious, if he really did plan to mark her paintings up that much, had she been a fool to sell for such low prices? Although she'd never thought the prices were low before. Even so, she felt worried. What if she'd left money on the table? Marley usually thought of herself as fairly well grounded and realistic, but now she felt giddy and slightly crazy. Was that what fame and fortune did to a person? Not that she had either, but there was that elusive potential, that promise of something more. But what if she hadn't been a very smart businesswoman about this whole thing?

Marley truly appreciated Jack on many levels, and she didn't want to be greedy. But when she subtracted his gallery consignment fee, calculating her actual earnings on the paintings, she couldn't help but wonder as she had so many times before, *What if I've sold myself short?*

CHAPTER 8
CAROLINE

Caroline couldn't believe that she'd spent the whole afternoon with Bonnie Boxwell. It had started when Caroline stopped by Bonnie's décor shop, and the next thing she knew, Bonnie was showing her a new line of cabinet hardware. "I love these handles," Caroline told Bonnie as she fondled a brushed-nickel bar. "But I have no idea what kind of cupboards would go with them. The truth is I'm pretty décor-challenged."

Bonnie laughed. "That's why you're here."

"Well, that, and because Paul Franklin won't work with me unless I hire a designer to help."

"Paul's a smart man. He doesn't want to waste time. And he knows I can stay several steps ahead of his game." Then Bonnie started speaking in what sounded like a foreign language, talking about base and wall cabinet installations, plumbing and electrical inspections, and all sorts of other technical terms that overwhelmed Caroline.

Caroline held up her hands. "My friends are all good at this," she confessed to Bonnie, "but I am hopeless. I even had to hire someone to help me stage my condo in LA, and all we did was rearrange furniture. The stager was nice enough about it, but I could tell she was stunned at my total lack of style." Caroline held up a finger. "Well, unless we're talking about clothes. I can hold my own with fashion. But houses — especially my mom's old ranch — just frustrate me."

"Don't worry," Bonnie assured her. "Lots of very stylish women need help with their homes."

The next thing Caroline knew, Bonnie had followed her over to her house and they were going through each room, and Bonnie was measuring spaces and showing Caroline samples of paint and wood and fabric and light fixtures and tiles and so many choices that Caroline felt her head was spinning.

"I like this," Caroline pointed to the cover of one of the design books that Bonnie had spread out on the fireplace hearth. "If this house could look even a little bit like this photo, I'd be over the moon."

"That's perfect for this house," Bonnie told her. "Mid-Century Modern." She looked at Caroline. "I can imagine you fitting in with that style."

Caroline chuckled. "Meaning I'm Mid-Century Modern too? I was born in the midfifties, so you could be right."

Bonnie wandered back toward the burned-out section of the house. "You can be thankful that this is the part of the house that was destroyed," she told Caroline.

"Whatever for?" Caroline frowned.

"Because your insurance money will help you to turn it into a real master suite."

"Really?" Caroline considered this. "With a master bath, too?"

"Absolutely. You'd be crazy not to. I assume that you'll want a good-sized walk-in closet in there too."

"That'd be great." Caroline nodded eagerly. Then she looked at the gutted space and just shook her head. "Although how that horrible mess could possibly be transformed into a livable room is beyond me. I honestly cannot begin to imagine it."

"Well, leave it to me and your contractor," Bonnie assured her. "I promise you, we'll get it done — and you'll be happy with it."

Caroline had felt a twinge of guilt that she'd signed the contract with Bonnie.

Although she wasn't eager to share this news with Abby, she reminded herself that she was providing Paul and his crew with a little work. Hopefully Abby would appreciate that.

Caroline had just emerged from the shower when Marley called, and Caroline was more than eager to go out and celebrate with her friend. Tonight would be a twofold celebration. First of all for Marley's success. But they could also celebrate the start of Caroline's adventure in restoring her childhood home.

"Here's to my talented friend, who's about to become a world-renowned artist," Caroline said as she and Marley held up their champagne flutes, clinking them together.

"Thank you." Marley beamed at her. "And here's to your house renovation — may it turn out to be as lovely as its owner."

Caroline laughed, then took a bubbly sip. "You're sweeter than usual tonight, Marley. I will chalk it up to your big sale. That is just so awesome — I can't even imagine how jazzed you must feel. Have you told Jack about it yet?"

Marley's smile faded a little. "No, but I will."

"Is it a problem?" Caroline studied her

face. "I mean, won't Jack be thrilled for you? And for himself, too, since it's his gallery?"

"I'm sure Jack will be happy." Marley set her glass down. "But between you and me and the lamppost, I'm questioning myself."

"Questioning *yourself?* Whatever for? The guy obviously loved your art. Surely you don't feel guilty for making such a great sale?"

"No, it's not like that." Marley told Caroline about the buyer's gallery in Santa Barbara and how he planned to resell the paintings at a higher price.

"Oh." Caroline nodded. "I'm guessing it's a pretty swanky gallery."

"I think so. Thomas told me that he could add an extra zero to the prices of my paintings and still sell them."

"You're kidding." Caroline was no math genius, but she knew what an extra zero could mean when a painting had previously been priced at more than a thousand dollars. "Oh, Marley, do you think he really meant *that?*"

Marley shrugged with an uncomfortable expression. "I don't know."

"Oh . . . wow."

"After I thought about that a bit, I felt kind of depressed. You know, like I had a winning lottery ticket but tossed it out with the trash."

Caroline didn't know what to say. But what had started out as a fun celebration was beginning to feel more like a wake.

"I know I should be happy that my paintings sold at all," Marley said in a somber tone. "Well, I'm only human. No one likes to be undersold."

"Maybe the guy was exaggerating," Caroline suggested. Although the more she thought about it, the more she realized that art would probably bring considerably more in a place like Santa Barbara. Especially considering how that area was known as a popular playground for some fairly rich and famous folks.

"Hey," Caroline said suddenly, "I think Oprah has a vacation home in Santa Barbara. Maybe she'll shop in that guy's gallery. What if she bought one of your paintings? Wouldn't that be cool?"

Marley brightened. "Yeah, I guess so."

"Think of it like this, Marley. Even if you sold your paintings for less than they're worth, that gallery owner might've just launched you into true art greatness. I mean, what if he hadn't stopped by the gallery tonight? You'd be sitting at home, and you'd still be thinking you were just some . . . well, no offense, but a small-town artist."

"That's true."

"But now your work will be hanging with the best of them. You should be happy and proud."

Marley smiled. "You're right! Thanks so much, Caroline! I knew you were the perfect person to celebrate with me tonight."

Caroline lifted her glass again. "Here's to you painting even more and raising the prices even higher in the future."

"Thanks." They clinked glasses again. "I should be thankful that my art is a renewable resource," she said. "I hope to get better with time, although I'm not sure when I'll actually be able to paint again."

"Why not?"

"I've been helping with Hunter," Marley told her. "It kind of eats into my day."

"Her mom is still gone?"

Marley nodded. "Jack's not even sure she's coming back."

"So she's really abandoned her child?"

"Oh, I don't think Jasmine thinks of it as abandonment. I'm sure she assumes that her dad will take care of everything just like he always does."

"That's so wrong." Caroline frowned. "And unfair. I mean, I think about how much other people would love to have children. Like me — I used to want a child so badly when I was younger, and, well, you know that sad story." Caroline really didn't want to think about that just now, especially since this was supposed to be a happy night. "But if I'd ever had a daughter as sweet and adorable as Hunter, I couldn't imagine abandoning her. It's just nuts."

"I know." Marley sighed. "I'm pretty sure Jack is going to end up raising Hunter, which won't be easy at his age. I mean, I just did the math — Jack will be in his mid-seventies by the time Hunter graduates high school. Can you imagine?"

"Wow." Caroline tried to wrap her head around that. "But you have to remember that the seventies, like the fifties, aren't as old as they used to be." She smiled. "Right?"

"Let's hope so." Marley changed the subject, asking about Abby's first official guests at the bed-and-breakfast.

"It's not going as well as Abby had hoped." Caroline filled her in on the grumpy guests. "I think it would've been better if they'd just checked out today like they'd threatened to, but Glen Hawley, who came to town to interview for the city manager job, decided to stick it out at Abby's inn. Now Abby is stuck with them."

"Poor Abby. But doesn't that come with the territory? I mean, you can't exactly handpick your guests."

"That's true," Caroline conceded. "But having to cohabitate with people like Glen Hawley — and we're hoping and praying he doesn't get hired — actually makes me want to look for new digs myself." Caroline told Marley her hopes of getting her remodel done before the Mexico trip. "To that end, I've signed contracts with both Paul Franklin and Bonnie Boxwell."

Marley looked surprised. "Really?"

"I know." Caroline offered a weak smile. "Abby doesn't know about it yet. I mean about the Bonnie part. I'm not eager to tell her, especially in light of her recent frustrations over her guest situation at the B and B. She doesn't need something else to stress about. Even now I'm thinking maybe I should call Bonnie and tell her I've changed my mind." She frowned. "But then I'll lose Paul, too."

"Why?"

So Caroline explained how Paul refused to work for her without a designer involved. "And he recommended Bonnie."

"That seems a little suspicious."

"Not really. I mean, it's not like this town is crawling with designers. The way they both explained it, it sounds like things will go a lot more smoothly. My problem is that I don't want Abby to find out, at least not for a while."

Marley made a zipping motion on her lips. "She won't hear it from me."

"This is one of the challenges of living in a small town," Caroline admitted. "Having to work around stuff with friends and personality clashes and trying to keep everyone happy."

"That's true, but don't you think the benefits outweigh the negatives?"

"Absolutely," Caroline agreed. "I adore Clifden. And I love living here. I'm even enjoying this rainy winter weather." She pointed to her heavy wool blazer. "I get to wear real winter clothes here. I couldn't do much of that down in LA. It's fun pulling out sweaters and boots and scarves and knowing that I really need them here."

Marley got a slightly dreamy look. "Clifden is a sweet place, but I have to admit that when Thomas — the Santa Barbara gallery guy — asked if I'd ever lived in a tropical place like Jamaica, well, I realized that it's something I would actually love to do someday. If it's possible."

"Really?" Caroline considered this. "You'd move away from here?"

"Not permanently, but maybe for a while. In my dreams, anyway." Marley laughed. "Like I can even afford that."

"If you keep selling paintings like you did tonight, you can."

Marley waved her hand. "This was probably a one-time thing."

"Don't be too sure."

"Besides," Marley added, "who knows if I'll ever have time to paint again?"

"Oh, you know you will. Even if you keep helping with Hunter, you could paint while she's in school."

"Maybe, but it's been pretty distracting. I want to get back into a groove again soon." Marley sighed. "Of course, by then Hunter will probably be home for winter break."

"What about babysitters?"

"I don't know. I hate making her feel like she's getting shoved off. I want her to know that I really do love her — you know, the way a grandmother would. She needs that. Poor little thing."

"I'll bet you're a really good grandma."

"I try."

"But maybe Hunter needs some aunties, too." Caroline got an idea. "In fact, I wouldn't mind helping out with her sometimes. I mean, if Abby wouldn't mind me having her at the inn. That is, until I get into something else."

"That would be wonderful," Marley told her. "So what are your plans? I mean as far as where you live? Will you move into your parents' old house once it's finished?"

"I don't know. I honestly can't imagine it. I mean, Bonnie was all enthused today, talking about Mid-Century Modern and how cool the house could be, but I'm just not seeing it. To me that sorry old ranch house is just a hopelessly run-down and depressing place full of way too many unhappy memories. I'm not sure I'll ever feel good about living there."

"I can understand that."

"Until my condo sells or I get a job, I can't really afford to invest in anything else. All my insurance money is going right back into my mom's house. I'm trying to think of it as an investment. Anyway, I guess I should be thankful that Abby's giving me such a good deal on my room, and, unless she gets a lot more cranky guests, I guess I can stick it out there as long as I need to. Really, it could be worse."

Caroline realized how pathetic her life sounded. Middle-aged and unemployed, living in a rented room . . . even her love life was unimpressive. But at least she had a dog. That was something!

CHAPTER 9
ABBY

If Abby had known that running a bed-and-breakfast was going to be like this, she never would've started one. By Tuesday, after four days of cleaning up after and fixing breakfast for one of the rudest men she'd ever met, she was seriously fed up. Glen Hawley was a jerk, and she didn't care who knew it.

"There's no such thing as guest confidentiality, is there?" Abby asked Janie that morning. She'd slipped down to Janie's office for some advice and sympathy.

"I'm not sure I understand."

"Well, I know doctors can't talk about their patients, and you're not supposed to discuss your clients. As an innkeeper, am I supposed to keep my mouth shut about my guests?"

Janie smiled. "Not legally. But, as a businesswoman, you'd be wise to respect your guests' privacy."

"Why?" Abby demanded. "My guests

don't seem to respect a thing about me."

"Mrs. Hawley seems nice."

"I'll admit she's okay. But her husband is a real piece of work, and I plan to do whatever it takes to make sure that man does not get hired as our city manager."

"Just be careful," Janie warned. "Or you could end up with serious legal troubles."

"How so?"

"Slander, libel, defamation of character."

"Define those terms," Abby demanded. "I mean in layman's words."

"Basically, if you say anything about anybody that's untrue, and if your comments cause that person some sort of harm, either personally or professionally, you could be liable in a court of law."

"If I say anything *untrue?*"

"Yes."

"Well, I don't need to lie about Glen Hawley, Janie. The guy is a selfish, narcissistic, arrogant —"

"Okay, let's start with that. Calling him narcissistic is your opinion, correct?"

"Yes, but he is."

"Are you an expert?" Janie asked. "Have you done a psychological evaluation of him?"

"All I know is that he treats me like I'm his slave and like this inn is a dump and he leaves messes wherever he goes and he's rude. I don't know how his poor wife can stand him."

"You're treading on shaky ground, Abby. If you go around town saying these things, including that he's a narcissist, it could backfire and —"

"Fine, he's not a narcissist. But he *is* a jerk. Even you have to admit that."

Janie held up her hands. "I'm just saying."

Abby leaned over Janie's desk, planting both hands on the edge. "Are you saying you'd like to see Glen Hawley hired as the city manager?"

"No, of course not."

"So do I, or do I not, have a responsibility to say something?"

Janie seemed to think about this.

"As a citizen of our fair city," Abby continued, "and as a friend to the late city manager — our dear friend Cathy Gardener — shouldn't I do something before it's too late?"

"Just go carefully, Abby, that's all I'm saying."

Abby frowned. "Paul told me to stay out of it."

"Paul might be right."

Abby stood up straight, folding her arms across her front. "Well, I'll take your advice,

Janie. I will go carefully, but I do intend to go."

"Just remember," Janie said as Abby was leaving, "when it comes to harsh assessments of character, less is more."

"Right." Abby nodded. "I'll keep that in mind."

Abby went back upstairs, where she put away the breakfast things, then cleaned the Hawleys' room, changing linens and replacing the missing toiletries, which she knew they couldn't have used up. How was it possible to use three whole bars of French-milled soap, no matter how small, in a single day? Not to mention the shampoo, body wash, lotion, and conditioner. She suspected the Hawleys were tucking these top-notch toiletries into their suitcases to take home.

Finally, with her work done, she headed over to talk to Jackie Day. For starters she asked Jackie if she had any idea what kind of guests she had referred to Abby.

"I honestly didn't know a thing about them," Jackie said, "except that he was coming to interview for a job."

"Well, he is the rudest young man I've ever met."

"Really?" Jackie looked alarmed. "I'm sorry. I had no idea." She broke into a slightly sheepish smile. "But I guess I'm glad you got him instead of me."

"You have no idea."

"Well, aren't they checking out in a couple of days?"

"Unless you have an available room here." Abby glanced hopefully around. "Seems pretty quiet here. Are you really still full?"

Jackie just shook her head. "Look, I'm sorry you got stuck with them, Abby. But sometimes that's the breaks. There are guests like that. You have to accept that it's part of this business. And then you have to learn how to handle them."

"How?" Abby asked. "I mean besides spitting in their coffee and short-sheeting their beds?"

Jackie blinked. "You did that?"

"Not really. I just imagined doing it."

"Oh, well . . . good."

"So, tell me, how *do* you deal with a cantankerous guest?"

"To start with, you remain a professional. You do everything for them that you do for any other guest. But you also avoid them as much as possible. Most importantly you don't let them get to you." She pointed her finger at Abby. "Because if you let them get to you, they've won the battle."

Abby knew that Glen Hawley had already gotten to her.

"And then" — Jackie smirked — "you put them on your bad list, and you never rent a room to them again."

"That's for sure." Abby lowered her voice. "There's one more thing I plan to do as well."

"What?"

"I'm going to get the word out about this guy before he gets hired as city manager."

"He's applying for city manager?" Jackie looked shocked. "Oh, my!"

"Marsha Lake just happens to be —"

"A very good friend," Jackie finished for her.

"As well as head of the finance department."

"You're going to tell her?"

"I am."

"Good for you, Abby. The last thing this town needs is a lousy city manager. We were barely rebounding from the economy when Cathy Gardener passed on. I sure do miss her."

"Out of respect for her memory and love of this town, I feel it's my duty to speak up."

"You go, girl." Jackie raised a defiant fist.

"Are you sure that your inn is really full?" Jackie just grinned. "It is now."

From her car, Abby called Marsha and

caught her on her lunch break. Abby asked if they could meet for coffee this afternoon.

"*This* afternoon?" Marsha sounded unsure. "We're kind of busy doing interviews for the manager job this afternoon."

"Yes, that's exactly why I want to talk to you."

"Really?"

"I have some insider information about one of your candidates," Abby said carefully. "I wanted to share it with someone and thought of you."

"Interesting."

"So how about meeting me for coffee?"

"Coffee this afternoon is impossible," Marsha told her. "But if you can meet me in my office, we don't head back into the interviews until one fifteen."

Abby looked at her watch. "I'm on my way."

As she drove the few blocks to city hall, Abby tried to formulate her thoughts. She planned to take Janie's advice. But she also planned to do what she could to paint a realistic image of who Glen Hawley truly was.

On her way into the building, Abby wished she'd dressed a bit more professionally today. Why hadn't she thought of that?

"Hey," Paul said as he emerged from the

building department, "what are you doing here?"

Abby felt a wave of guilt. "Just having coffee with Marsha Lake," she said quickly. "How about you?"

He held up some papers. "Just getting the building permit for Caroline's house." He frowned at her. "Why are you having coffee with Marsha?" he asked suspiciously.

"Because we need to catch up." She glanced at her watch. "I need to hurry." She took off, but she could feel him watching her and knew he was jumping to conclusions. She'd have to deal with him later.

"Hey, Abby." Marsha smiled as Abby came into her office. "Take a seat."

"Thanks for seeing me on such short notice." Abby started to go into a lengthy explanation about her inn and how Jackie had referred guests to her.

"Yes, congratulations, Abby. I was pleased to see we have another B and B in town. I'm surprised you didn't have some kind of official grand opening, you know, to show the place off to the public. It's such a lovely old home."

"Maybe I'll do that." Abby made a mental note to remember this idea.

"So what's your big insider tip?" Marsha leaned forward with a curious expression.

"Glen Hawley is a guest at my inn and —"

"Oh, isn't he great? And so qualified, too. I think he's a shoo-in."

"Oh." Abby frowned. Apparently she was too late.

"And that's a problem?"

"Well" — Abby thought about her words — "I'm sure that Glen Hawley is putting his best foot forward for the interview process, but I've been around him a lot these past few days — you know, up close and personal — and I have to say that I'd be hugely disappointed if he gets hired to replace Cathy."

"Why?"

So Abby carefully explained how rude he'd been, trying to avoid words like narcissistic and jerk, which wasn't easy. "He just doesn't seem like a Clifden sort of guy."

"Really?" Marsha looked slightly skeptical.

"I wouldn't make this up," Abby said. "In fact, it's not easy coming in here and saying this, Marsha. But I really think our city would be better served with someone else — someone a bit nicer, if you know what I mean. I hate to imagine how someone like Glen would run roughshod over everyone once he got in here. Really, his people skills, when his guard is down, are atrocious. You could even ask Caroline; she's renting a room from me, and I'm afraid if he was around much longer, she'd move out. Or you could talk to Janie, although Janie, being an attorney, might not be willing to speak out."

"So what exactly am I supposed to do with this information?"

"I don't know." Abby shrugged. "I figured you could put it to use."

"Seriously, Abby, what am I supposed to say? That Glen Hawley doesn't pick up his socks? That he steals complimentary toiletries? Or complains about breakfast? Maybe I should tell the committee that he doesn't like that your inn because it has no ocean view, which is true — it doesn't have a view."

"I know that. But most people wouldn't be so ill mannered about it."

Marsha nodded.

"Have his references been checked?"

"Of course."

"Maybe someone should probe a little deeper. Maybe there are folks in his town who'd be happy to spill the beans on Glen Hawley."

"Maybe, but I'm not sure how we'd go about finding them."

Abby held up her hands. "Well, all I can

say is I tried, Marsha. Don't come crying to me if you hire him and discover on down the line that he's a total jerk." Abby regretted this last bit, but there it was.

Marsha smiled. "I'll keep what you said in mind. And if you come across something really useful, let me know. Otherwise, I think my hands are fairly tied." She looked at the clock on the wall. "It's time to resume our interviews."

Abby thanked her for listening, then left, but as she was going out, she ran into Glen Hawley. "Oh, hello," he told her with a surprised expression.

"Hello, Mr. Hawley," she said crisply.

He looked curiously at her, taking in her casual jeans and sweatshirt, as if trying to figure out why she'd be here at city hall.

"Just visiting with a friend," she told him with a fixed smile. "Have a good day."

"You, too," he called as she continued on her way.

Back at the inn she found Mrs. Hawley comfortably settled in the living room with a thick paperback. Abby went into the room, taking her time to check the water level of the fresh flowers and straightening a stack of magazines. "I saw your husband at city hall," she said casually. "He must be doing more interviews this afternoon."

Mrs. Hawley smiled and nodded. "Yes. For a small town, they certainly do a lot of interviews."

Abby knew that the Hawleys came from a town about ten times as large as Clifden. "I'm surprised that you and your husband want to relocate to such a small town," she said as she fluffed a pillow.

"It'll be something to get used to," she admitted. "But so far I think it's a charming town."

"I'd think there might be a reduction in salary, too," Abby pointed out.

"I don't really know. Glen handles all that." Mrs. Hawley smiled. "I just try to stay within the means of my household budget, and everyone is happy."

"It must be hard to leave your friends behind." Abby hoped her fishing wasn't too obvious.

"Not as hard as you'd think."

"I'm such a hometown girl. I'd hate to leave my friends and my house and everything." Abby shook her head. "You're a brave woman."

"Oh, you get used to it after a while."

"So you've made moves like this before?" Abby tried to appear impressed. "I'll bet you get really good at it then. I've only moved once, and it was incredibly difficult."

Mrs. Hawley talked about some of her packing techniques and tricks. "It's a great way to keep from accumulating too much junk. I do a thorough clean-out every time we move."

Abby asked about other towns that they'd lived in, reacting as if their lives were truly remarkable. As Mrs. Hawley listed off places, Abby noted them in her head. Then she looked at her watch. "Oh, dear, I nearly forgot that I have an appointment," she said. "Please excuse me." Then she hurried out to her car and, pulling out a notebook, wrote down the names of the cities that she could remember.

Once she got home, she did something that she knew could get her into trouble, but she just couldn't help herself. She started calling up the various towns, saying in a roundabout way that she worked for the city of Clifden (and her rationale was that she *was* working for the city, just not getting paid for it, because she had the best interests of Clifden in mind). As she made inquiries about Glen Hawley's previous employment history, she was pleased to find a few opinionated people who were willing to talk. Taking furious notes, she later condensed these into an interesting and informative document that she prepared to email to Marsha — but then she stopped herself. An email could come back to haunt her.

Instead, she reminded herself of Janie's counsel and simply made an anonymous copy and dropped it by Marsha's office. What Marsha did with this information was up to her. At least Abby had tried. Maybe, if this whole inn-keeping idea didn't work out, Abby would become a detective. She'd heard about some female private eyes who were quite successful. Remembering how she and Marley had cracked the case against Caroline, helping to prove their friend's innocence in regard to the house fire, Abby thought perhaps she was getting rather good at this.

CHAPTER 10
MARLEY

As hard as she tried, even getting up extra early to make more time in her day, Marley felt challenged to get back into her painting. By the end of the week, she had to finally acknowledge that her most creative time of the day had always been in the afternoon. It was just the way she was wired. Until this situation with Hunter was resolved, which seemed unlikely to happen soon, it would be hard to reclaim those hours. The only news from Jasmine came to Jack in the form of a brief email, as if taking off was completely acceptable and expected.

"It's like she's blamed me for this," Jack had told Marley on Wednesday night as they caught up in another one of their afterhours phone conversations. "Like if I'd been a crummy excuse of a grandpa, she never would've done this."

"Well, that's just ridiculous."

"I emailed her back saying pretty much

the same thing. Although I don't expect to hear from her. Not for a while anyway."

"Did she say where she went?"

"Just that it was sunny there, and that it was what she needed. Jasmine has always claimed to have seasonal affective disorder."

"SAD." Marley sighed. "I can relate."

"Really?" Jack sounded slightly alarmed. "You suffer from that too?"

"I've never really been officially diagnosed or treated, but living in the Seattle area for as long as I did, I think the gray skies took their toll on me."

"I'm afraid it won't be much better here."

"It is, a little." She paused, weighing her words. "Did I tell you that Thomas Hatfield assumed that I'd spent some time in the tropics? Like Tahiti or the Caribbean?"

"No, really?"

"You know, because of my paintings."

"Oh, yes. They do have that warm tropical feel. One would assume the artist had spent some time there. But you haven't, have you?"

"No, I've never lived in any of those places." She sighed. "Although I've often dreamed of it."

"You've dreamed of it?"

"Oh, sure, haven't you? I mean who doesn't dream of a sunny beach, palm trees swaying in the breeze, a warm ocean to swim in . . . doesn't it sound lovely?"

"I guess."

Somehow — maybe it was the serious tone of his voice — she thought he hadn't really felt like that. And that made her wonder. Maybe she didn't know Jack as well as she'd assumed. Or maybe Jack was just feeling stressed.

He had seemed thrilled, initially, when she'd told him about selling all her paintings. But then, after she'd mentioned what Thomas had said about marking the prices up, Jack, like her, had seemed saddened. She wasn't sure if he felt guilty for her sake, or regretful that he had missed out on a bigger profit margin. Oh, she would never say as much to him. The poor man already had his hands full with his runaway daughter and the responsibility of Hunter. Still, Marley couldn't help but feel a little out of sorts.

"You have no idea how excited I'm getting about our cruise," Marley told Abby on Friday when they met for coffee. "I even plan to do some painting on board if I can find the time. Anyway, thank you so much for inviting me. It really gives me something to look forward to."

"Me, too." Abby looked down at her mocha. "Although I've skipped out on the fitness club this week, so it's doubtful that I'll be getting into a swimsuit anytime soon."

"You and me both," Marley told her. "But we can sport around in shorts and tank tops. Let Janie and Caroline squeeze into their string bikinis if they like. I'm willing to accept that those days are long gone for me."

"Can you believe the kinds of things we used to wear?" Abby chuckled. "It was downright scandalous."

"It sure would be now — at least with my fifty-five-year-old body. Actually it'd be worse than scandalous. It would be disgusting."

"Sometimes I envy my mother's generation," Abby said sadly.

"Why?"

"They were allowed to grow old gracefully."

"And we're not?"

Abby shrugged. "Well, in some ways, we are. But there's also this expectation that we should look younger and stay fitter like Caroline and Janie. You should see them at the fitness club. They fit right in with the thirtysomething crowd."

"Well, that's because they've stayed fit.

You can't really fault them for that."

"I don't fault them." Abby frowned. "I guess I'm just jealous."

"I do understand wanting to grow old gracefully, though. I don't want to give in to things like plastic surgery and all the rest of the Hollywood nonsense. Even though I can see more gray hair every day, I think I'd like to go with nature."

"Some people look good in gray hair." Abby touched her own hair. "I still can't decide which way to go. Caroline and Janie keep encouraging me to hide the gray, and I have to admit it was fun getting the highlights. My girls liked it too."

"You have to do what makes *you* happy, Abby. I'm not saying we should all just let ourselves go, that everyone over fifty should be gray and wrinkled. I'm saying that if we want to be gray and wrinkled and saggy and baggy and frumpy, then we shouldn't let anyone guilt us out of it."

"You're lucky," Abby told her. "Jack's so much older than you that you'll always be young in comparison. Sometimes people assume that I'm older than Paul, which Paul thinks is hilarious, and then I want to smack him."

"I'm afraid having Hunter is going to prematurely age both Jack and me."

"Or else keep you young," Abby suggested.

"How so?" Marley was curious.

"Well, I always feel younger when I'm with my granddaughter. A tired sort of younger maybe, but somehow seeing Lucy enjoy making cookies or sandcastles or seeing *Mary Poppins* for the first time . . . it's like a new lease on life for me." Abby sighed. "They're coming for Christmas too. I'm going to let all my kids stay in the inn. It's going to be wonderful."

"Sounds delightful. Speaking of the inn, have your cantankerous guests checked out yet?"

Abby's eyes got wide. "They left yesterday. I cannot believe what a relief it was to see the last of them. Oh, Mrs. Hawley was fine, but that Glen . . . he's something else."

"Hopefully he won't get hired by the city."

Abby gave her a sly grin. "I think he's out of the running."

"Seriously?" Marley studied her. "Why's that?"

"Can I trust you?"

Marley chuckled. "I'm a Linda."

"Yes." Abby nodded. "Well, the truth is I did a little investigating of Mr. Hawley."

"No! You did?"

"Uh-huh, and I turned up some rather

143

interesting things. Things I doubted were included in his résumé or mentioned in his interviews. Things I thought the city needed to be aware of, so I made it aware."

"You didn't."

Abby chuckled. "I most certainly did."

"What did you uncover about him?"

"Mostly there seem to be a lot of unanswered questions, generally related to city finances and private contracts. But most interesting is how Glen almost always gets terminated, and always before his contract expires. Then he gets the city to give him a severance package, as well as sign a document with Glen's lawyer not to slander his reputation, so legally they can't say anything."

"You're kidding."

"No. Can you believe it? It was so fun finding this all out. It reminded me of the time we did our detective work for Caroline. Remember how fun that was?"

"It was kind of exciting."

"I decided that if running a B and B doesn't get better, I might start my own detective agency. Maybe you'd like to work for me."

Marley laughed loudly. "Okay, if I can't get myself back into the swing of painting, I might just take you up on that."

Abby waved her hand. "Oh, don't be silly. Your painting is going too well to quit now. Honestly, if I had talent like yours, they wouldn't be able to keep me away from my easel."

Marley explained how Hunter's needs were carving into her painting time. "I feel so selfish for even saying that. I mean, poor Hunter has been dumped by her mother, and I'm moping around because I can't seem to get into my creative groove."

"What would get you into your creative groove?"

Marley considered this. "Probably having a whole day without interruptions. Actually, I could use several days like that."

"You have Hunter after school every day?"

"Yes. I keep telling myself that it's not that big of a deal, but it's like I use up all my creative energy coming up with activities for her. Of course, she loves that. And she needs it." Marley sighed. "It's really a small price to pay for a child's happiness."

"Caroline mentioned wanting to have Hunter come visit us at the inn," Abby said. "At the time I was a little distracted with my, uh, guests. But I think it would be delightful to have a child around there. Why don't you let Caroline and me give you a hand with Hunter?"

"Really?" Marley wanted to hug Abby.

"Sure. We can make Christmas cookies to put in the freezer and do some small sewing projects, or I can teach her to crochet. It'll be great fun."

"That would be fantastic." Marley paused to think. "How about if we start next week? I already promised Hunter I'd take her to the aquarium tomorrow. And I'd actually like to see it too. Then she and I will probably help Jack out at the gallery on Sunday. Also, there's a Christmas craft fair in town."

"So Monday then?" Abby asked.

"Monday would be perfect. If you're sure you don't mind. Hunter is actually really easy and quite mature for seven. Still, it's a responsibility."

"I promise you, we'll take good care of her."

"Of course! I know you will."

"Either Caroline or I will pick her up after school. Or else she could ride the school bus. It still goes right down the street."

As they discussed the details, Marley felt a mixture of relief and regret. On one hand, she knew she had to get back to work. On the other hand, it would be hard to give up being with Hunter. Even for just a few days. It troubled Marley to think she'd gotten so attached to the little girl. It was as if they were really becoming family. More than once, Hunter had asked if Marley was ever going to marry her grandpa. She'd even suggested that Marley could move in with them.

"Grandpa's house is bigger than yours," she'd pointed out, and rightly so. "Why don't you just live there with us? Then you wouldn't have to drive so much."

Marley had laughed, then attempted to explain that she wouldn't move in with Jack unless they got married.

"But aren't you Grandpa's girlfriend?" Hunter persisted.

"Well, yes. I suppose."

"So why don't you just live with him?"

Marley tried to think of an explanation suitable for a seven-year-old.

"My mom's boyfriends lived with us before," Hunter continued. "And they weren't married."

"Well, I would prefer to be married."

"Then why don't you and Grandpa just get married?" Hunter had pressed.

To that, Marley had simply changed the subject by mentioning how much she wanted to see the aquarium. Naturally, Hunter had gone for the bait, and they were instantly talking about stingrays and dolphins and sharks. But even after Marley had dropped Hunter off, the young girl's words continued to echo through Marley's head.

Why don't you and Grandpa just get married? As much as Marley cared about Jack, perhaps even loved him, she wondered how she'd actually respond if he popped the question. Mostly she hoped that he wouldn't. Not yet anyway. She knew she wasn't ready to go there, and she hated the idea of having to turn him down. Perhaps he even felt the same way. He was a sensible man. He probably knew that, at least for the time being, they should not consider it. Really, they both had enough on their hands, trying to figure out how to run their lives as well as to care for Hunter. They just needed more time.

Chapter 11
Janie

Janie was surprised at the progress that had been made in Caroline's house. In less than two weeks, the whole place had been gutted, the rough plumbing and electrical was nearly finished, and the drywall was starting to go up.

"This is looking fantastic," she told Caroline on Saturday. "At this rate you might be in here by Christmas."

"Don't count on it," Paul said as he came in from where he'd been checking on something in the master bathroom. "It's the finish work that slows everything down."

"Well, anyway, it looks great. And I think it's nice you're helping Caroline out." Janie made a face at him. "Even if you did refuse to help me."

He just laughed. "Hey, it's all about timing. I was too busy when you needed help. But December is slow. Slower than usual even."

"Lucky for you," Janie told Caroline.

Caroline just made what seemed a stiff smile. "Uh-huh."

"Okay, ladies." Paul nodded briskly. "I'll let you get back to your sewing circle."

Janie laughed. "Yeah, right."

"See you later, Paul," Caroline called out as he left. She went over to the door, as if to be sure it was closed, then turned to Janie. "I have a problem," she said in a serious tone.

"What?"

"Paul."

Janie blinked. "What do you mean?" Had Paul put the move on Caroline? In a way, it wouldn't surprise Janie. Paul had always been a bit of a flirt. And yet it would be so incredibly low. Surely Paul wouldn't go after one of his wife's very best friends. Really, that would be almost unforgivable.

"I mean I walked in here yesterday, and Paul and Bonnie were standing right over there in the kitchen and . . ." Caroline held up her hands in a frustrated gesture.

"You mean they were *together* — in a compromising position?" Janie waited.

"No, not exactly. Not like that. But they were standing *very close* together. You know, the kind of close that gets your attention . . . too intimate for just business associates.

150

And then when they realized I was in the house, they stepped apart real quick. You know, like they felt guilty."

"Oh." Janie shook her head. "Oh dear."

"Yeah."

"Are you sure that is was . . ." Janie's voice trailed off. "Of course you're sure."

"I wish I was wrong, Janie. I really do. But I just don't think so."

"So now what?"

"I don't know." Caroline looked close to tears. "I feel like this is all my fault, Janie. Why did I hire Paul and Bonnie? I should've known better. I am the worst friend in the world. Abby should hate me." Caroline was crying.

"It is not your fault," Janie told her.

"But I hired Bonnie behind Abby's back."

"Because Paul insisted you hire her."

Caroline sniffed. "Yeah. That's true. Even so, Abby doesn't deserve this."

"Don't blame yourself for Paul's stupidity." Janie opened her purse, pulled out a tissue pack, and handed it to Caroline.

"Unless I'm wrong." Caroline blew her nose. "Maybe I saw something that really wasn't there. And if I looked at them, you know, in that way — like they were guilty — maybe they acted that way. Do you think?"

"I don't know what to think. But I do

know this is not your fault, Caroline. Paul and Bonnie are adults who make their own choices. They work together a lot. Everyone in town knows this. Abby knows this."

"Does she?" Caroline cocked her head to one side.

"I don't know. I guess I assume she knows it."

"Anyway." Caroline let out a loud sigh. "What do I do now?"

Janie pressed her lips together, thinking. "I'm not sure. But maybe you do nothing."

"Nothing?"

"Well, what can you really do? Do you want to fire them in the middle of your remodel? If you cancel their contracts for personal reasons, you could be held responsible for paying them anyway. Can you afford that?"

Caroline shook her head.

"And what good does that do Abby?"

She shrugged.

"It's not like you caught them actually doing something. I mean if they'd been embracing or kissing, I think you could make a case of it. I'd even help you with it. But if they were only standing too close — how do we define *too close*? I mean, some people have closer boundaries than others. As I recall, Bonnie is one of those people whose comfort zone is a lot more intimate than mine."

"That's true." Caroline nodded. "She does get close when she's intense about something."

"So it's possible that she'd done that to Paul," Janie reasoned. "And maybe he was uncomfortable too, and that's why he backed up."

"Do you think?" Caroline looked hopeful.

Janie shrugged. "I think it's all we have to go on."

"Okay." Caroline blew her nose again. "That's what I'm going to tell myself."

"If you walk in on something that's — well, more obviously wrong — then we'll confront Paul. Together."

"Really?" Caroline smiled. "You'd do that for me?"

"Of course I would."

Caroline came over and hugged Janie. "You are such a good friend! Thanks."

As Janie drove over to Victor's, where he was fixing her dinner, she wondered if that was true. Was she really such a good friend? To Abby?

CHAPTER 12
ABBY

She couldn't believe that Paul had forgotten their counseling appointment — again! He'd missed it last week due to a double booking with his cardiologist. Although irritating, it was understandable, especially since Abby had decided to put aside her codependence some time ago, meaning she'd implored Paul to manage his own life, schedule his own medical appointments, and oversee his own fitness program. The fact that he overlooked some things to see to his health was entirely forgivable. In fact, it was to be expected. After all, he was a man! But two weeks in a row was just too much.

Embarrassed to be at the counseling center alone, she paced impatiently in the lobby, waiting for him to answer his cell phone. Adding insult to injury, her call went to voice mail. Instead of leaving him a message like a sane wife would do, Abby hung up. "Would you like to reschedule?" the receptionist asked Abby.

"No," Abby retorted. "I will let Paul take care of that."

The receptionist smiled. "Good idea."

"If we don't make it back here before the holidays, merry Christmas." Abby forced a smile, then left. She didn't want to be angry — she knew it would only add to her suffering. Really, it was Paul who should feel bad. But she just couldn't help herself. Didn't he care about her? Or their marriage? How hard was it to remember a silly appointment? If he needed to meet with a plumber or a building inspector or the kid who mowed their lawn on Saturdays, Paul wouldn't blow it off. No, she was the only one who got the short end of the stick, and that was unfair.

Instead of going home, Abby stopped by the inn. She knew that Caroline was watching Hunter today. Abby had taken care of the child yesterday and actually enjoyed herself. The prospects of hanging with Caroline and Hunter seemed preferable to going home to her big lonely beach house and stewing over her husband's selfish neglect.

"I thought you had counseling today," Caroline said as Abby joined them in the dining room, where it looked like Hunter was doing homework.

"We did." Abby set her purse down. "But *someone* forgot."

"Oh."

"Hi, Abby." Hunter smiled up at her. "I'm doing homework."

"I see that," Abby observed. "But what I want to know is how did Auntie Caroline get you to do it?" Abby had tried to talk Hunter into doing her homework yesterday, but Hunter had weaseled her way out of it. Or maybe Abby had simply given in too easily. Really, making cookies seemed a lot more fun than doing second-grade arithmetic.

Bribe, Caroline mouthed to Abby. "I told Hunter we'd take Chuck for a walk on the beach if she finished her homework first."

"Well, don't let me disturb you." Abby went into the kitchen and got herself a glass of water.

Caroline followed her in there. "So are you pretty mad?"

Abby just nodded, took another swig of water, then plunked the glass down into sink so hard she was surprised it didn't break. "Two weeks in a row."

"Maybe you should've reminded him."

"Or maybe he should take some responsibility and remind himself." Abby scowled. "Good grief, he has a five-hundred-dollar watch that's got all these alarms and things — and an iPhone as well. He's got the technology to deal with this. The problem is he just doesn't want to."

"I'm sorry, sweetie." Caroline put a hand on her shoulder. "You need to talk to Paul about this. He needs to hear how you're feeling."

Abby firmly shook her head. "No. If Paul wants to know how I'm feeling, he needs to talk to me."

Caroline just stood there with a frustrated expression as if she had no more answers.

"Aren't you glad you're not married?" Abby challenged her.

Caroline seemed to consider this. "Sometimes I am. Sometimes not so much."

"That's only because you idealize marriage, Caroline. If you knew what it was really like — I mean years and years of being married to the same man. If you lived day in day out with a man who acts like it's your only job to pick up after him and fix him dinner, then you'd be singing a different song."

"Maybe so . . . and my experience with marriage was pretty brief, not to mention unconventional."

"I've got a mind to just start staying here at the inn," Abby continued. "That'd teach him."

"What would it teach him?"

"Not to take me for granted."

"Oh." Caroline nodded. "Hey, we missed you at circuit training again yesterday. You said after your guests checked out you'd be coming back."

Abby sighed. "I decided that circuit training is not for me."

"But what about your club membership?"

"What about it?" Abby glared at Caroline.

"Well, you shouldn't waste it, Abby. Even if you don't like circuit training, there are lots of other fun ways to work out."

"Fun?" Abby rolled her eyes.

"Exercise is fun after you get used to it, Abby. Really, I promise you it is. Your body releases endorphins and you get in shape and you feel better about yourself in general."

Abby thought about this. She would love to feel better about herself. She just didn't buy that exercise was going to get her there.

"You just need to find something you like to do," Caroline encouraged.

"Like what?"

"How about the recumbent bike?"

"Huh?"

"You know, a stationary bike. You always liked biking when we were girls, Abby. Remember?"

Abby nodded. "That's true. I have a bike that I keep meaning to get out and ride. But it's a little overwhelming to imagine myself riding all the way to town and then being too tired to get back home."

"See!" Caroline exclaimed. "A recumbent bike would be perfect."

"I don't know."

"I do." Caroline was actually pushing Abby out of the kitchen. "Please, Abby, for your own good, I'm begging you to go over to the fitness center, get on a recumbent bike, and just ride it for, say, thirty minutes. And remind yourself as you're riding it that you are burning calories, and that if you do that every other day up until our Mexico cruise, you could lose — I don't know — maybe five pounds."

"Five pounds?" Abby felt hopeful.

"Maybe more. If you really set your mind to it, Abby." Caroline patted her nice flat stomach. "You don't think I could stay in shape without working out, do you?"

"I don't know." Abby shrugged. "I always just figured you had some kind of magical DNA."

Caroline laughed. But Hunter was calling,

asking for help with a problem. "Just go," Caroline urged her. "If nothing else, it's a good way to blow off steam. A good workout will help you to deal with Paul."

"Well, my gym bag is still in my car," Abby admitted.

"So *go!*" Caroline pointed at the clock. "If you leave now, you'll be early enough to beat the after-work crowd."

Abby knew she might regret this, but she decided to take Caroline's advice. Within fifteen minutes, she was seated on a stationary bike, and, after some brief instruction from a trainer, she was pedaling away. To her surprise, it was kind of fun. Not only that, but the club wasn't too crowded, and the woman two bikes down from her appeared to be in similar shape — make that out of shape.

"This is my first time doing this," Abby told the other woman.

"It's only my second week," the woman huffed. "But I think it's helping me."

"Really?" Abby smiled. "That's nice to hear. I'm Abby, by the way."

"My name is Ginger."

They made a bit of breathless small talk as they congenially continued to work out, side by side, together. And Abby started to feel a tiny bit hopeful. Perhaps she'd been too hasty to give up on the fitness club. Maybe Caroline had been right about those endorphins. Abby could certainly use some happy vibes today.

"After the bike I do some stretches," Ginger told Abby. "Do you want to join me?"

"Sure." So after about thirty minutes, Abby followed Ginger over to a stretching area and tried to imitate her.

"The trainer said stretching is as important as working out." Then Ginger told Abby how she planned to start aqua aerobics next week. "You should come too."

"I don't know." Abby frowned. "The idea of getting in a swimsuit . . . I'm just not ready for that."

"If you saw the other old ladies in the class, you might not be so worried," Ginger told her.

Abby chuckled. "I hadn't thought of it like that. You could be right."

Then, realizing what time it was, Ginger explained she had to pick up her daughter from basketball practice. "Maybe I'll see you around here another time." Ginger waved and headed off toward the locker rooms. But Abby, feeling surprisingly strong and energized from the success of her workout, decided to stick around and see if there were any other exercise machines that would appeal to her.

She was just getting into a bit of rhythm on some kind of stationary climber machine when something caught her eye. The climbers were situated to overlook the lobby below, and if she was not mistaken, that was Paul down there. Although she had to admit that it didn't look quite like him. He had on navy sweats, and his paunch belly seemed to have shrunk — or perhaps his shoulders were wider — but on closer inspection she saw that it really was her husband . . . and he looked pretty good.

She was about to call out and wave to Paul when she noticed a petite blond woman walking directly to him. The woman had on a pink warm-up jacket and very short white shorts. And, just like that, the two were engaged in what looked like an animated and pleasant conversation.

Abby struggled to dismount from the machine, nearly falling on her face. She fought to get her feet under her, catching her balance by grabbing hold of the balcony ledge, then leaned over to get a closer peek at what was transpiring below. Completely unaware of Abby's presence, Paul was leading the attractive blonde over to the tables by the juice bar, and the two were sitting down together. Paul even pulled out her chair!

But as they sat down, Abby got a good look at the woman's face. She could not believe it. That was none other than that conniving, husband-stealing Bonnie Box-well — going after Abby's husband right here in broad public daylight!

Abby inched her way along the edge of the balcony, moving toward the stairs and trying discreetly to watch the unfortunate tryst while determining how to handle this. What should she do? Should she storm down there and confront the pair — shake her finger at the two of them and publicly accuse them of infidelity? Or perhaps she could just silently stand there, looking wounded and betrayed, waiting for their guilty expressions or lame excuses to give them away? Or should she simply wander down there and act nonchalant? She could just casually say hello, then give them an innocent look and leave. Maybe that would give them something to think about.

While trying to decide, Abby caught a glimpse of something else — there, not far from her, stood another frumpy, dowdy middle-aged woman with frowsy hair and baggy paint-splattered sweats and really poor posture. Another poor fitness-club

163

misfit. But then Abby realized she was actually seeing her own reflection in one of the floor-to-ceiling mirrors so prevalent in this club. She stared at herself with real disgust. Was that *truly* what she looked like? Or was this just a case of bad lighting — a bad hair day and no makeup?

She turned and peered back down at where Paul and Bonnie chatted amicably together, still oblivious to Abby's presence, and she experienced a fresh wave of horror. Of course, it all made sense. Why wouldn't Paul prefer someone like Bonnie to his old worn-out wife? Not only did Bonnie look good, she was looking at Paul like she thought he looked good too. And she was listening to him as if he were the most entertaining thing since color TV. No wonder Paul had blown his counseling appointment with Abby today. He had simply wanted to spend time with Bonnie.

Her eyes blurred with tears as, gripping the railing for support, she hurried down the stairs and around the corner, rushing directly to the women's locker room, where, instead of showering, she simply gathered her things and, using a side exit, scurried away, got into her car, and drove — not home — but back to the inn. Her old home, which would now become her new home.

CHAPTER 13
CAROLINE

No matter how hard she tried, Caroline could not convince Abby to speak to Paul. Abby was ignoring his calls on her cell, while Caroline got to deal with the landline. Caroline didn't want to say this to Abby, but the whole thing was starting to feel a whole lot like high school.

"Tell Paul to stay away from here, too," Abby told Caroline after the second time she came up to the master suite, begging Abby to at least talk to her frustrated husband. "I do not want to be within a mile of that evil man!"

"He's not evil, Abby." Caroline sat down on the edge of the king-sized bed where Abby had appeared to have taken root. "You two have too much history to throw it all away like this."

"I'm done with him," Abby declared. "I'm finished, Caroline. And I mean it this time."

"Oh Abby." Caroline sighed. "That's just

your hurt talking."

"Maybe so. But this time I'm listening."

So Caroline returned to the landline and attempted, again, to explain what was troubling Abby.

"It's like I already told you. Bonnie and I were just talking business," Paul insisted. "That's all it was. I swear!"

"Maybe so, but Abby doesn't believe it."

"Why? Why won't she believe me?"

"It would've helped if you'd made the counseling appoint—"

"I already told you I had the wrong day down. Abby can look at my Day-Timer in my office if she doesn't believe me. The appointments used to be on Thursday, and it caught me off guard to have it on —"

"I know, Paul. You already told me that."

"Well, it's just so frustrating. I don't understand my wife."

"Her feelings are hurt, Paul. Can't you get that? She sees you having your little tête-à-tête, and it looks bad. You even admitted that yourself."

"Yes, but I explained that it was innocent. *Bonnie is a business associate.* It's perfectly normal to have an impromptu meeting with a business associate at the fitness club."

"You're talking to the wrong woman."

"I know." He let out an exasperated sigh.

"But the right woman won't listen."

"Because she's hurting right now. Can't you understand that?"

"Not really. Abby *knows* that I love her."

"Really? You honestly believe that? She knows you love her?"

"Of course. I tell her that all the time."

"You tell her that?" Caroline was skeptical.

"Well, not always in words. But I show it to her every day. I built her this great house, and I work —"

"You built Abby that house, Paul? Really? That's not the way I heard it."

"Okay. Fine. I wanted the house too. But I've been with Abby all these years. If I didn't love her, why would I still be with her?"

"Wow, those are some romantic words. Just what a girl wants to hear."

"Right. I didn't mean it like that."

"I think your heart's right," Caroline said carefully. But the truth was, she wasn't positive about this. "But you really need to work on your delivery."

"So what do I do?"

"I'm not sure. This is kind of new territory to me."

"But you're her friend. Can't you talk to

her and find out what she expects me to do?"

"I'm trying."

"Just tell her I'm sorry, okay?" His voice softened. "Tell her I want to talk to her."

"I'll do that, Paul. In the meantime, can I give you a bit of advice?"

"Sure. What?"

"Well, there are women out there — I'm not saying Bonnie is one of them; in fact, I like Bonnie and she's been great to work with — but there are women out there without boundaries when it comes to other women's husbands. Do you understand what I mean?"

"Sure. Abby and I have talked about this. We've been down this Bonnie road before. And I've assured Abby over and over that Bonnie and I are nothing more than business friends. That's it."

"Well, Abby isn't as sure as you think."

"Obviously."

"I've seen Bonnie look at you, Paul. And Abby saw it today. As your friend, I'm warning you, Paul. Bonnie might think that you are up for grabs."

He laughed.

"Don't laugh, Paul. I'm being serious. Some women have no respect for the bonds of marriage. They wouldn't think twice about snatching up a good man."

He chuckled. "So you think I'm a good man?"

Caroline considered this. "I'd like to think so, Paul. Why don't you prove it to all of us by winning your wife back?"

"Fine. Maybe I'll just do that."

"Great. I hope you do."

"You're a good friend," he said in a more gentle tone. "To Abby and to me. Thanks, Caroline."

"You're welcome. And you take care, Paul."

She felt hopeful as she hung up the phone. Maybe Paul really wasn't the dirtbag that Abby claimed he was. The question now was how to convince Abby.

By Friday afternoon, Caroline felt desperate. Abby seemed to be slipping into a real depression. Still refusing to speak to Paul, she was barricaded in the master suite, where she spent most of her time either crying or sleeping. Even more troubling, for three days Abby had refused to eat. Finally, Caroline couldn't take it anymore. For that reason, she called an emergency meeting of the Lindas on Friday at five. Janie and Marley already knew what was going on and, in their own ways, had tried to comfort

Abby. But all of them felt frustrated — they were not getting through.

"She needs help," Caroline told them as they gathered downstairs. "But I'm just not sure what kind of help."

"She's so down on herself," Marley said. "As much as she says she hates Paul, I think she hates herself just as much."

"But why?" Janie asked.

"So many reasons," Caroline explained. "She feels like a failure. Like she's failed as a wife. And she's certain her B and B is going to fail too. Did you guys hear about what happened with Glen Hawley, the grumpy guest who was applying for the city manager job?"

"You mean the guy Abby exposed for who he really was?" Marley added.

"I told her to be careful about that," Janie said.

"She *was* careful," Marley explained. "She sent an anonymous letter to city hall. She did the city a favor."

"So what happened?" Janie asked.

"Hawley must've found out that it was Abby."

"How is that possible?" Janie demanded.

"I'm not sure." Caroline's brow creased. "But he must've known because he wrote this nasty review on the B and B website that Abby belongs to. Posted for everyone to see. He blasted her. He even said she had bedbugs!"

"Bedbugs? That's slanderous — Abby could sue him." Janie pulled out her iPad. "Tell me the name of the website again. I need to see this."

Caroline told her, and Janie pulled it up, reading the review out loud.

"Oh, dear." Marley shook her head. "That's terrible."

"Well, I'll warn the website that they have to remove it," Janie declared. "Unfortunately Glen Hawley's name isn't attached to it, so I won't be able to do anything more than send him a warning letter."

"That's better than nothing." Caroline smiled. "It's sure great having an attorney for a friend."

Janie shrugged. "It's nice being able to help someone who really needs it. I'm just not too sure about the rest of my practice. I'm finding out that it's not exactly what I'd hoped it would be. Sometimes I wonder if I should go in a completely different direction."

"You probably just need to give it time," Caroline told her.

"But back to Abby," Janie said. "Has this Glen Hawley business really derailed her?

Because we should be able to shut that down by the end of the day."

"It's more than just that." Caroline glanced toward the stairs. "She's so buried under it all. From her perspective she's got a ruined marriage, a failed business, she hates her body, and then there's Christmas."

"Christmas?" Marley frowned.

"What's wrong with Christmas?" Janie asked. "Abby has always loved Christmas."

"That's the problem. She feels like she's ruined Christmas, too." So Caroline told them about Abby's plans to have all her kids stay at the inn. "She wanted to have a great big gathering, pulling out all the stops. You know, Abby-style. But now that she thinks her marriage is on the skids, Abby says she's calling Christmas off."

"Poor Abby." Marley shook her head.

"So?" Caroline looked hopefully at them. "What can we do to help her?"

The room got quiet. Everyone just looked at each other, but no one came up with a suggestion.

"I realize we all have our own stuff to deal with," Caroline said a bit helplessly. She looked at Marley. "You've got your hands full, trying to help with Hunter and stay on top of your paintings." She turned to Janie. "You're trying to get your law practice up

and running. And it's almost the holidays."
She held up her hands. "But I just didn't
know who else to turn to."

"What can we do?" Marley asked.

"What does Abby need?" Janie leaned
forward. "Can we make a list?"

"Sure." Eager for any suggestions, Caroline jumped up and got the little tablet by
the phone, then hurried back. "Okay, I'll
play secretary. What does Abby need?"

"She needs to talk to Paul," Janie said.

"She needs to feel good about herself
again," Marley added.

"She needs to figure out a way to get rid
of that bad B and B review." Janie frowned.
"I wish we could take legal action. Are we
sure it was written by that Hawley guy?"

"Who else?" Caroline said. "The Hawleys
are the only guests she's had."

"Unless you count Victor's ex," Janie said
quietly. "But I don't really think she'd do
that — not to Abby anyway. And Victor said
she's getting some good help."

"You know what I think Abby needs?"
Caroline said. "A slumber party! A real old-
fashioned, honest-to-goodness slumber
party — you know, like we used to have.
Sometimes right here in this very house."

Marley and Janie looked at Caroline like
she had totally lost it.

"Hear me out." Caroline held up the list. "I'm not saying this list isn't worthwhile. But the question is — how can we help Abby out of her funk *right now?*"

"With a slumber party?" Marley frowned. "Aren't we a little old for that?"

"No." Caroline stood. "We're as young as we feel. But right now Abby feels like a hundred-year-old woman. She said as much this morning."

"Okay, if we did this slumber party . . ." Janie's brow creased like she was trying to analyze this idea. "What *exactly* would we do?"

"The same things we used to do," Caroline explained. "We'd eat junk food, watch silly old movies, do each others' hair and fingernails, talk about boys." She clapped her hands. "Hey, maybe we could even talk some of the guys into coming over here and sneaking in —"

"Caroline," Marley said with a little exasperation. "Jack is a grandfather with a wooden leg. I cannot imagine him climbing up the trellis to sneak in here."

"And I doubt Victor will want to come over and toilet paper the shrubbery," Janie added.

Caroline laughed. "Yeah, I get that. I was actually thinking maybe Paul would crash."

"Seriously?" Janie frowned. "Even if Paul was willing, Abby would probably throw a lamp at his head."

"Maybe, maybe not." Caroline looked hopefully at them. "Are you girls in?"

To her relief they agreed. Instead of listing the practical steps Abby might take to feel better, they began to list what they needed for a rip-roaring slumber party. "I've got all the beauty products," Caroline told them.

"I can go out and gather up the junk food," Janie offered. "Does it have to be real junk food?"

"Just make it fun food," Caroline told her. "We don't really need to make ourselves sick. Just don't make it too healthy."

"How about margaritas?" Marley suggested.

"Why not?" Caroline told her.

"And we need some good old funny movies," Janie said.

"Chick flicks," Marley stated.

"Like *Overboard*," Caroline suggested.

"Or *What Women Want*," Marley added.

"Or *The Women*," Janie said. "The original one from the thirties. I just got it on DVD."

They shot out some more ideas, including old music and old photos. Then, with a plan in place, they all hurried off on their various ways to gather the miscellaneous ingredients for a successful slumber party. Caroline knew her crazy idea could flop badly, but it could also be exactly what Abby needed. It was worth a shot.

It was about seven thirty by the time they had everything ready to go. Dressed in their goofiest pajamas with beauty products spread about like a Mary Kay party on steroids, and with sixties music playing, they set out old yearbooks and bowls of popcorn, chips, and a big selection of chocolate, as well as a fruit and veggie platter. They had a diverse selection of chick flicks ready to go. Finally, ready to take it to the next level, they invaded Abby's bedroom.

"Time to get up and *par-tee!*" Caroline announced as she flipped on the light.

"Wh-what?" Abby sat up, looking disheveled and shocked and confused.

"Slumber party!" Marley shouted. "Up and at 'em."

"Come on, Absters," Janie said. "We've got a big night ahead of us, girlfriend."

"What are you guys —" But before Abby could protest, they had her by the hands and were pulling her out of bed.

"Girls night in," Caroline said. "And we need all the girls present."

Before long they were all downstairs, eating junk food, giving each other facials and pedicures, singing old songs, playing cards, watching movies, and acting like teenagers. Although Abby seemed to have no idea that they were doing this party for her benefit, it didn't take long before she was starting to act and look a lot more like her old self.

"So what do you think about the idea of having Paul crash?" Janie whispered to Caroline while they were replenishing some of their junk food in the kitchen.

"I don't know." Caroline frowned. "We're having so much fun already. I'd hate to spoil it."

"I agree." Janie nodded.

At Janie's insistence, they watched *The Women,* the original version, and they laughed so hard that Abby had tears running down her cheeks. Caroline gave Abby a pedicure, and Marley took it a step further by painting little daisies on her toes. So their slumber party continued on into the night. And although no one really had the energy to pull a true all-nighter, they did keep it going until the wee hours of the morning, watching *Overboard* until after two, when Janie drifted off in a chair and Marley wandered off to sleep in one of the guest-room beds. After thanking Caroline, Abby excused herself to bed too. Caroline couldn't fault her friends for crashing, since she was sleepy too. Slumber parties in her fifties weren't quite the same as when she was younger and had slept in sleeping bags on the hard floor.

All in all, as Caroline got into her own bed, she thought it had been a very good night. And she hoped that, even if it wasn't exactly what Abby needed, it was enough to remind Abby that she was needed and loved by her girlfriends. Before she dozed off, Caroline decided that she would write her own review of Abby's B and B — a five-star review about the most comfortable beds, the finest linens, delicious French-milled soaps, and the best cuisine imaginable!

CHAPTER 14
MARLEY

Abby's mom had been Marley's inspiration since childhood. Independent, outspoken, and an artist, Doris had been ahead of her time. Sometimes Marley marveled at how different Abby was from her mother.

"Oh, I wasn't always like this," Doris told Marley as the two shared coffee the morning after Doris had returned from a trip to New Mexico. "I actually started out a bit like Abby — content to be a homemaker and mother. But I realized that wasn't enough, and that's when I began to paint."

"Did you ever feel guilty about painting?" Marley asked a bit tentatively.

"Guilty?" Doris's brow creased. "Whatever for?"

"Perhaps you thought you were stealing time from your family?" Marley remembered feeling like that when Ashton was young.

Doris laughed. "Well, my family — particularly Abby, since she was the baby and a bit spoiled — sometimes resented my art. But I think if they'd understood how much it improved the quality of my life, and hence the quality of theirs, they would've supported me wholeheartedly." She leaned forward to peer at Marley. "Why are you asking me about that? Surely, you have no reason to feel guilty about your own work. Especially now that you've gotten that impressive Santa Barbara gallery interested in you." She grinned. "That's just the best news, Marley."

"It was good news. But it's ironic, because it feels like I've been unable to paint much of anything since then."

"Do you think the idea of getting more recognition has intimidated you?

"I suppose that's possible."

"Sometimes I worry that I'd stop enjoying pursuing my art if someone raised the bar for me. But I like to paint for the fun of it."

"I can understand that, but I don't think that's my problem." Marley hadn't told Doris about Hunter yet. And so she decided to spill that story — the short version anyway. "I want to help out," she said finally. "Jack certainly needs it. But it's as if I've gotten stuck. Even with others helping to watch Hunter for me, it's as if I can't really create anymore. I feel distracted and edgy and worried, and as a result I'm not painting."

"That's not good." Doris got a thoughtful look. "Do you pray about it?"

"About what?"

"Your art."

Marley considered this. "I don't know. Not really, I guess. Not specifically anyway. I pray about a lot of other things though."

"That's good. But you should pray about your art, too, Marley. God gave you the gift to paint and create. It only makes sense that you should commit that gift to him. Don't you think?"

"Probably so." Marley nodded. "I'll try to do that."

"Now, tell me how Abby is doing. I haven't talked to her since I got home yesterday, but she left me a couple of odd messages this past week. And she hasn't returned my call. Is she really living at the inn?"

"Yeah, she is." Then Marley told her about how Abby saw Paul and Bonnie together at the fitness club.

"Naturally, she jumped to the obvious conclusion." Doris made a *tsk-tsk* sound.

"Naturally."

"But the obvious conclusion isn't always the right one."

"Paul claims he's innocent." Marley still wasn't convinced of this. Based on her own history, it seemed entirely plausible that Paul could be cheating on his wife. Still, she planned to keep her opinions to herself.

Doris shook her head. "Poor Abby."

"Did you know she wants to cancel Christmas?"

Doris chuckled. "Well, my daughter always did think she was the center of the universe, but to cancel Christmas? That seems a bit much."

"Well, you know how she wanted to have her girls stay at the inn and all that. Now she just wants to hide out and avoid everyone."

"Why on earth should Abby hide out?" Doris demanded. "What did she do that was so bad?"

"That's what we've been trying to tell her." Marley told Doris about the slumber party. "At first we thought that perked her up. But by Sunday she was down again."

Doris thrust her fist in the air. "This is just all wrong. I didn't raise Abby to give up so easily. And I wonder if she's forgotten that Nicole comes home from Europe this week."

"Really? I haven't heard Abby mention it."

"Well, I guess it's time for me to put on my mother hat and go over and pay that girl a little visit."

Marley smiled. "Good for you."

Doris wagged her finger at Marley. "I expect you to start praying about your painting. It's a God-given gift, and you should be taking it seriously."

"I plan on it."

Doris's countenance softened. "But I do understand you being distracted by Hunter. That must be very hard on everyone."

"At first I was impressed with how well Hunter was holding up. But the last few days, she's seemed a little depressed. Like the reality of what happened is sinking in — and that it's possible her mom isn't coming back."

Doris sighed. "That's so sad. Poor little thing."

"Jack's actually handling everything pretty well. I can tell he's stressed out, but he still manages to be a very sweet grandpa as well as run his business fairly smoothly. Fortunately Jack hired someone else to help out part-time at the gallery, and Janie is helping him to file for custody of Hunter. I suppose we're settling into something of a routine, although with having Hunter out of school, well, it's a bit of a challenge. In fact, I promised to pick her up at the gallery at eleven. So I should probably get moving."

"You do have your hands full."

Marley went over and rinsed her coffee mug, placing it in Doris's sink. "But there are worse problems, aren't there?" She looked at Doris. "I mean, what if I was still stuck in Seattle? Living alone miserably. No Lindas. No Jack. No Doris next door. And no Hunter." Marley smiled. "Really, I should be counting my blessings."

"As should we all, dear. Maybe you could convey that little message to my daughter next time you see her."

Marley hugged Doris. "Well, it's sure good to have you back home. Tell Abby that Hunter and I will probably drop by the inn to say hi this afternoon."

"If she's still at the inn." Doris reached for her jacket. "I plan on sending her home today."

Marley chuckled. "Well, if anyone can do it, I suppose you can."

"Don't be too sure. Abby never listened to me before; I hardly think she'll start listening now."

As Marley drove to town, she wondered about that. Why was it always so hard for women of all ages to listen to their mothers? As a teen, Marley rebelled against everything her mother said. And yet Marley's friends loved her mother, and her father, too. Marley's friends always thought her laid-back parents were pretty hip and cool. Marley had thought them pretentious and somewhat negligent. Of course, she changed her way of thinking later. After she'd been married with a child of her own, she grew to appreciate her own parents a bit more. Although she didn't agree with all they'd done, she knew they'd been trying, just as she tried with her own son. She made her own mistakes, like staying too long in a rotten marriage. But at least she and Ashton were still close. That was something.

Thinking about mothers and daughters simply made her think about the situation with Hunter and Jasmine again. As usual, the more she thought about it, the worse she felt. She was about to turn off the beach road and go toward town when she decided to stop. She parked in a beach-access lot, got out of the car, and walked over to look out over the ocean. The wind was picking up, and it was tempting to go back to the warmth of her car. But she felt like she needed to deal with this. She remembered what Doris had said about Marley's art — that it was a gift. But what about Hunter? She was a living being and a small child.

Wasn't she a gift too? Before Marley could commit her art to God, she knew she had to commit Hunter.

"Dear God," Marley started to pray, "I need help with this situation with Hunter. Every time I think about it I get so frustrated, so sad. I pray about it, but I don't ever feel like it changes anything." She zipped her jacket up higher, turning up her collar against the wind as her short hair whipped around.

"I know she's not mine, but I feel like I'm carrying the weight of this child. So today, here and now, I commit Hunter to you, God. You created her. You know what's best for her. I place her in your hands, God. Please, help her through this time. And please, show me what my role should be in this situation. I do love this little girl, but I realize that without you, I can't do much for her."

Then, almost like an afterthought, she committed her art to God as well. Really, painting seemed secondary to the life of a poor motherless child. She knew then that she would put her art aside indefinitely if that's what it took to help Hunter through this. And, for the first time since Jasmine had left, Marley felt a sense of peace about everything. With a much lighter heart, she drove on into town and went into the One-Legged Seagull, ready to play a stronger and more vital role.

"Hey, Marley," Jack said as she came into the gallery. "I was trying to call you, but I think your phone must be turned off."

"Oh, yeah." She nodded with realization. "I must've left it in the charger at home." She glanced around the shop. "Where's Hunter?"

"That's what I was calling about. I found someone else to watch her."

"Oh?" Marley wasn't sure how to respond. She should've been relieved, but instead she felt somewhat let down.

"Words can't express how much I appreciate how you've helped with her," Jack said kindly. "I don't know what I'd do without you."

She waved her hand. "You know I enjoy being with her."

Jack tipped his head toward the back room. "I'd like you to meet Sylvia," he told her.

"The woman you hired last week?"

"Yes, it's her first day. But she used to work in a framing shop, and she's jumped right into a project." He smiled. "I feel like I hit the jackpot."

She chuckled. "Jack's jackpot."

Soon she was meeting a tall brunette woman who appeared to be in her forties. "I just moved to town last week," Sylvia told Marley. "I feel so fortunate to have found a job so quickly." She turned to smile at Jack. "And to work with such a great guy and doing something I love."

"Sylvia's daughter Leah is babysitting Hunter," Jack explained. "It's a perfect situation."

"Leah graduated from high school in the spring," Sylvia told Marley, "and she's just not sure where or if she wants to go to college." She sighed. "I think the divorce has really rocked her world. So having a babysitting job is perfect. And Leah is great with kids. She always has been."

"Hunter was thrilled with the setup." Jack smiled happily. "Sylvia dropped Leah at my house this morning, and I'll bet you that Hunter's still in her pajamas, eating her cereal and watching cartoons." He laughed. "In other words, she's in hog heaven."

"That's great," Marley told him.

"I'm sorry I couldn't reach you," he said, "to save you the trip."

She waved her hand. "That's okay. I actually grabbed a nice little moment at the beach on my way into town. And I need to get some groceries anyway."

"Now you have no excuse not to get back to painting again." Jack patted her on the shoulder. "You have no idea how much that troubled me."

"You're an artist?" Sylvia asked with arched brows.

"I was."

"Don't let her kid you," Jack told Sylvia. "It took me a couple days to rearrange the blank wall after this big-time California dealer bought every piece she had."

"Wow." Sylvia nodded at Marley with a curious expression, almost as if she couldn't quite believe that someone like Marley could produce worthwhile art. "Well, lucky you!"

Marley wanted to point out that she may have been lucky, but her success was also the result of a lot of hard work.

"I'm just hoping Marley won't get the big head and refuse to consign her work with me anymore." He gave her a wistful look.

"Oh, Jack." Marley shook her head. "You know that won't happen."

"So go home," he told her. "Back to work."

She forced a smile. "Okay, I'll get out of your hair." She wanted to ask if he'd call her later, the way he usually did every evening to chat and catch up and exchange information about Hunter and how to best coordinate her care. Instead, she just went out and walked toward her car. As she drove to the grocery store, she felt a sad pang of emptiness inside her. She realized how much she'd looked forward to having Hunter with her today. After she'd said that beach prayer, she'd assumed that God was setting her up to play a more permanent role in Hunter's life. Now she felt like she'd been removed from it. Not only that . . . but there was something about Sylvia that nettled her. The woman seemed nice enough, maybe too nice. Maybe Marley was simply being paranoid. Jack was right — she needed to get back to work!

CHAPTER 15
ABBY

Her mother's pep talk would've been useless except for the fact that she reminded Abby that Nicole would be home from Europe in two days.

"Two days?" Abby stood and started pacing. So much to do, so little time. "I need to make a to-do list." She headed over to the inn's registration table and pulled out a tablet. *"Two days!"*

"Yes." Doris came over and placed a hand on Abby's shoulder. "And I'm sure it will come as a bit of a shock for Nicole to discover her parents are separated."

"Separated?" With the pen in hand, Abby turned and stared at her mom. "Who said we're separated?"

"Maybe not legally. But you are living apart."

"I just need a break," Abby said in a dismissive way.

"I've heard the whole story, Abby."

Abby frowned. "So what are you saying, Mom?"

"I'm saying you need to deal with your life, not run away from it."

"And that's exactly what I intend to do."

"I don't mean the peripheral parts of your life, Abby. I mean your relationship with Paul. Do you really think he's been unfaithful?"

Abby bit her lower lip. "I'm not sure. Naturally, he denies everything. But you know what they say about smoke."

"Smoke?"

"Where there's smoke . . ."

"So what are you going to do about it?"

"For now I'm going to get through Christmas. But first I'm going to have a homecoming dinner for Nicole — you'll come won't you? And I'm —"

"Are you just going to sweep everything under the rug? Pretend that everything between you and Paul is fine? Or are you going to sit down and have a rational conversation with him?"

"I don't know." Abby shook her head.

"I can tell you from experience that sweeping problems under the rug isn't the best way to go. I learned my lessons the hard way. But that was partly due to my generation. You have more choices nowa-days."

Abby had only recently learned that her father had cheated on her mom long ago. She'd been shocked at first, but in retrospect it made sense. "Seemed like you had choices back them, Mom. And you certainly kept Dad under your thumb. Was that your way of punishing him?"

"I suppose so. His infidelity changed who I was. I started speaking out more, pursued my own interests, including my art. Those were good changes, but looking back, I wish I'd done things differently."

"Do you wish you'd left him?"

Her mother's expression was thoughtful. "No, I don't think so. I did love him. But I wish we'd gotten help. I think we would've enjoyed our marriage more."

"But you seemed compatible. And, until I heard the truth last fall, I always assumed you guys were happy."

"And your daughters probably think the same thing about you and Paul. I guess my question is, are you satisfied with that?"

"No, of course not."

"Then you need to be willing to work on your marriage."

Abby was about to tell her about how Paul blew off their counseling appointment, except that she knew he honestly had mixed up the dates. Besides that, she had a lot to get done. "You're right, Mom. And I am willing to work on it. That is, if Paul is. But for now I've got a whole lot to get done." She smiled at her. "Thanks for coming over to light a fire beneath me, Mom. I needed that. I have to get busy."

And that's exactly what Abby did. Kicking in the afterburners, she straightened up the inn, wanting it to be perfect for Christmas and the kids' visit. Then she went grocery shopping and headed for home. She knew she should've given Paul a call, just to let him know what was up, but there just wasn't time.

Hauling in an armload of groceries, Abby let herself into the house and then stopped in the foyer, staring out into the great room, which was not looking too great. The place was a total mess. She nearly dropped the bags, which would've resulted in broken eggs and even more mess. But she did let out a loud shriek, along with a few choice words for Paul, as she carried the bags into the kitchen. It too was a mess — a big fat mess. If Paul had been there just then, she might've picked up the greasy cast-iron frying pan — complete with several cold burnt strips of bacon — and let him have it.

Enraged, she put the groceries back in her car and drove straight back to the inn, and began putting them all away. Slamming cabinet doors and talking to herself, she was nearly done when Caroline came in.

"What's going on?" Caroline asked.

Abby quickly filled her in on Nicole's impending arrival, her decision to go home, and what she found there. "Seriously, it's like Paul did it on purpose, like he wanted to teach me a lesson for leaving him like that."

"Oh." Caroline grimaced. "I'm sorry."

"There I was, ready to make up and try again." Abby could feel the tears coming, but she was determined not to give in. She would rather be enraged than cry. "And that's the thanks I get. Paul destroyed our lovely house."

"Destroyed?" Caroline looked confused. "I thought you said it was just a mess. Do you mean he actually broke things or —"

"No, I don't think he went that far. But he's like a dog marking his territory. He wanted me to know that it's his house and that he can turn it into a filthy disgusting dump if he wants to."

"Did Paul *know* you were coming home today?"

"No. But that's no excuse."

"Maybe you should talk to him," Caroline suggested. "He's working at my house. Why don't you go over and — ?"

"No way!" Abby shook her head in anger. "If I saw Paul today, I couldn't be responsible for what I might say or do. I could end up in jail, asking Janie to defend me."

"Right." Caroline looked uneasy. "So what about Nicole? You said she'll be here in two days?"

"Yes." Abby sighed. "I guess she'll just have to hear the truth. They all will."

"And the truth is what?"

"That Paul and I are through."

Caroline's eyes got big. "Are you sure about that, Abby? I can understand that you're upset. You have a right to be. But it seems a little unfair not to at least talk to Paul. I could be biased — I mean since he's working on my house right now — but he's been pretty busy lately. And he's been stressed over having you gone and —"

"He talks to you about that?"

"Not exactly. But I can tell. And I think he's sorry —"

Sorry? Abby shook her head. "You should've seen my house, Caroline. That was not the way to convey an apology."

"But Paul's never been good at that sort of thing. You know that, Abby. He's always been used to you taking care of everything in the home. Maybe if he'd known you were coming home, he would've cleaned —"

"He *wanted* me to see that mess!" Abby shoved a carton of orange juice into the fridge, then slammed the door hard. She turned and shook her fist at Caroline. "Paul is sending me a message loud and clear. He doesn't respect me or our marriage. He never has, he never will. I'm done trying to hold everything together. I'm finished with his games, and I'm sick of picking up after him." She looked around her old-fashioned kitchen, not nearly as tricked out as the one she was leaving behind, but at least this one wasn't trashed — and it was hers. "I'm just thankful I have this place. Even if it never makes it as an inn, I will do everything I can to hang on to it. Maybe I'll get Janie to sue Paul for alimony. That'd help."

Caroline nodded, but she seemed uncomfortable, like she was trying to think of something encouraging to say but couldn't. Really, there was nothing Caroline could possibly say to change how Abby felt. She was finished with Paul, and that was that.

After Caroline left, Abby decided to do some baking. Cooking and food had always soothed her in times of stress — probably one of the main reasons she was packing on these extra pounds. With Christmas around the corner, it would be nice to have some cookies and specialty breads tucked away in the freezer. Plus, she could make some preparations for meals, too. Her revised plan was to remain at the inn. Nicole could have her old room, and then when the other girls and family members got here for Christmas, they would keep all the festivities here. She would put up a tree, and she'd sneak over and get the gifts she'd purchased last summer and bring them back here.

Paul could have his trashed house all to himself. Maybe he'd like to have the kids out to see what he'd done with the place. Now that would be interesting!

She was just pouring fudge into a glass baking dish when she heard the front door open and close. Assuming it was Caroline, she called out to her. "I've got goodies in here." She licked the chocolate-coated wooden spoon. "You might want to check it out."

"Abby."

She dropped the spoon and turned to see Paul standing in the doorway to the kitchen. "What are you doing here?"

"Caroline told me —"

"She had no right to —"

"She told me because she was trying to

help, Abby."

She glared at him.

"We need to talk." He took a step toward her.

"Go ahead." She took a step back, and, folding her arms across her front, she waited. "Talk."

"I'm sorry, Abby. I know I've told you this already. But I really am sorry."

"Sorry for which part? Specifically?"

"I'm sorry you felt betrayed when I spoke with Bonnie. But, like I told you, it's business. That's all."

She gave him a skeptical look.

He shrugged. "It's your choice whether you believe me or not. But I'm not interested in Bonnie. I love you, Abby."

"And you show your love to me by trashing our house and —"

"I planned to clean it up. I just didn't have time."

"Seriously, *you* planned to clean it up?" She frowned in disbelief. "Get real, Paul."

"Okay, I was going to call someone to help."

She rolled her eyes.

"I was!"

"Well, don't bother. At least not for my sake." She bent down to pick up the fudge spoon from the floor.

"That looks good." Paul leaned forward, looking at the pan of fudge like he wanted a sample.

She quickly moved it away. "Not for you."

"You're just plain mean, Abigail."

"Mean?" She shook her finger at him. "Just because I care about your cholesterol and triglyceride levels, *I am mean.*" She took the pan of fudge and shoved it toward him. "Go ahead, eat the whole blasted thing. See if I care. And if you end up in ER again, don't expect to see me sitting by your side."

He stepped back. "So now you're trying to kill me?"

She closed her eyes, slowly counting to ten. But when she opened them, Paul was no longer in the kitchen. She heard the closing of the front door, and she knew he was gone. And although she felt guilty for being so hard on him, she also felt that Paul was getting exactly what he deserved from her. If anything, he deserved worse. He was lucky she hadn't thrown something at him.

It wasn't until the following evening that Abby realized she'd forgotten to slip back over to the beach house and gather up her stockpile of Christmas presents to bring back to the inn. Amazingly, she'd accomplished everything else on her list — well, except for sending Christmas cards, which she'd decided to skip this year, but she'd even managed to get a Christmas tree up. She wanted to get her tree decorations as well as her family's presents. She'd hoped to get them all wrapped before Nicole arrived tomorrow. Not only would this make the tree prettier, it would allow more free time for her to spend with her youngest daughter.

Abby had a sneaking suspicion she was handling this all wrong — doing everything backward. Just this morning her mother had called, reminding Abby that she needed to value people over perfection, and yet Abby wanted this distraction, bordering on obsession, because she believed the hyperactivity kept her sane. Unfortunately, it had also eaten up the entire day. She looked at the clock to see it was nearly seven. In all likelihood, Paul would probably be home.

However, Caroline hadn't come back to the inn yet, which suggested she was still at her house, and that meant Paul might be there as well. Caroline had mentioned he was working hard to get things done. So Abby decided to drive by in the hopes that she'd spy Paul's pickup and be able to make a fast dash home to pick up the gifts. As she drove to Caroline's she made a plan. She'd grab laundry baskets, go directly to the gift cupboard, fill the baskets, grab some wrapping paper, and get out of there. The tree decorations could wait. Obsessed? Perhaps, but sometimes a girl had to do what a girl had to do.

To her dismay only Caroline's car was there, but Abby decided to go inside and check on the progress just the same.

"Wow," Abby said as Caroline let her into the house. "This is really coming along."

Caroline nodded with a big smile. "I was just sweeping up. Come see how the master bedroom looks. The drywall guys are nearly done in there."

"This is going to be nice," Abby said when the tour ended. Then she asked if Caroline knew where Paul was.

Caroline shrugged. "At home?"

"That's what I was afraid of."

"Why?"

Abby explained her plan. "But I guess I'll just forget it."

"Why?" Caroline challenged her. "Are you afraid to go into your own house?"

"It doesn't feel like my house anymore."

"Maybe you just need to give him a second chance." Caroline's voice sounded a little stiff, as if she too was growing weary of Abby.

"A second chance?" Abby scowled. "Try a

hundredth chance. All I do is give that man chance after chance after chance. And what does he give me in return?"

"He built you that fabulous beach house, Abby. Most women would appreciate that."

"Guess I'm not most women." Abby sighed. "But I really wanted to pick up some things over there. You know, before Nicole gets here."

"Just go over and get them," Caroline said with impatience. "Don't be such a chicken, Abby."

"Fine," Abby snapped back at her. "I will."

Caroline grinned. "Good for you."

Abby just shook her head and left. It was easy for Caroline to goad her into this. But what if the shoe were on the other foot? However, Caroline had always had an easy way with guys. Whether that was because of her good looks or some secret formula was a mystery. But maybe Abby should ask Caroline to give her lessons someday.

The lights were on in the house, and Paul's pickup was in the driveway. Abby braced herself as she walked up to the front door. She was tempted to just let herself in — and why shouldn't she? Instead, she rang the bell.

Paul opened the door and just looked at her. She had no idea what his expression meant. Was he surprised, miffed, bored? But she heard music in the background and suddenly she wondered if he was alone.

"I came to get some of my things," she said stiffly.

"Come in." He opened the door wider. The first thing she noticed was the smell, kind of a sweet, fruity smell. Was there a woman here? Bonnie perhaps?

She peered beyond him into the great room and saw that it had been straightened — a lot! There was even a fire in the fireplace. But even more surprising than that was the fresh bouquet on the foyer table — red and white mums with some ivy tucked into one of her crystal vases. Flowers were something Abby usually did herself, but she'd never ever seen Paul do it. She wondered if he was even capable. Her suspicions increased by the second.

"What is going on here?" she demanded.

"What do you mean?"

"I mean, *who's here,* Paul?"

He held up his hands. "Just me."

"Right." She pointed at the flowers and then at the fire. "You go to this much trouble for yourself?"

He made a nervous smile. "No, not usually. But I have to admit it's kind of nice. I suppose I missed it."

She pushed past him, going into the great room, looking around for any traces or clues of Paul's mystery guest, whom she knew was here. She even peeked in his den and then the powder room.

"I swear, Abby, there's no one else here."

"But there was?" She opened the door to the spare bedroom, actually sniffing the air like a bloodhound.

"No. Just me."

She turned and studied him closely. "So tell me, why does this place look like this, Paul? And tell me the truth."

He sighed. "I was hoping you'd come home, Abby. I thought if I cleaned up some and made it nice again, you'd —"

"You did this for me?"

He gave her another nervous-looking smile. "For *us*."

She frowned. "That's the truth? You don't have some woman hiding in a closet somewhere?"

He laughed. "Why do you always go there, Abby?"

"Because . . . because . . ." She held out her hands, looking down at herself in dismay. "Because I know you'd like someone younger, prettier, thinner —"

"That is hogwash, Abby. I love *you*. I want to be with you. I'm married to you, and I like it like that. What does it take to convince you?"

She felt tears coming. Then Paul came over and took her in his arms and she just let the tears fall. He held her tight, and, stroking her hair, he told her he was sorry and, despite all her previous misgivings, she believed him.

Finally, as she was blowing her nose and checking out the condition of the rest of the house — all of which was spotless, sweet smelling, and frankly amazing — she asked him how he had managed to do all this in such a short amount of time.

He held up two fingers. "Two words."

"Huh?"

"Merry Maids."

She laughed. And then they hugged again, and eventually she called Caroline and told her not to expect her to return to the inn tonight.

"You made up with Paul?" Caroline asked hopefully.

"I think so." And although Abby knew she might be sorry about this by tomorrow or next week or even next year, tonight she didn't really care. If ignorance was bliss, she wanted some.

CHAPTER 16
JANIE

Just three days before Christmas, Janie thought she heard something at her front door. It had been one of those dark rainy days, the kind that made Janie want to hole up and go to sleep. In fact, if she could just hibernate through Christmas, she would be perfectly fine. Oh, she'd told Matthew she understood his choice to spend the holidays with his girlfriend's family. But not having family around — especially her children — made Christmas lonelier than ever.

But there was that sound again — either someone was knocking on her door, or the wind was stronger than she'd assumed. Feeling uneasy, she set down her book and reached for her phone and almost wished she had a watchdog. Not that she was frightened, exactly. But it was past nine o'clock, and she couldn't imagine who would be calling at this time of night, and in this weather. When she turned on the porch light, peeking through the side window, she was stunned to see what looked like a homeless person. A pitiful person with dripping hair stood on the porch, head hanging. A soggy denim jacket, holey jeans, and rubber flip-flops suggested this person either lacked common sense or was hard up on luck. As Janie's initial surprise subsided, she was hit with a wave of shocking realization. This poor waif was Janie's daughter.

"Lisa!" Janie exclaimed as she jerked the door open wide. "Come in!"

Lisa stepped into the house, and Janie threw her arms around her, pulling her close and holding her tight. Despite being cold and wet, Lisa felt stiff and bony. And she didn't return the hug.

"Oh, sweetie, we need to get you dry," Janie said as she stepped back, noticing that her own blouse was fairly soggy too. "Come on," she urged Lisa. "You need to take a hot shower and change into some dry clothes."

Lisa looked down at herself, then slowly shook her head. "These are the only clothes I have."

"Oh." Janie nodded. "Well, that's okay. You can wear something of mine. But let's get you warmed up before you catch pneumonia. Come on." She led Lisa to the guest bath and pointed out where shampoo and soaps and towels were stored, produced a fluffy terry robe, then left her alone. Closing the door, Janie took in a deep breath and steadied herself. For about a minute, she just stood there in the hallway, trying to soak this in. Lisa was here! Really here — right here in Janie's home. But how had she gotten here? Why had she arrived with only the wet clothes on her back? How long would she stay?

Janie waited, wishing she'd hear the sound of the shower. Then she decided to busy herself by finding some warm pajamas and socks for Lisa. Then she put on the teakettle. Still not hearing the shower water, she tapped on the door, then called out Lisa's name. When Lisa didn't answer, Janie felt a rush of fear. What if Lisa had snuck out while Janie was distracted by gathering clothes and things? It wouldn't be the first time.

"Lisa?" Janie called again, opening the door and bracing herself for the worst. But Lisa was still there. She'd made some progress. Her soggy jeans and jacket were in a pile, but Lisa was just standing there in a dirty-looking pink T-shirt and underwear.

"Come on, Lisa." Janie set the pajamas on the counter, then turned on the water in the shower, adjusting it to the right heat. "You need to get in here." She reached over and touched Lisa's arm. "You're freezing, honey." Janie noticed the telltale tracks of past drug use on her daughter's thin arm, and it took all her strength not to fall apart. For Lisa's sake, Janie had to be strong.

She peeled off Lisa's T-shirt, trying not to gasp at the bony ribcage, and gently pushed her daughter into the shower stall and under the flow of warm water. Lisa still had on her bra and panties, but Janie didn't care. She just wanted to get Lisa warmed up.

"Do you need me to help?" Janie asked Lisa.

"No." Lisa shook her head. Janie wasn't convinced. She wasn't sure if Lisa was high or depressed or just suffering from hypothermia. But Janie decided Lisa really did need her help. And so Janie removed her own shoes, and since she was already fairly wet, she just stepped into the shower and began washing her daughter. Using shower gel and a washcloth, Janie rubbed vigorously over Lisa's pale back, wishing she could rub more than just warmth into her daughter. If she could, she would rub hope and strength and health into Lisa. But first she had to get her warm.

Finally, with Lisa out of the shower and

her hair in a towel and the terry robe tied snugly around her, Janie could hear the teakettle whistling in the kitchen. It had been full, so it couldn't have boiled dry yet.

"Come on," Janie told Lisa. "You can put your pajamas on in the bedroom." Then she led Lisa to the guest room. "I'll be back in a minute."

Janie made a cup of instant cocoa and returned to see that Lisa had the pajamas nearly on. That was progress. Janie set the steaming cocoa on the bedside table, then handed Lisa the woolly socks. "Put these on too."

Lisa frowned at the socks as if she wondered what they were for.

"Unless you'd rather have some slippers." Janie waited.

"No." Lisa barely nodded. "These will be fine."

"I'm going to go change into something drier too," Janie said lightly although she was starting to shiver. "Then I'll be right back. Okay?"

Lisa didn't even look at her. Still worried that her unpredictable child could pull a disappearing act, Janie hurried to her room and pulled on a set of sweats, then hurried back to discover Lisa sitting in the living room. On the couch, with her feet tucked under her and her hands cupped around the mug, she was sipping her cocoa.

Feeling relieved, Janie sat down in the chair adjacent from her and just stared. "I can't believe you're here," she said quietly. "I'm so glad to see you."

Lisa continued to sip.

"How did you get here?"

Lisa looked up with a blank expression, like she didn't intend to answer.

"I mean I would've sent you a plane ticket or come and picked you up. But how did you know how to find me here in grandma's house?"

"I've been here before."

Janie cocked her head to one side. "Yes, a long time ago. You were a kid."

"I remembered where it was."

Janie smiled. "Obviously. I'm so glad you did."

Lisa looked around. "You changed it."

"Well, yes. I wanted to make it my own."

"I liked it better before."

Janie told herself not to take offense. It was only natural that Lisa would say something like that. She and Lisa had been at odds for years.

"But I guess it's okay." Lisa looked up at the painting Marley had done. "That's nice."

So Janie filled the air by telling Lisa a bit about Marley and her other Linda friends.

"Really?" Lisa looked confused. "There were four girls named Linda in your school?"

"Weird, huh?"

"And you're still friends with them?"

"More so than ever before."

Lisa slowly nodded. "That's cool."

"Are you hungry?" Janie asked.

Lisa shrugged with that faraway look in her eyes again.

"Do you remember when you last ate?"

Another shrug.

"Do you still like oatmeal?"

Lisa looked up with a bit of interest.

Janie stood. "I'm going to make some. It actually sounds kind of good to me, too. I've been eating it with nuts and dried berries lately."

Using the still-hot water from the teakettle, Janie made what looked to be about four helpings of oatmeal. "Do you still like it with honey?" she called.

"I guess so."

Before long, they were seated in the kitchen, eating oatmeal together. And Lisa, in Janie's blue and yellow April Cornell pajamas with her hair wrapped loosely in a white towel and a bit of color reappearing in her cheeks, was starting to look almost normal. However, Janie was no fool. She knew that looks could be deceiving. Still, she was glad that Lisa was here. Despite the odds, Janie felt hopeful.

The next morning, Janie couldn't wait to call Victor — except that she knew he was on his way up to Portland to pick up his son Ben. Victor's older son, Marcus, as well as Marcus's fiancée, had opted to spend Christmas split between their moms, both of whom were more conveniently located in the Chicago area. But Victor had made it clear that Marcus would've preferred to come out here. "But he's feeling sorry for his mom," Victor had told her a couple of days ago. "I guess Donna's been depressed."

Janie wasn't surprised, given all that had transpired around Thanksgiving. Even though Victor's ex was seeing her therapist again, it would probably take time and meds to undo the damage of that ill-fated visit. Plus, a lot of people got blue at Christmastime. In fact, Janie had been a little down before Lisa showed up. Now she was mostly just nervous. More than anything, she wanted Lisa to stay with her. But knowing Lisa, that could be a challenge. Lisa had a history of showing up unexpectedly, getting what she wanted, and taking off again. Janie prayed that this time would be different.

For that reason, she called her son. "Hey, Matthew," she said cheerfully into his voice mail. "You'll never guess who showed up at my door last night." She chuckled. Well, knowing her smart son, he would guess. "Anyway, I sure wish you could come out here and be with us for Christmas. I know you have other plans, but if you change your mind, I'll be glad to spring for your flight." Of course, she knew the chances of this happening were minimal. Matthew wouldn't be willing to expose his girlfriend to Lisa, and even if he was willing to leave Cassie behind, getting tickets at this late date would probably be next to impossible. Still, it didn't hurt to ask.

Then she decided to call Victor's home phone. That way she could at least leave a message. She wanted him to be aware of what was happening, especially since Victor had been planning to have her and Ben at his house for Christmas Eve. She hoped he'd be okay with another guest — and that Lisa would be okay with going.

With those two calls done, Janie considered fixing breakfast. Except she had no idea how long Lisa would sleep. As worn out as she'd appeared last night, Janie wouldn't be surprised if she slept until noon. Mostly, Janie was glad that Lisa was still here. She'd checked to be sure. However, what would happen later today or tomorrow remained to be seen.

CHAPTER 17
CAROLINE

Caroline considered herself to be a fairly understanding person. At least she tried. But sometimes Mitch stretched her patience a bit. To be fair, she probably stretched his, too. He'd surprised her by flying into Clifden this afternoon, just two days before Christmas. Shortly after she picked him up at the airport, it became clear that their holiday plans were not quite melding. Because she hadn't heard anything specific from him, and that had been an issue in itself, Caroline had agreed to celebrate Christmas with her friends.

"I'm sorry you're disappointed," she apologized again. "I didn't know what else to do. It's not like I wanted to just sit by myself throughout the holidays."

"But I told you I was coming."

"I knew you were coming, Mitch." She wondered if that was really true. He'd been so vague. "I just didn't know exactly when, or how long you'd stay, or much of anything specifically."

"Yes, and that's my fault and I do understand you making other plans. But it's just that I had something else in mind." Mitch gave her a slightly hangdog look.

"What sort of plans?" She pulled in front of the hotel where, unbeknownst to her, he'd booked a room.

"Different ones." He grinned.

"You made plans for right here in Clifden?" she questioned. "I mean, you do realize there's not a whole lot to do in town on Christmas, right?"

He shrugged.

"And you know that I don't have a real home at the moment, so I can't exactly invite you into my house for hot buttered rum." She explained how Abby's family was already filling up the inn and Caroline was starting to feel slightly in the way. "In fact, I'd even considered camping at my house during the holidays, although Abby keeps telling me that's unnecessary."

"You can always stay here at the hotel." He arched a brow. "I hear they have plenty of rooms."

"Thanks just the same." She smiled and shook her head. "But I'm sticking to my guns on this." She knew he knew what "this" meant. They'd discussed this topic via email several times already, and she'd made her position clear: She was not going to indulge in premarital sex, and that was that. They'd been there and done that before, even if it was a long time ago, and she was not going there again. Not without a marriage certificate this time. They say you can't teach an old dog new tricks, but Caroline was not an old dog!

He nodded. "Okay. I get it."

"Anyway, Janie is in a situation and she needs our help." Caroline turned off the car's engine. "Plus, Marley is having a bit of a go of it right now. And for that matter, Abby and Paul need a little support too, which is why she wanted everyone at the inn on Christmas day."

"Are *all* your friends falling apart?"

"No." She frowned at him. "They're just having some challenges."

"And their challenges control your life?"

"No. But they've stood by me in my times of need, and with my mom I had plenty of needy times." She didn't point out that Mitch had not been around then.

"So what's so wrong in the world of the Four Lindas?" he asked.

"Well, this Linda is just fine, thank you."

"Okay, the other three Lindas. What is

troubling them?"

She peered curiously at him. "You really want to know?"

"Sure, why shouldn't I?"

She started by explaining Paul and Abby's recent marital difficulties. "Even though they kind of patched it up, Abby said she feels like they're both walking on eggshells. With their kids all here, she just wanted some friends around to buffer things a bit. That's why I committed to spend Christmas day with them at the inn, and I hope you'll want to join us too."

"Because Abby and Paul need buffers?" He frowned.

"Because they are my dear friends," Caroline clarified. "Besides being my friends, Abby has given me a place to live, and Paul is the reason my house is being finished. And, as I mentioned, I hadn't made any plans for Christmas day." She controlled herself from shaking an accusatory finger at him.

"Okay, fine. But what about Christmas Eve? Are you telling me that's written in stone too?"

"Well, yes, sort of. You see, Janie's daughter, Lisa, just showed up in town yesterday right out of the blue." She quickly filled him in about Lisa's drug addiction problems.

"As if that's not enough, Lisa has taken a strong dislike to Victor. Janie said that the instant Lisa met him this morning, she started acting strangely."

"What kind of person doesn't like Victor? He's one of the nicest guys around."

"I know that. You know that. But I think Lisa feels threatened by him. Or she's jealous of him, or maybe she thinks he's trying to replace her father or something just as irrational. That's why Janie begged me to join them for Christmas Eve tomorrow night. And it would be lovely if you wanted to come too."

"So for Christmas, we get stuck playing buffers and counselors to a bunch of dysfunctional people."

"That's not very nice, Mitch. We're talking about my friends here. Even if some of them are having a hard time, what's the big deal? I mean don't we all struggle sometimes? What do you think Christmas is supposed to be about anyway?"

He sighed. "I don't know. Happy times, snuggling by a crackling fire, watching *It's a Wonderful Life*."

Caroline laughed. "Yeah, we could sit around and watch an old flick about make-believe people with make-believe problems, or we could go be with real, live people and some real, live problems."

"Now that you put it like that . . ." He offered a crooked smile. "Okay, you didn't tell me what's wrong with your artist friend yet. Or is she okay?"

"Marley? Well, she's a little out of sorts too." Caroline explained about Jack and Jasmine and how Marley had been helping out, but that now Sylvia and her daughter were filling in the gap. "Jack arranged it like that so Marley could spend more time painting." She told him about the Santa Barbara art connection.

"Hey, I'll bet I've been in that gallery. Marley should be thrilled. And I'd think she'd be thankful that this other woman and her daughter are giving her a break."

"Marley would agree with you . . . mostly. But she really enjoyed helping Jack and Hunter. I think she liked being needed. Now she's worried that Sylvia might be developing a romantic interest in Jack."

"What makes her think that?"

"Marley said Sylvia seems to be catering to his every whim. She picks up his dry cleaning and runs his errands. She brought him homemade pumpkin muffins yesterday."

"Sylvia sounds nice."

"Except that she's his employee, not his

wife." Caroline scowled. "I'm a little suspicious myself. I went in there the other day, and I saw Sylvia in conversation with Jack and she was standing pretty close."

"Standing pretty close? That's grounds for suspicion in this town?"

"It was her body language," Caroline tried to explain. "I can read women. I haven't told Marley — she has enough to worry about — but I think she might be right about Sylvia."

Mitch laughed. "Your charming Clifden is like a regular little Peyton Place."

"Very funny."

"So thanks to your frazzled friends, you don't get to do what you want for Christmas."

Caroline pressed her lips together. She wanted to tell him, in no uncertain terms, that she was doing exactly what she wanted to do for Christmas and that he could take it or leave it, but that would probably sound too harsh. After all, he'd gone to a lot of effort to be here with her. Maybe she should try harder to make him happy. Or not. At the moment, she had no response to what seemed like pure selfishness on his part.

"I'm sorry," he said quickly. "I really should've given you more warning. I just thought you'd like the surprise." He looked out to where the fog was rolling into town. "If the weather were better, I'd consider hopping back in my plane and just heading back down to —"

"No, you would not." She let out an exasperated sigh. "We're just talking about a couple of days, Mitch. You're staying stateside until New Year's, right?"

"Yeah. That's true."

"And" — Caroline gave him a sly smile — "I'm not busy tonight. And it is our first night back together. And it is pre-Christmas Eve. That should be worth celebrating, don't you think?"

"You're right." He looked hopeful. "Any chance I could take you out?"

"Oh, I think that could be arranged."

He leaned over and kissed her. "Sorry, I sound like such a spoiled brat. I guess I just missed you."

She smiled. "I missed you, too!"

"And I would like to see your miraculously transformed house." He reached over the backseat and tugged out his bag. "I still find it hard to believe you've made as much progress as you claim."

"Then prepare to be amazed."

"How about I check in at the hotel and drop off my stuff? Then you can take me over there and give me the grand tour."

While Mitch was in the hotel, Caroline tried to figure out what was bugging him. Was he really that upset that he couldn't have Caroline all to himself? While that was sweet, it was a little claustrophobic, too. Didn't he understand that Caroline had been single for a long time, that she was used to coming and going and doing with friends as she pleased? Perhaps she'd gotten selfish over the years. Maybe they both had. She reminded herself that it was Christmas, and he probably did have some expectations. Maybe she wasn't being fair to him. Maybe her Christmas plans were all wrong.

She was tempted to call Janie for advice. Of the Four Lindas, Janie seemed to disperse the soundest advice when it came to marriage and relationships. But Janie had her hands full. Caroline knew that Janie had taken Lisa shopping today. It sounded as if the poor girl showed up with nothing but the ragged clothes on her back. Janie was very anxious that one misstep might cause Lisa's visit to blow up in her face. After inviting Caroline for Christmas Eve, Janie had asked her to pray specifically for Lisa. "Pray that she doesn't bolt and run while we're out shopping," Janie had quietly told Caroline this morning.

So, while waiting for Mitch, Caroline

prayed again. She prayed that Lisa would realize how dearly her mother loved her, how no one on this planet loved Lisa more than Janie. She prayed that Lisa would choose to stay here in Clifden and choose to get the help she so desperately needed, and finally that Lisa would seek out God and get healthy from the inside out. Janie had told Caroline that she was already scouting out nearby rehab places, and Caroline knew that money would be no object in getting care for Lisa. Janie would probably do anything to help her daughter. Caroline just hoped (and prayed) Lisa would accept it.

"All right," Mitch said as he hopped back into the passenger seat. "All set."

"Oh." Caroline blinked and sat back.

"Napping?" he asked.

"No. Praying actually."

He looked worried. "Uh-oh. I really must've stuck my foot in my mouth even more than I realized. I'm sorry."

"No, it's not about you, Mitch." Then as she drove to her house, she explained how she'd promised to pray for Lisa. "I have a lot of empathy for Lisa. I can't explain it, but I think it's almost like I'd feel for a child of my own, even though I never had kids. But you know all about that."

He sighed, then slowly nodded. "Yeah, I know."

He and Caroline had already discussed the one and only child she'd carried — his child — and how she'd given up the chance to be a mom for him. Or so she'd thought at the time. Although Caroline had mostly resolved that pain, she still felt a pang deep inside of her at times. She thought she would've made a good mother.

"Anyway, Janie feels as close as a sister to me," Caroline confessed as she turned onto her street. "So I guess I feel a special protectiveness toward Lisa."

"Have you actually met her yet?"

"Not yet. But I'm looking forward to it. I kind of understand how it feels to be a lost girl. I mean, I never got seriously into drugs, but I was quite the party girl back in my day. Well, you probably remember. I felt pretty lost during my twenties and even into my thirties. So I feel for Lisa. And I'd like to help her if I can." She pulled her car into the driveway.

"That might be tougher than you think, Caroline. Addiction is pretty complicated. Some people don't want help."

"Maybe." She got out of the car. Unreasonable as it was, she wished she hadn't told him about her feelings. It felt like he was just brushing it all aside — like Lisa didn't really matter, like she wasn't worthy of Caroline's love. That bugged her.

"Well, it still looks pretty much the same from the outside," he said as they stood in the driveway. The light was dusky, and she supposed the house didn't look much different to him, although she could point out every single improvement.

"The windows are new," she told him. "The doors, too. And I'll get the siding replaced later on." She didn't mention that she was running out of funds and couldn't afford to have the exterior completely finished until her condo sold. As they got closer to the front door, the new porch light, complete with a motion sensor, came on.

"Oh, yeah." He made what seemed a stiff smile. "They look like good windows too. Nice."

"Well, they're just vinyl, but they're a lot better than the old aluminum ones, and I'll get a tax rebate for the energy efficiency." She went ahead of him and unlocked the door, opening it wide for him to go in first. "There's still a lot to do, but as you can see, it's changed a lot too."

He slowly walked through, taking it in, making a comment here and there. But for the most part his reaction seemed unenthusiastic to her, sort of ho-hum.

"I know it's just a little old ranch house," she said in a forced dismissive tone, acting like it wasn't a big deal. "It's not like there's a whole lot you can do architecturally speaking. But when it's all together, the décor and everything — the designer says it'll look pretty cool. Mid-Century Modern, you know." She showed him the sample board that Bonnie had put together, explaining what would go where.

"That'll be nice, Caroline. I hear a lot of twentysomethings are into the whole retro sixties thing. This would be a great little starter house for a young couple, so I'm sure you'll have no problem selling it."

Caroline took in a long slow breath. "*If* I sell it."

"If?" He looked confused. "I thought you said you were going to sell —"

"I honestly don't know, Mitch. I kind of go back and forth on it. But I have to admit: The more progress the house makes, the more I wonder if perhaps I could be happy here after all."

With a grim expression he shook his head. "It seems like a bad idea, Caroline."

"Why?"

"You've said yourself that the place is full of bad memories. And do you really want to

be tied down to a house? What about freedom and traveling?"

"I can travel," she said defensively. "Don't
forget, I'm going to Mexico in January."

"Don't remind me."

Out of habit, she picked up the broom and
started pushing a pile of sawdust toward
the wall, but with each sweeping movement,
she felt herself getting more irritated. Why
was Mitch acting like this? "What's the
problem with Mexico?" she asked in a calm
voice.

"Well, how do you think that makes me
feel?"

She stopped sweeping to look at him. "I
have no idea. How *does* it make you feel?"

"Like you'd rather travel with your friends
than with me."

"Oh." She leaned the broom against the
wall. "But it's a girls' trip. Abby won the
tickets . . . and . . ."

"I know, I know. I probably sound petty
and jealous and childish. But how many
times have I asked you to travel with me,
Caroline?"

"Mostly you asked when Mom was still
alive," she reminded him, "and you knew it
was impossible."

"But it's possible now."

"It's only been about a month," she said

quietly. "I've had a lot going on."

"I know." He slipped a hand around her waist and pulled her close. "I'm sorry I sound like such a spoiled brat, Caroline. I don't know what's gotten into me today. I guess it's just that I've missed you so much." He kissed her again.

"I've missed you, too," she murmured.

"And I'm a little disappointed that I have to share you with all your friends during Christmastime. So I guess you'll have to cut me some slack for being a brat."

"Brat slack." She smoothed her hand over his cheek. "Now remember, you promised me dinner and since I missed lunch, I'm starving. If we go now, we can get the early-bird special at the Lighthouse."

Fortunately, Mitch was hungry too. They beat the dinner crowd and were seated in a cozy booth near the fireplace. Before long they ordered the captain's platter to share and were sipping some good California pinot gris that Mitch had picked out. After a while their conversation lightened up. They shifted away from the earlier stresses and even shared some laughs. By the end of the meal, Caroline thought this was more like it.

"This was really nice," she told him after he paid the bill. "Thanks for a lovely evening."

"But the night is still young." He pointed to his watch. "What now, my love?"

She considered this. "Well, Abby's family has pretty much taken over the inn, and you saw what my house is like." She thought hard. "We might be able to catch a movie. There are some new holiday releases out."

He frowned. "That sounds a little dull."

"If it wasn't so foggy, I'd suggest we drive over to look at the Christmas lights on the lighthouse. As it is, I doubt we could even see it."

"Maybe another night." He looked into her eyes with longing. "But what about *to-night?*"

"Bowling?" she said in a teasing tone.

He laughed. "No, thanks."

"We could grab a newspaper and see if there's any live music anywhere, but since it's early in the week, I don't —"

"I feel like we're in high school," he said with disappointment. "In a small town with nothing to do." He brightened. "Hey, maybe we should go find a place to park and make out."

She laughed. "No, thanks. I've been there and done that — in this very town for that matter."

"Why don't you show me your favorite

make-out spots?"

"Seriously, Mitch. Can you imagine having a cop tapping on our steamed-up windows and seeing how old we are? It would be humiliating."

"Or just plain funny."

"Maybe another time. A warm summer evening perhaps."

He grimaced. "And you're sure I can't talk you into coming back to my hotel with me?"

"I'm positive."

"I wish I'd rented a house. I was so eager to see you that I just wasn't thinking straight."

She reached over and grabbed his hand, squeezing it. "I'm so glad you came, Mitch. I'm sorry that you got stuck with my Christmas plans, but I think we'll have fun. Just wait and see."

"Maybe we can plan something more exciting next year," he suggested. "Skiing in Aspen perhaps?"

She smiled. "That sounds wonderful."

"You think you'll be able to tear yourself away from your girlfriends by then?"

She made a tolerant smile. "My girlfriends have been my lifeline, Mitch. I'd think you'd appreciate that."

"Oh, I do. It's just that . . ." He made an apologetic shrug.

"Yeah, I know. I understand." She was beginning to think this whole situation with Mitch resenting her friends was a lot bigger than she realized. She felt bad, but what did he expect from her? Did he think she should choose between him and her Lindas? That was ridiculous.

"I've stuck my foot in my mouth again, haven't I?"

She sighed. "I have a feeling we're both more tired than we think. I know I had a long day between helping Abby at the inn and cleaning up the construction mess at my house." She pointed at him. "I'll bet you're having some serious jet lag, too."

"Probably so." He stifled a yawn.

"So maybe we should just call it a night and start out fresh tomorrow. I promise I'll have a whole list of great things to do right here in town. We'll do a real Clifden Christmas, and you'll see exactly why this little sea town is so charming."

He agreed, and she drove him back to his hotel, where in the parking lot, she refused, again, to join him in his room. "Just to watch old movies," he said enticingly. "There's popcorn in the lobby."

"Thanks," she said lightly, "but no thanks." Then they kissed good night. As she drove back to the inn, she had to

234

wonder. As much as he claimed to understand where she stood on this issue, he certainly didn't give up easily. While she knew he was just being a normal guy, she also had to ask herself — did he really get it? And what about her hints? What if his thoughts on marriage had changed? What if he wasn't looking for a life mate as much as he was looking for a playmate? She'd been down that road before and had no intention of going back there now.

CHAPTER 18
MARLEY

The Christmas season had always been hard on Marley. She had rationalized it was simply the by-product of a loveless marriage. After all, who wanted to sit around a Christmas tree and pretend that all was well when she could still smell another woman's perfume on her cheating husband's shirt? But after putting those years behind her and finding real faith, Marley had truly expected this Christmas to be much improved. Yet here she was making a fast getaway on Christmas Eve just to escape a man.

She'd told Jack and her friends that she was worried about Ashton and hated to think of him being alone during the holidays, so soon after his breakup with Leo. In truth, Ashton had been quite convincing, assuring her that he had plans to go to a Christmas Eve concert tonight and a Christmas dinner with friends tomorrow.

Even so, when she'd called him this morning, she had insisted on coming to visit. She hadn't told him when exactly, but she explained that she was coming to give him his Christmas present, which she hadn't had time to mail. That was partly true. She hadn't had time to mail it. In fact, the paint was barely dry on the piece she'd been working on these past few days. Distracted by Jack and Hunter (actually by Sylvia and Leah), Marley had felt uninterested in painting. But with Ashton as her motivation, she'd managed to get a painting started and finished.

It wasn't a large piece, but she thought Ashton was going to like it, and she could imagine it hanging in his apartment. Maybe in his tiny dining area. As a child, Ashton had loved toucans. At first she'd assumed it was simply thanks to his brief addiction to Froot Loops, but when his love of the tropical bird outlived his interest in the cereal, she realized it was more than just a passing infatuation. Anyway, she hoped Ashton would be pleasantly surprised by Walter. For some curious reason she'd named the colorful bird *Walter Cronkite*. Maybe it was a flash from the past, from back when Ashton was a toddler picking his Froot Loops from the tray of his highchair while she caught up with the evening news. Who knew?

237

Just as her son had needed her then, she had convinced herself that he needed her now. But as she checked into the hotel a few blocks from Ashton's apartment, telling the clerk that, yes, she was here to see family, she felt like the world's biggest phony. Really, who was she kidding? Running off like this to deliver a toucan to her son just to get away from Jack and his new little "family" was truly pathetic. And yet she couldn't seem to stop herself.

"You need to grow up," she told herself as she hooked the strap of her overnight bag over one arm and pressed the number 7 button in the elevator. Of course, she could always wait until after Christmas to grow up. Really, what would it hurt? Besides, she told herself, after all she'd done to help Jack and Hunter, she needed a vacation, which she could afford thanks to selling those paintings. But why here? Didn't she know how pitiful she looked right now?

It had all started when Jack called her late last night. She'd actually been surprised to hear from him, since they hadn't spoken for several days. Although she knew he'd been busier than usual at the gallery, she was nearly convinced that he'd forgotten all about her. And she couldn't believe how much that hurt.

"I'm sure you can understand how, being so new in town, Sylvia and Leah are at loose ends," Jack had begun tentatively, after some initial small talk. "So I thought you wouldn't mind if we invited them to join us for Christmas. Naturally, Hunter thinks it's a great idea."

"Yes. It's a *great* idea," she'd agreed quickly, trying to sound enthusiastic rather than panicked. "But I'm going to Ashton's for Christmas."

"Oh?" Jack had sounded surprised. "You never mentioned it."

"Actually, it just came up." She immediately regretted the lie. But feeling trapped, she rambled on, reminding him of all that Ashton had been through. "You know how holidays can be for people when they're alone. That's just one more good reason for you and Hunter to reach out to Sylvia and Leah like you're doing."

"But what about tomorrow?" Jack asked. "I thought we were going to go to Abby's together and —"

"And you should still go," she insisted. "Take Sylvia and Leah with you. It's a good way for them to meet people. I know Abby will be happy to have them. It's not a sit-down meal, so the more the merrier."

"Oh, I don't know. Maybe we should just

stay here and —"

"You'll enjoy the festivities. And I know Hunter is looking forward to playing with Abby's granddaughter, Lucy."

"But it won't be the same without you there." He sounded a bit sad, although it could've been politeness.

"I'm so sorry," she told him. "But Ashton has been through so much recently. And he's my only child and it's Christmas and . . . well." She ran out of words.

"I do understand, Marley. I just wish you'd talk Ashton into coming back here with you. He seemed to enjoy Thanksgiving. It would be great to see him again."

"I'll try."

Jack let out a long, weary sigh. "I had a phone call from Jasmine earlier this evening."

"Really?"

"Yes, but nothing has changed."

"Oh."

"She was just calling to say she'd forgotten to send Hunter a Christmas gift. She wanted me to pick up something for her."

"You're kidding! Jasmine called to ask you to buy Hunter a present and then pretend that it was from her?" She wished she hadn't said it. Jack didn't need a double dose of pain.

"I know it sounds a bit strange, but for Hunter's sake, I'll do it. She needs to be reminded that her mother loves her."

Marley bit her tongue. "Well, you know what they say, Jack . . . Christmas is really for the children."

"Who says that?"

She forced a laugh. "I have no idea, really. Maybe it was my parents. Or maybe it's what I used to tell Ashton."

"I've always enjoyed Christmas — as a child, as an adult, and even more so as a grandpa. I think Christmas should be for everyone."

Then she'd explained that she wanted to drop some presents for Hunter by the gallery before she left. She'd done so this morning, quickly and discretely, while Sylvia was helping a customer. Marley had gone in and placed the large brown bag, clearly marked with Hunter's name, behind the counter. Marley hadn't mentioned that the gifts weren't only for Hunter, although most of the packages did have Hunter's name on them. However, she'd written "from Santa" on a number of them, just to keep from overwhelming the young girl. For Jack, Marley had splurged on a silver and brass chess set she'd seen him admiring in the antique shop across the street several weeks ago. She knew how much he'd love it.

As the Christmas song in the elevator crooned "if the Fates allow," Marley wondered if she'd get the chance to play a game of chess with Jack, or if he'd break in the chess set with Sylvia. She didn't want to think about that.

As she went down the deserted hallway, letting herself into the hotel room, she knew that she was pitiful and sad and just plain silly. And as she dropped her bag, then sat down in the chair by the window and stared out over the gray, gloomy cityscape, she felt certain she'd been a fool to run away — a childish, immature, juvenile fool. Yet she didn't think she could have done anything else.

Really, when it came to relationships with men, Marley had never been terribly savvy. And at her age, it seemed unlikely that she was going to get any smarter. She picked up the television remote and clicked the TV on. She didn't get TV reception in her beach house, so this felt like a novelty. It took her a bit of time to figure out how to make the complicated thing work.

She just needed to get herself through Christmas, she decided as she leaned back into the chair, even if all she did was sleep and eat room-service food and watch this silly TV. She would sort out the rest of her life afterward.

By the next morning, thoroughly sick of her pity party of one, as well as the stark hotel room and obnoxious television, Marley put together a plan. She asked at the hotel desk where she might find an open grocery store, then she drove over and gathered up some breakfast ingredients. At a bit past nine o'clock, she surprised Ashton by showing up at his door. "Merry Christmas," she said as she handed him the bags. "I bring you good tidings of great joy! I'm here to fix you Christmas breakfast."

He laughed and set down the bags and hugged her. "Merry Christmas, Mom!"

"I'll be right back with your present," she told him.

It was a perfect morning. Ashton loved Walter the toucan. And he gave her a hand-made drum, which she promised to treasure forever. "I plan to play it on the beach," she told him as they were finishing up a delicious breakfast of French toast made from artisan bread, fresh fruit, and Black Forest ham.

"I'm so glad you came," Ashton told her as they washed up the breakfast dishes. "It makes it seem more like Christmas. I know you'll be welcome at the Christmas dinner this afternoon, but I think I should give my buddy Laurence a call, since he usually plans this amazing gourmet, sit-down feast."

"It sounds lovely," she told him. "But I think I'll pass."

"Are you sure?" He sounded a little disappointed, but she could also see relief in his eyes. He probably didn't really relish the idea of dragging his mother along.

"Positive." She smiled. "Abby is having a big shindig at the inn."

"Oh, yeah, kind of like Thanksgiving. That was fun."

"Yes. And this time her family's there too."

They finished up and hugged again, and although she knew she was leaving him with the impression that she was driving back to Clifden to spend the rest of the day with her friends, she consoled herself with the fact that she had never actually lied about it. She had simply said that Abby was having a Christmas dinner. He had assumed that meant she was going. How she actually spent the rest of the day was her choice.

CHAPTER 19
ABBY

Although Abby knew she'd overindulged during the holidays as usual, and she knew her jeans were starting to feel snug again, she did not want to go work out at the club on Monday morning. "You take Nicole in my place," Abby told Caroline. "I'm sure she'll enjoy it more than I possibly could." She nodded to the inn's messy kitchen. "Besides, I need to clean this up. That'll be exercise enough for me today."

The truth was, Abby knew that Nicole would prefer Caroline's company to her own. So far her reunion with Nicole had been a great big letdown. Nicole seemed so much older than before, so independent and wise, almost as if she'd outgrown Abby. It was as if Nicole related more to Abby's friends than she did to her own mother. Perhaps she fit in with Abby's friends even better than Abby did. All in all, it was just one more pathetic piece of Abby's depressing life.

"Okay." Caroline glanced around the kitchen. "If you're not done, I'll help you when I get back." She lowered her voice. "I'm surprised your daughters didn't help you out more, Abby."

Abby waved her hand, trying to look nonchalant. "It's okay. Like I told them, they were guests."

"Guests should help too, Abby, especially when they're your own kids anyway."

"Both Jessie and Laurie had to go back to work today," Abby defended. "Plus Laurie has Lucy and Brandon to take care of. I don't mind letting them just relax a little. Don't you think it's nice for them to have some downtime?"

Caroline shook her head. "I think you might need some downtime too. Why don't you take a break? Go put your feet up."

"Go on." Abby pointed to the clock. "You don't want to be late for your class."

After Caroline and Nicole left, Abby did take a break — or rather a breakdown. Tired of her perfect-mommy act, exhausted by her wonderful-hostess routine, and sad about Nicole outgrowing her, Abby sat down and just cried. No one in her family had really appreciated all the work she'd gone to, trying to make their holidays special. No one in her family knew the stress she was under these days, trying to pretend like her marriage wasn't in serious trouble. No one really understood the pressures heaped upon her with this inn. Even her friends seemed a bit weary of her mood swings. Abby felt trapped, partly by life in general, partly by herself, and partly by this inn. What was she going to do? Who could she talk to?

Suddenly she remembered how Marley had gone MIA during Christmas. Abby suspected something was amiss there, but no one had said a word. Maybe it was true that misery loved company, but it was even more true that Abby was genuinely worried about her friend. So with her own tears barely dried, she went back to the kitchen and dialed Marley's number. She might not be in control of her own life, but she was determined to help Marley. If there was nothing else she could be good at, she could try at least to be a good friend.

"Are you okay?" Abby asked Marley with genuine concern.

"I'm fine. Why do you ask?"

"Because I'm worried about you, that's why." Abby poured herself a cup of coffee. "And because I miss you."

"Really?" Marley sounded touched.

"In fact, you should come over here and have a cup of coffee as well as . . ." Abby began to list all the delicious leftovers.

Marley laughed. "It sounds like you want to fatten me up."

"Maybe I do. After all, the Mexico trip is only a couple of weeks away. I don't want to be the only chubby Linda."

"I'm on my way," Marley said.

Before long the two of them were sitting in the living room with their coffees and a big platter of Christmas goodies on the coffee table. "So how is Ashton?" Abby asked. "Did you cheer him up?"

Marley's brow creased. "Want the truth?"

"Of course."

"Ashton was just my excuse to run away from home."

Abby leaned forward with interest. "Because of Sylvia?"

Marley nodded, taking a second piece of pumpkin-nut bread.

"Do you really think Jack is interested in Sylvia?"

Marley shrugged. "What do you think?"

Abby thought hard about her answer. "Oh, I really don't think so. I mean Sylvia is pretty enough, and she's certainly friendly toward Jack. But I've seen Jack look at you,

248

Marley. He gets that look in his eye." She sighed. "Paul used to have that look for me."

"He still does."

"I'm not so sure." She shook her head, determined not to hog the spotlight this time. "But we were talking about you, Marley. You and Jack and Sylvia."

"Yes." Marley took a slow sip of coffee.

"So what good do you think it did to run away?"

Marley shrugged. "Avoidance."

"Yes, I know about that." Abby considered how she'd used busyness to escape the pain in her own life.

"I admit it wasn't terribly mature on my part. But it just feels as if Sylvia is moving in, you know, just inserting herself into Jack's life like she belongs there. He doesn't really seem to mind much."

"Well, that's because she's working for him, Marley. That lightens his load a lot. And then Leah is taking care of Hunter. In a way, it's like having Jasmine back, only twice as good."

"I suppose. But at the same time it makes me feel displaced."

"Yes, I know that feeling."

"It's hard getting old." Marley picked up a ginger cookie, then made a sly smile. "But I guess if it's hard to be old, we might as well get fat, too."

"Or we could go take a walk." Abby set her coffee down.

"The weather seems to have cleared up some."

"I'll bet Chuck would be glad to join us." Abby stood.

Abby left Caroline a note saying she'd dognapped Chuck, and before long, she and Marley were walking down the beach, talking about getting older and how to do it gracefully.

"I read this article a year or so ago in the *New York Times* about French women," Marley told Abby. "It was about their attitude toward aging and beauty, and it was actually quite inspiring."

"How so?"

"For one thing, it said French women don't like fitness clubs. They prefer to get their exercise by walking."

"Like us," Abby proclaimed.

"And French women enjoy their food —"

"Like us!"

"Yes, but in smaller portions."

Then Marley explained how French women took a great interest in caring for themselves, investing in good skin and hair products. "And they dress stylishly."

Abby looked down at her faded Blazers

sweatshirt and saggy jeans. "Well, you had me with the walking and eating part, Marley. After that I felt a little lost." She brightened. "But now that I think of it, Nicole has been singing a similar tune. It seems she learned about a lot more than just art in France."

"Anyway, the point of the article," Marley said, "and the point I think I'm trying to make is that French women seem to accept aging better than American women. And they seem to it with a bit more style. I guess we could learn something from them when it comes to pampering and caring for ourselves." Marley held out a hand. "Like these fingernails — I sure could use a manicure."

"You know the cruise line has a lot of spa and beauty treatments available," Abby said. "Maybe we should indulge ourselves a bit."

"Come back as new women," Marley said in a teasing tone.

Abby thought about that as they walked quietly together and Chuck raced back and forth between them and the surf. She wondered if making some improvements to herself would improve her marriage. Paul kept claiming she was just fine, but she'd seen him look at women like Bonnie or Caroline or even Sylvia, and she just wasn't sure. Most of the time she didn't give aging a second thought, and she even liked the idea of being a grandma in a rocking chair. But seeing others, ones who seemed more adept at holding back the clock, made her wonder.

"So tell me how everyone is doing," Marley said, breaking the silence. "How are Caroline and Mitch? Did he pop the question yet?"

"No. In fact, Caroline is starting to wonder if Mitch isn't thinking along those lines at all."

"Really? I'd been under the impression that once she was free of her mother, he planned to whisk her away to some exotic foreign locale like Bali."

"Me, too." Abby bent down to pick up Chuck's ball, then gave it a hard toss. "But according to Caroline, he hasn't mentioned the marriage part yet — just the whisking her away part. In fact, it sounds like he's a little put out with me."

"What on earth for?"

"For inviting Caroline to go to Mexico. Mitch seems to think that her going to Mexico means she prefers her girlfriends to him."

"Well, that is just perfectly ridiculous." Marley shook her head.

"Yes. But then men can be perfectly ridiculous."

"So how did Janie and Lisa seem, and how was Lisa treating Victor?"

"Oh, you didn't hear?"

"Hear what?" Marley looked worried.

"Lisa picked a very ugly fight with Victor on Christmas Eve. They were having dinner at Victor's house, and Lisa just blew up. Janie said there was absolutely no reason for it — except that Lisa is, you know, out of sorts."

"Well, that's reason enough. Her perspectives are skewed by drugs."

"Besides that, Janie feels sure that Lisa sees Victor as an intruder," Abby added.

"I'll bet there's some jealousy too. Lisa probably wants Janie all to herself."

"Or she might think Victor is replacing her dad." Abby paused to pick up a sand dollar. "Anyway, Victor didn't even come to the inn for Christmas. After the showdown at his house, he felt it best if he and Ben did something else."

"Oh? What did they do?"

"They went sailing, just the two of them. The weather was actually pretty decent here on Christmas day."

"So how were Janie and Lisa? Could you tell?"

"Well, Lisa seemed pretty quiet and subdued. Nicole really went out of her way to make her feel welcome, and we invited Janie and Lisa to lunch tomorrow. It was Nicole's idea."

"Does Nicole know about Lisa?"

"No." Abby shook her head. "I didn't think I should mention it."

"Right."

"I just thought a mother-daughter lunch might be fun. You know, to help Lisa feel like she's fitting in here better."

"Has Janie had any success talking Lisa into rehab?"

"I don't know." Abby threw the ball for Chuck again. "But Jessie told Janie about a place down in the Bay Area that sounds quite good."

"Doesn't Janie want to keep Lisa closer to home?"

"Yes, I think so. Although I wouldn't think it would matter. Don't patients get locked in for a long time?"

"That depends."

"I just hope Janie gets it figured out before it's time for the cruise." Abby frowned. "She told me she might have to back out if Lisa isn't squared away by then."

"Then we'd better hope and pray that Lisa agrees to some sort of treatment program."

"You know, I just don't understand how some kids grow up to be such a mess." Abby slowly shook her head. "Not that my daughters are perfect — they're certainly not. And until recently, Jessie and I had been in a rough spot, but at least she's talking to me."

"Was it nice having your family with you for Christmas?"

"It wasn't as great as I hoped it would be," she admitted. "I'm afraid I set my sights too high."

"Not your picture-perfect Christmas," Marley teased.

"Well, my girls enjoyed being together again. Everyone was so happy to see Nicole. And it is fun to see the girls getting along, seeing how well they've all turned out. Then I think about poor Lisa, and it just doesn't make sense. How could someone as smart as Janie have raised a girl like that?"

"Are you saying it's Janie's fault that Lisa got addicted to drugs?" Marley sounded slightly indignant.

"I don't know. It's not that I'm blaming Janie for Lisa's problems. But parents do have some responsibility for how their children turn out, don't you think?" Abby wasn't going to say it out loud, but she did credit herself for some of her daughters' successes. Why shouldn't she?

"So you probably think my son is . . . well,

the way he is . . . because of me?" Marley was walking faster, as if she was upset.

"No, no, not at all." Abby held up her hands.

"Because I am very proud of Ashton," Marley continued defensively. "He is a fine young man with wonderful qualities and the kindest heart imaginable. But I don't think it's because of me. I think it's because he is who he is."

"Yes, he is a fine young man," Abby echoed. "But don't you want to take just a smidgeon of the credit for it?"

Marley firmly shook her head. "No. The more I think about it, the more I think our children are going to be who they're going to be no matter what we do."

"Oh, I can't agree with that," Abby said. "What about children who are neglected or abused? What if they turn out to be serial killers?"

"Or what if they turn out to be like Caroline or Janie?"

Abby stopped walking and looked at Marley in wonder. "You know, you're right. Those girls didn't have very good child-hoods, and yet they turned out to be won-derful women."

"So do you credit Caroline's abusive

father for that? Or Janie's neglectful parents?"

"I guess not." Abby thought about this as they continued to walk. "I suppose I have a tendency to oversimplify sometimes," she admitted. "I want everything to be black and white and clear-cut. Maybe life's not really like that."

"Not usually. At least not for me."

"Not for me either," Abby conceded. "You'd think that by my age, I would've had that figured out."

Marley chuckled. "Well, I'm glad we still have some things to learn."

"And you know what I want to learn?" Abby said eagerly.

"What?"

"How to start thinking like a French woman!"

Marley nodded. "You know where I think it might begin, Abby?"

"Where?"

Marley pointed to her chest.

"We need to work on our bust lines?" Abby looked down at her own ample bosom and sighed. "I'm not sure there's much I can do about —"

Marley was laughing. "No, Abby, not our bust lines. We need to work on our hearts — our interior selves. Your mom told me

257

recently about how Jesus said we need to love our neighbors in the same way we love ourselves."

"Yes, of course. I know that."

"You may know that, Abby, but do you practice it?"

Abby thought about it and suddenly felt confused. "Maybe I don't know it as well as I thought. What do you think it really means?"

"I think it's like putting on your own air mask first," Marley told her. "You know the emergency warning the flight attendant gives before every flight, about securing your own air mask securely you before you help those around you?"

Abby had a good idea about where this was going.

Marley pointed at Abby. "You're one of the worst ones about this. You get so caught up in caring for everyone else — like your daughters or guests at the inn or your friends or even Paul — that you completely neglect yourself. You're like that passenger who's getting everyone's air mask safely on, and then she falls down dead in the aisle."

"That's a bit harsh."

"But it's true, Abby. We've told you this very thing before: You've got to start taking care of yourself *first*. That way you'll be in better shape to help someone else. Because how can you really help anyone if you're about to die of suffocation yourself?" Marley paused like she needed to catch her breath. "You know what? I think I'm preaching to myself, too. So maybe you and I need to make a pact to help each other remember this." She pointed to her chest again. "We need to take care of ourselves — we need love ourselves — even more so as we get older. And if we do, if we really do love ourselves, we'll be in a lot better shape to help someone else. Don't you think?"

Abby nodded dismally. "I suspect you're right."

Abby and Marley stopped walking and shook hands, right there on the beach, promising to be accountable to each other when it came to loving themselves. Really, the more Abby thought about it, the more sense it made. When Abby took a little extra time for herself, whether it was to indulge in a bubble bath or a good book or a walk on the beach, she usually did feel stronger and better equipped to help someone else. Once again — and her mother would laugh to hear Abby admit this — but it really did seem that Jesus knew what he was talking about.

CHAPTER 20
JANIE

Most people thought of Janie Sorenson as levelheaded, sensible, and in control. Right now she felt like anything but. At the moment, Lisa was in the guest room, crying. As unbelievable as it seemed, the reason Lisa was crying was because Janie had refused to give her twenty dollars. Twenty miserly bucks. And the reason Janie had refused to give Lisa that bit of money was because she knew — Janie absolutely knew — that Lisa would use it to buy drugs.

It wouldn't buy much, but it would buy enough. Then Lisa, having made a drug connection, would begin to slip back into the dead-end life that Janie so wanted her to leave behind.

"I'm done with that," Lisa had told Janie the day after Christmas. After several good talks, Janie actually believed she was starting to get somewhere with her confused daughter. Then today, after having lunch with Abby and Nicole, which had been strange but interesting, Lisa had opened up even more to Janie. For the first time ever, they both spoke openly about Lisa's dad, Phil, and how hard his cancer and death had been on them.

"I just couldn't deal with it," Lisa had admitted earlier this afternoon. "I felt so lonely at the time. I didn't know what to do, you know, to make the pain go away."

"I'm so sorry," Janie told her. "I realized too late that I should've been more available to you. All I can say is that was the hardest time of my life. Because you were older than Matthew, and because Matthew seemed to be dealing with it, I assumed you were too. I know how wrong I was to assume that. Please forgive me."

They had hugged, and Lisa had cried and said she did forgive Janie. And they had talked until Lisa was so exhausted that she wanted to take a nap. But after about an hour, Lisa was up and prowling around the house in a way that made Janie nervous. When she'd asked Lisa if she was looking for something, Lisa claimed she just wanted to walk to town.

"I just need some fresh air," she told Janie.

"Why don't we walk together?" Janie offered. "I could use some fresh air too."

"No. I need some time to myself," Lisa insisted. "I'm not used to all this hovering."

So Janie agreed, although secretly she planned to follow Lisa. But then Lisa casually asked for money, and when Janie questioned why, Lisa seemed sincerely hurt that Janie didn't trust her.

"Just twenty bucks," Lisa pleaded. "Surely you can spare that."

Janie had tried to tell her it wasn't about the money, but Lisa, being an expert in smoke screening, refused to budge from the accusation that her mother was a selfish tightwad and a few other choice labels that Janie felt shocked to hear come out of her daughter's pretty mouth.

As Janie sat in the living room, she found it difficult to believe that the angry young woman in the guest room had once been her sweet, tenderhearted little girl, and that they used to have such good times together. Janie even remembered times when all four of them — Phil, Matthew, Lisa, and Janie — had been out doing something, and people would look and sometimes comment on what a nice family they were. What had happened? And where could she go to undo it?

Janie had been trying to avoid the rehab conversation, at least until after the holidays were behind them. Mostly she just wanted to show Lisa how much she loved her, accepted her, and was glad to have her back in her life. So many times before, Janie had brought up rehab and Lisa had flown into a rage, claiming she didn't have a problem and accusing Janie of always thinking the worst of her. But perhaps the time had come to gently bring it up.

The attorney side of her brain said to do it and get it over with. The mother side of her brain was frightened. She didn't want to lose Lisa again. Finally, she decided to call Victor and see if he had any words of wisdom. So far, he'd been a rock regarding Lisa. Despite Lisa's chilly treatment toward him, Victor hadn't spoken one bad word against Lisa. Janie knew she could trust him. "I'd like to do an intervention," Janie quietly told him. She was standing outside in the front yard, afraid that Lisa might eavesdrop in the house and equally afraid that Lisa might sneak out and disappear altogether.

"An intervention with just you and Lisa?"

"I guess so."

"I don't know much about interventions, but wouldn't it be helpful to have a group?"

"Maybe so. Except that Lisa doesn't really have family or friends here."

"You have your friends, Janie. As much as we all love you, Lisa should be able to see that we care for her, too."

Janie told him a bit about lunch. "It was weird. I mean Lisa and Nicole couldn't be more different. And Lisa's a few years older than Nicole. But in a strange way they kind of hit it off. I think Abby was even surprised." Janie laughed uncomfortably. "Probably worried, too."

"Worried?"

"Oh, you know, that Lisa might corrupt Nicole."

"I seriously doubt that."

"Don't be too sure."

"Well, I'm not afraid to bring Ben over there. I'm sure he'd be willing. In fact, Ben had a buddy who went to rehab a couple years ago. Ben might even have a good perspective on it."

"If we did something like this, it would have to come across as really positive, I think. I mean Lisa is so negative and down on herself. So often she thinks her life is useless and wasted. We need to remind her that she's worth rescuing."

"Absolutely. Knowing how Lisa feels about me, I'd be fine staying in the background."

"That might be good. I do think Lisa

respects some of my friends. She and Caroline hit it off. And I noticed her talking to Sylvia's daughter, Leah, at the Christmas party and —" Janie stopped herself as she spotted Lisa furtively emerging from the front door. "Oh, dear. I may have to do an intervention right now."

"What's going —" Victor began to ask.

"She seems to be making a fast break. I'll see what I can do to encourage her to stick around — long enough to hear what I'd like her to do, anyway."

"I'll see who I can round up to back you up."

"Thanks." She shut off her phone and slowly walked toward Lisa. "Hey," Janie said in a friendly tone. "Still want to take that walk?"

Lisa scowled. "No. I just want a cigarette."

"Oh." Janie nodded. "Where is it?"

"What?"

"Your cigarette."

"I'm out."

"Oh." Janie didn't like that Lisa smoked. But cigarettes seemed minor in comparison to illegal drugs. "Want to go get some more?"

Lisa brightened. "Sure."

Before Lisa could suggest Janie give her money, Janie just started walking. "There's a market not far from here," she explained. "I'm sure they have cigarettes. Maybe we can get some pop and junk food too. For some reason I'm craving chips and chocolate." Lisa cast a suspicious glance her way, but Janie just kept on rambling. She felt like she was running on nerves as she walked and talked about the slumber party they'd had for Abby and how they'd eaten junk food and watched old movies. She talked nonstop until they were at the little convenience store.

Then they went in, and she and Lisa picked out all kinds of crazy stuff like canned cheese and Fritos and Blow Pops and Cheetos and Twizzlers and canned bean dip — the kinds of foods that Janie had given up back in college — and she even let Lisa buy a whole carton of cigarettes, which was surprisingly expensive. Because she didn't want Lisa to see how much cash she had, Janie used her debit card to pay for the purchase.

"It's getting cold again," Janie said as they went back outside. She waited while Lisa opened the carton, removed a pack of cigarettes, shook one out, and, with jittery fingers, lit it. Lisa closed her eyes and took a long slow pull on the cigarette, like she thought it was going to make up for whatever substance of choice she was missing. Maybe it was. Janie had read that chemicals like nicotine, caffeine, sugar, and salt were sometimes used as replacements for illegal substances.

"I guess we should've worn warmer jackets," Janie said as they started to walk again. On the return trip she talked about weather, asking Lisa if she remembered the times they'd all gone to the mountains together, and the first time Lisa and Matthew had snowboarded. Lisa smoked and Janie talked. She told Lisa about Matthew's new girlfriend and how they were snowboarding. "Actually, they're probably finished for the day." She looked at her watch. "Good grief, it's past seven o'clock on the east coast."

To her relief, they were soon back home again. Even better, Victor wasn't there yet. Although Janie did want him to come, she really hoped that he wouldn't arrive until she had Lisa safely back inside the house. Not that she could forcibly keep Lisa there. Janie continued to chatter at Lisa, hoping to hide her impatience as they stood on the front porch and she waited for Lisa to finish her fourth cigarette. "Let's go get warmed up," Janie said as she flung open the door.

Soon their odd assortment of purchases was splayed across the kitchen counters like a convenience store had exploded. Lisa began ripping into the bags and boxes, sampling as if she hadn't eaten in days. Janie hoped this substitute for drugs might have a placebo effect or at least calm Lisa enough to listen to reason and buy them some time. Janie prayed silently as she made a pot of strong coffee.

While Lisa visited the bathroom, Caroline arrived. Janie was so glad to see her that she threw her arms around her and pulled her inside. "Come in, come in. Welcome to the crazy house."

"Victor called," Caroline said quietly. "And Mitch is in the car, if you want him to join —"

"Not yet," Janie decided. "But it's perfect that you're here. I need you."

"Abby and Nicole are on their way. And Marley and Doris, too."

"Doris is coming?" For some reason it touched Janie to think that Abby's mother would care enough to come.

"Hey, Lisa," Caroline said casually as Lisa joined them in the kitchen.

"What're you doing here?" Lisa grabbed a handful of cheese puffs.

"I thought I'd crash your junk-food fest." Caroline picked up the box of Twinkies. "My favorite, by the way."

"Help yourself," Lisa told her. "We can all get sick together."

"I've got coffee brewing," Janie said.

Lisa didn't even seem suspicious when Abby and Nicole showed up. They claimed they were in the neighborhood, saw Caroline's car, and decided to pop in. "It's like a party," Abby said as she poured herself some coffee. Then when Doris and Marley arrived, Janie offered to order pizza for everyone. It wasn't until Victor and Ben arrived, bringing Mitch in with them, that Lisa seemed a little curious.

"Did you invite them?" she asked Janie.

"I think this is just serendipitous." Janie made what she hoped was a believable smile. "Maybe it's a pre–New Year's Eve party. Anyway, let's just go with it."

They were all in the living room, sitting in a circle like it was going to be a real intervention. Janie worried. What if Lisa got angry and decided to bolt? Janie exchanged glances with Victor, and he tipped his head in a very subtle nod, as if to say, *Go for it.*

Janie stood, and out of habit, from years of playing the attorney, she went into her legal mode. "Thank you all for coming here tonight," she told the group. "I know that reason you're all here is because you're my friends and you care about me. And on the

269

same token, you care about my daughter." She looked at Lisa. "We are here because we love you, Lisa. And we want to talk to you about your life and about how —"

"What is this?" Lisa's eyes narrowed.

"It's our way of telling you we care about you," Janie continued. "You are an intelligent and beautiful young woman with so much potential, but we're concerned for your welfare. And we're here tonight to tell you that we want to help you get your life back on track, and we have some ideas —"

"You're doing an intervention?" Lisa stood, glaring at Janie. "I can't believe this." Then she let loose with some language, though no one seemed offended. Janie attempted to speak again, looking directly into Lisa's eyes.

"I love you so much, Lisa. And it breaks my heart to see you —"

"I'm outta here!" Lisa took off toward the front door, but before she got there, Victor and Ben were up and blocking it.

"Just take it easy," Ben said calmly. "No one is going to hurt you. Trust us, Lisa, you're among friends."

In the meantime, Mitch had gotten up and was keeping guard in the kitchen near the back door. Janie looked around nervously, but her friends all seemed to be just fine, smiling at her, nodding as if all this was just perfectly normal.

"Hey, sweetie," Caroline said gently as she went over and put her arm around Lisa. "Come back in here and at least hear what we have to say. Ben is right. No one here is going to hurt you. We all love Janie, and we all love you."

"That's right," Abby chimed in. "You may never find a roomful of more caring people than what you have right here. Come back and listen to your mother."

Even though Lisa had the look of a scared rabbit, she allowed Caroline to guide her back into the living room. "It's okay to need help," Caroline was telling her. "Everyone needs help sometimes." She looked around the room. "Right?"

"That's right," Marley said. "And that's what friends are for."

"Lisa," Nicole said as she stood and went over to stand in front of her. "You told me on Christmas Day that you've been un-happy. You said you want a fresh start in your life. Remember?"

Lisa nodded.

"You said you wish you could go to France like I did, just to get away from everything."

"I'd like that," Lisa mumbled.

"I want to give you that," Janie said

271

eagerly. "Oh, honey, I would gladly pay your way to France if I thought it would help."

Lisa looked hopeful. "You would?"

Janie nodded. "Yes. I absolutely would. With all my friends here as witnesses, I promise to pay all your expenses to France if . . . if you get yourself completely clean and free from drugs."

"I am clean." Lisa nodded eagerly. "I haven't been using at all, Mom."

"For how long?" Janie asked quietly.

"I don't know." Lisa looked desperate. "A long time though."

"It's only been a few days."

"How do you know that?"

"Because I saw you when you got here, Lisa. I'm not blind."

"Yeah, but I haven't been using," Lisa persisted. "I've been clean the whole time I've been here."

"Really?" Janie peered intently at her.

"Well, yeah, I mean mostly."

"Here's the deal," Janie told her. "You have to be clean for a whole year before I can send you to France. And to do that you have to go in for treatment."

"Rehab?" Lisa frowned. "You want me to go to rehab?"

"Yes." Janie nodded firmly. "Because I love you."

Lisa began to fight back. Not physically, but with words and arguments and pleading. "You *don't* love me — you just want to control me. If you loved me, you'd trust me, Mom. You wouldn't be thinking the worst of me. You wouldn't be trying to send me away."

"I don't want to send you away, Lisa. I wish I could keep you here. But I can't help you. You need more —"

"How can you possibly know what I need? You're trying to force what you think I need, shoving it down my throat." Lisa started pacing again. "I can deal with this myself. All I wanted from you was a place to stay, Mom. Is that too much to ask?"

"You can't expect Janie to keep you here when you need real therapy," Abby said.

"How do you know what I need?"

"Everyone in this room can see what you need, honey." Caroline stood up and put a hand on her shoulder. "Everyone but you, Lisa. Sometimes it's like that. We all have blind spots, things about ourselves that we can't accept. But you just have to trust someone else. Do you believe your mother loves you?"

Lisa shrugged.

"I do love you, Lisa. All I want is what's best for you." Janie continued trying to

273

reason with her. But it was feeling more and more useless. Even when others stepped in, speaking truth to Lisa, it was like her ears were blocked. Finally, after almost two hours, Janie felt like giving up. She knew the others were tired too. She had to put a stop to this.

"I give up," Janie told Lisa. "As usual, you will get your way. Go out there and do your drugs and sleep with strangers and end up in a morgue somewhere. You win, Lisa!" Janie sat down next to Abby, and, holding her head in her hands, she started to sob. Abby slipped her arm around Janie and held her.

"Lisa." Caroline was speaking. "Your mom just told you that you won. But do you realize what that really means?" There was a long pause.

"Lisa, *you lost*," Nicole declared. "I can't believe you're going to throw it all away. I can't believe you'd be that stupid."

"Just go to rehab," Ben urged. "Like I told you, my best friend went, and it totally changed his life. You could have a life, Lisa. A real life."

Just like that, the others stepped in all over again, challenging Lisa, telling her not to pass on this opportunity.

"Lisa." Victor spoke up in a firm voice.

"You obviously have a choice to make. No one can make this choice for you. No one, unless you wind up in a court somewhere, will force you to go to rehab."

Janie looked up. "He's right, Lisa. It's your choice. No one will force you."

"Your mom is offering you an opportunity to get out of a lifestyle that will kill you," Abby said urgently. "Why won't you accept it?"

"Because it *will* kill you," Nicole said with emotion. She told Lisa about a friend of hers who died from an overdose. "He was only eighteen," she said finally, "with his whole life ahead of him too. But just like that it was gone. He doesn't get a second chance. You do."

Lisa's hands were shaking, and she was beginning to cry. Janie went over and wrapped her arms around her. "We want to help you, Lisa. We want to take care of you. Please, let us. All you have to do is agree that you need help. You do need help, don't you?"

Without speaking, Lisa nodded.

Several others came over and gathered around Janie and Lisa, speaking encouraging words, and some even prayed. Janie thanked them, and slowly they began to leave until it was only Victor, Ben, Janie, and Lisa.

"Do you want us to stick around?" Victor offered.

"No," Janie told him. "We'll be fine. Lisa has made her decision, and I think she's going to stick to it."

"Well, it is her choice," Victor reminded Janie. "No one can force her."

After they left, Lisa and Janie went to bed. As she'd done before, Janie tried to pray for her daughter, and as usual, it wasn't easy. When she said amen, she realized that Lisa might still change her mind, might even run away in the middle of the night. Really, what could Janie do about it? She considered trying to stay awake. She could go out in the living room and keep watch over the door. But the truth was, she was too exhausted — too emotionally spent from the past several days. Maybe Janie would regret it tomorrow, but Lisa was on her own tonight.

CHAPTER 21
CAROLINE

It had only been just over a week, but it was the longest time Caroline had spent with Mitch — well, at least since they'd been together back in the eighties, which seemed like another lifetime ago. Since his arrival, Mitch had been forced to mingle with her friends, spend time in her town, help sweep up construction dust in her house, walk her dog on the beach, and even participate in last night's intervention.

That was still the hot topic at the B and B's breakfast table the next morning.

"I feel like I've been initiated," Mitch told Caroline as he buttered his toast. "By the way, have you heard how Lisa is doing?"

"I saw her this morning," Nicole said as she set a platter of eggs and sausage in the center of the table. "I was jogging by, and Lisa was sitting on the porch puffing on a cigarette."

"Is she still agreeing to rehab?" Caroline

asked eagerly.

"Seems like it." Nicole sat down. "But she was in a rather nasty mood."

"Drugs will do that to you," Mitch said soberly.

"So is everyone coming to our New Year's Eve party tonight?" Abby asked as she joined them. "I didn't ask anyone to RSVP, and now I'm starting to worry. What if no one shows up?"

"Oh, so last night really wasn't a New Year's Eve party after all?" Mitch said in a teasing tone. "I thought maybe that's how you Clifden folks celebrated."

"Very funny." Caroline made a mocking smile.

"You've got to come," Nicole urged them. "Dad's gotten fireworks and everything."

"You're not supposed to tell anyone, Nicole," Abby chided.

"Yeah." Nicole nodded eagerly. "They're *illegal* fireworks."

"But Paul's very careful," Abby assured them. "He shoots them directly over the ocean. No one gets hurt."

"That sounds like fun." Caroline glanced over at Mitch, but his expression was impossible to read. "Doesn't it?"

He nodded in a reserved sort of way. "Sure, we'll come."

After breakfast, Caroline went into the kitchen to help Abby clean up. "It was sweet of you to come in to town to fix breakfast," she told her, "but you really didn't have to."

"Well, Mitch is a paying guest," Abby reminded her. "I don't want to get a reputation for being a slacker innkeeper. Especially since we barely got that bad review taken down."

"No worries there. And Mitch is very impressed with your master suite," Caroline said quietly. "He really wanted me to come check it out too."

Abby's brows arched.

"Of course I didn't." Caroline frowned. "Not only because of Nicole either. You know where I stand on that."

"How is it going with you two anyway?"

Caroline shrugged. "Sometimes he's hard to read."

"I hope I didn't twist his arm about coming tonight," Abby told her.

"But we didn't have any other plans." Caroline scrubbed a frying pan. "And getting a reservation anywhere, this late in the game . . . well, I think we're lucky we can come celebrate at your house. Fireworks over the ocean? Count me in."

"It's kind of a weird this year."

"What's weird?"

"This party." Abby shook her head. "Paul's determined to have it, but at the same time he's complaining about money right and left."

"Well, you know that business has been slow for him. Maybe he's feeling financially stressed, Abby."

"Yes, that's my point. He's financially stressed, and yet he's spending all this money on this party. It doesn't make sense."

"Paul always liked to throw a good party."

"And he's invited a bunch of people," Abby said in an unenthusiastic way. "A bunch of his friends too."

"Well, he should invite his friends, Abby."

"I know, but I have a feeling that means Bonnie."

"Oh." Caroline nodded. "Well, Bonnie is just a part of Clifden life. I guess you should get used to her."

"I was praying for Lisa last night," Abby said quietly. "I was thinking about how it must feel to be addicted and having to choose what's best for your life even if you think you want the other thing more."

"Uh-huh." Caroline dried the pan, hanging it on the rack over the stove.

"I realized it's probably like that for Paul, too."

Caroline didn't know what to say.

"I mean . . . I don't know. He might be attracted to Bonnie. It's only natural."

"But he's told you he's not —"

"Yes, yes. But I'm not dumb. And I have a point here, Caroline. Sometimes we're faced with tough choices. I realized that, just like Janie can't choose for Lisa, I can't choose for Paul."

Caroline nodded. "Yeah, and I can't choose for Mitch."

Nicole joined them. "I'm taking over for Caroline," she told them. "Mitch just told me that tomorrow's his last day in Clifden." She took the dish towel from Caroline. "He just told me he's flying to New Zealand in a few days. Lucky duck!"

"Mitch travels a lot for work," Caroline explained. "He spends most his time out of the country."

"Well, I want his job." Nicole grinned at Caroline. "Anyway, I figured you should be making the most the little time you have left with him, right?"

Caroline thanked them and went back out to where Mitch was standing in the living room, staring at the Christmas tree. "Looks like it's starting to dry out," he observed. "Guess the holidays are coming to an end."

"Do you mind going to Paul and Abby's?" she asked. "Because I'm happy with whatever we do. I just thought if we didn't have plans . . . Abby will understand if we have something else to do."

"No. I'm fine with that. Fireworks on the beach sounds like a kick."

"I'd like to take Chuck out to the beach while the sun's out," Caroline said absently.

He shrugged then looked out the window.

Suddenly she felt uncomfortable, the way one feels after having had a houseguest too long, like she was stumbling over manners and words, unsure of the right thing to do, and almost wishing the guest would just go home. Of course, that was ridiculous. This inn was not her house. Mitch was not her guest.

"Or maybe you'd like to do something else," she said lightly. "I've kind of been towing you around, haven't I? Forcing you to do what I normally do. Feel free to do as you like, Mitch. This was supposed to be your vacation, too, right?"

He made what seemed a tolerant smile. "I've enjoyed being with you."

She nodded. "And I've enjoyed being with you. Now Chuck would enjoy a run on the beach. Feel free to come . . . or not."

He looked over at the easy chair and otto-man. "You know, I think I'll just hang out here and put my feet up and read, if you don't mind."

Her smile felt a little stiff. "Sure."

Out on the beach, she tried to figure out what was going on with Mitch. At times he seemed resentful of her close relationships, like he wanted more of her attention and time, like maybe he wanted to be the center of her life and universe. Yet he didn't put any energy into planning things for them to do together, and when she did make plans, he seemed to resent it. And sometimes he seemed distant, like he wanted his space. Although some of his needs made sense, she wasn't sure that she was completely comfortable with them.

On the one hand, she had almost expected a proposal from him this week. On the other hand, she was hugely relieved that she hadn't received one. Really, what was the hurry?

Just when she got Chuck loaded into the back of her car and rolled down the windows to keep his hot panting breath from steaming up the windows, her phone rang. It was Bonnie, and she sounded happy. "Oh, Caroline," she exclaimed, "you have got to see this."

"What is it?"

"A surprise."

"Really?" Caroline started the car.

"Can you come over to your house?"

"I'll be there in ten minutes," Caroline promised. As she drove, she wondered what was going on. She hoped it was a good surprise. She'd been pleasantly surprised that the wooden floors were installed yesterday, although she'd barely seen them before someone covered them with brown paper. "To protect them," one of Paul's guys had assured her. Hopefully nothing had happened to mess them up.

When she got to her house, she realized what was going on — the cabinetmaker's truck was in the driveway. She hurried to put Chuck in the backyard, then went into the kitchen and couldn't believe her eyes when she saw the sleek maple cabinets partially installed.

"Oh, Bonnie!" she cried out. "They are beautiful."

"Remember when you picked out that hardware?" Bonnie said as she opened a gorgeous wooden door. "It's perfect in here."

"I absolutely love them." Caroline ran her hand over the smooth finish. "They're so pretty."

"And look at this." Bonnie pulled back a bit of the brown paper to show the wood floors where they met the cabinets. "Check out the contrast. Isn't it gorgeous?"

"Ooh, I can't wait to see the whole room put together. This will be the prettiest kitchen I've ever had." She slowly shook her head. "My mom would fall over if she could see it. I mean if she were in her right mind. Back when she was younger, she liked a pretty house and pretty furnishings too. She would've loved this."

"Well, we should get out of their way," Bonnie told Caroline. "I just thought you'd like a peek."

"Thanks."

"I've got to call and check on the counters and the plumber and . . ." Bonnie waved her hand. "Well, you don't need to concern yourself, Caroline. That's why you have me."

Caroline couldn't stop herself from hugging Bonnie. Oh, she knew Abby would be hurt if she could see this, but Bonnie deserved it. "Thanks, Bonnie. You're a miracle worker."

Bonnie looked pleasantly surprised. "It's my job."

"And you do it well."

"I enjoy seeing happy clients."

Caroline thanked her again. "I've got to go, and I'm going to leave Chuck in the backyard," she told her. "I want Mitch to see this. I'm sure he'd like to see me drooling over the cabinets." The workers laughed, and Caroline promised to bring some donuts for them.

She didn't tell Mitch why she wanted him to come to her house, and she supposed that he assumed she wanted him to help her clean something up. So when she took him inside and said, "Ta-da," she was hoping for more of a reaction than the one he gave.

"What are we looking at?" he asked.

"The cabinets," she told him. "Aren't they fabulous?"

He nodded. "Oh yeah. New cabinets. Very nice."

She felt embarrassed and glad that the workers were on their lunch break. "I guess I thought it was a bigger deal than that," she said quietly. "Sorry to drag you over here." She turned and gave him a very forced smile. "So what would you like to do today?"

"How about if we talk?"

"Okay." She looked around the room. Other than a couple of sawhorses and giant paint buckets, there wasn't much to sit on. "Want to go out in back?"

So, with their coats on, they sat in her backyard. "What do you want?" Mitch asked Caroline in a very serious tone.

"Want?" She studied him. "I'm not sure

what you mean."

"What do you want?" he said again. "I mean in life. What is it you're looking for, Caroline?"

"Looking?" She considered this. "I'm not even sure that I'm looking for anything."

"Meaning you've found everything you want?"

"No." She shook her head. "Of course not. But I guess I'm happy, if that's what you mean."

"Happy? As in content with your lot in life?"

"My lot?"

"You know." He waved his hand toward the backyard, where Chuck was contentedly chewing on the soup bone she'd picked up for him yesterday. "Clifden . . . your friends . . . your dog . . . your house. *This.*"

Caroline felt confused. "The way you say 'this' seems like you think it's not enough. Is that what you're insinuating?"

"I'm not sure." He leaned toward her, taking both her hands in his. "I love you, Caroline. I think you know that."

She just nodded.

"But I'm not sure that *this* is enough for me."

"*This* as in Clifden and everything that goes with it, or *this* as in me?"

His brow creased like he was thinking about it. And as she sat there, looking at him, she suddenly saw how different they were. Mitch, in his Italian shoes, cashmere sweater, and neatly pressed khakis — he looked like a million bucks. She knew that his bank account was worth a whole lot more than that. She looked down at herself — her dusty jeans, sand-encrusted running shoes. What a mismatch they appeared to be on the surface. But underneath all that, weren't they the same? Or had she simply been fooling herself? Maybe you could take the girl out of Clifden, but you couldn't take Clifden out of the girl.

"Being here with you this past week . . ." He sighed. "It's been interesting. Maybe even eye-opening."

"What were you expecting?" she asked quietly. "I mean, when you came this time. How did you think it would be?"

"Well, to be honest, I probably had been daydreaming about something that doesn't even exist."

"Such as?"

"You finally being free. I mean, it sounds corny, but I think I'd been thinking of you as my lovely princess who was trapped in the dungeon. Not that your mother was a dungeon — I don't mean that. But it seemed that you'd been under her spell. Like you were unable to leave her, to travel with me, to be free."

"That's kind of true."

"But then I got here, and it seemed like you were still trapped, Caroline."

"Trapped?"

"Yes. Like Clifden and your friends, and even this house. It's all got a hold on you."

She took in a deep breath, held it for a few seconds, then slowly let it out. "Wow."

"Can you see it now?"

"Sort of." She shook her head. "It is weird if you think about it. I mean, I ran away from here years ago planning never to come back. I wanted a bigger life." She made a weak laugh. "I wanted stardom. And more. I wanted it all."

"And now?"

She looked directly into his eyes. "Oh, don't be fooled, Mitch. I still want it all."

"Oh?" He looked hopeful.

"I'm just not sure what *all* is anymore."

"You know, Caroline, I came here with an agenda."

"An agenda?"

He nodded. "I wanted to ask you to marry me."

She took in a quick breath.

"But the timing just hasn't been right."

She nodded, slowly letting the breath out.

"I wanted to talk you into zipping over to Reno with me, getting married, and then going to New Zealand with me."

"Really?"

"Yes. But I kept seeing these flags. Or maybe they're stop signs. I'm not sure. But what I want to know is . . . are you really sending me some signals? Or am I imagining them?"

"I'm not sure, but I think I've seen some flags or signals too, Mitch." She looked directly into his eyes. "I do love you. And I suspect if you'd asked me to marry you — as soon as you'd arrived — I would've said yes."

"Really?"

"I think so."

"But not now?"

"Now, I'm just not sure. In fact, I've been rather relieved that you didn't bring it up."

He was still holding her hands in his. "So where do we go from here?"

"I don't know."

"I'm sure I can't talk you into coming to New Zealand with me, can I?"

"I — I just don't see how."

"No. Once again, my timing seems to be off." He let go of her hands.

"It's not that I'm rejecting you, Mitch.

It's just that I have commitments here. I promised to go on the cruise with my friends."

"Yes, I know." He looked slightly hurt again.

"And I need to be around to see that my house gets finished."

"Which you are never going to sell, are you?"

"I don't know. But I can't just walk out on it, can I? I mean it's my responsibility to complete what I started."

He looked skeptical.

"I feel like you're offering me the world on a silver platter," she said slowly. "And, believe me, it's very tempting. Just a few years ago, maybe even a year ago, I would've jumped at it."

"But not now?"

"It's not as tempting."

"Why not?"

"Because it's your world and your silver platter."

"But I'd gladly share it with you."

She smiled. "I know you would. But maybe I'd like to share my world with you, too."

He nodded, but his expression seemed to confirm that her world really wasn't big enough for him. They both just sat there.

The only sounds were a far-off siren and Chuck chewing on his bone. "I think I'm going to go home today instead of tomorrow," he said slowly.

"Because of me?"

"Because I need some time to think. Maybe we both need some time." He peered up at the sky. "And because the weather is clear today, and tomorrow is supposed to get foggy again."

"Oh."

"Will you be terribly disappointed if I don't go to the party tonight?"

She shrugged. "I think you would've enjoyed it, Mitch."

"Yeah, you're probably right." He stood and pulled her to her feet and into his arms. "But what would we do if I got too caught up in the moment — too much champagne, the fireworks over the water, my beautiful girl in my arms — and I proposed? Then where would we be?"

Caroline kissed him. "Maybe you're right, Mitch. Maybe you should go home today. We both need some time. Some time to think."

They were quiet on the ride to the municipal airport, and they kept their good-byes short and sweet, but his plane looked blurry as it shot up into the clear blue. For a moment, Caroline thought the fog was rolling in after all. But then she realized it was just the tears filling her eyes. She waved wildly with both arms, knowing he probably couldn't see her from up there. And as she walked back to her car, she wondered if she'd made a huge mistake.

CHAPTER 22
MARLEY

Perhaps it was romantic frustration, or just a matter of financial planning for her old age, or maybe her pump had been primed by *Walter Cronkite,* but Marley was painting again — and it felt good. She was in the zone. It showed not only on her canvases, but in her bungalow, where her bed was unmade, the kitchen a mess, and the garbage can overflowing. Plus, she was sorely in need of provisions. And a shower. She was so obsessed with her art, she hadn't even answered her phone.

At least that's what she told herself as she ignored its ringing. Later, when taking a break, she would check for messages and, if she was so inclined, return a call. However, she hadn't returned Jack's calls. Whether it was hurt feelings, immaturity, or just plain confusion was unclear. But Marley knew she was in avoidance mode.

When she heard someone knocking on her

door, however, she had to set down her brush. Thinking it was probably Doris, she yelled, "Come in!" as she wiped her paint-smeared hands on a rag.

"Marley!" cried Hunter as she came into the house. "Are you okay?"

"Oh." Marley stared at the little girl. "How did you get out here?"

"Grandpa brought me." Hunter tipped her head over to where Jack was still waiting outside.

"Oh. Well, come in, both of you." She offered a feeble smile, holding up her hands. "I'm a mess and my house is a mess, but welcome."

"I called you on the phone," Hunter told her. "But you never answered. And I told Grandpa I was worried about you."

Marley knelt down and looked in Hunter's eyes. "You are such a darling — I'd hug you except that I'd probably get paint on you."

"That's okay. These are just play clothes anyway." Hunter hugged Marley.

Marley hugged the little girl back. "I missed you," Marley whispered in her ear.

"I missed you, too." Hunter looked over to the painting Marley was working on. "Wow, that's pretty. Is it going to be a boat?"

Marley showed Hunter the photo that was the inspiration for her piece. "I guess it doesn't look much like this, but it is going to be a boat."

"Nice." Jack came closer, rubbing his chin in the way he did when he liked something.

"Thanks." She smiled at him. "How are you doing?"

"It's been busy."

"But that's good thing."

"Yep." He frowned slightly. "How are you?"

"Well, I finally emerged out of my creative slump. But I think I've been kind of obsessed lately." She ran a hand through her uncombed hair. "At least I haven't cut off an ear yet."

Jack made an uncomfortable-sounding laugh.

"You're going to cut off your ear?" Hunter asked with concern.

"No, darling, I'm just kidding. There was an artist a long time ago who did that. I made a bad joke." She turned back to Jack. "I'm sorry you felt like you needed to drive out here to check on me. It's just that I've been so absorbed with painting." She waved her hand. "As you can see, I've let everything else go." She kicked a pair of clogs out of the way, tossed some pillows that had fallen on the floor back onto the sofa. "I suppose it's time to take a break and clean this place up."

"I can help you," Hunter offered.

"Really?" Marley patted her head. "You'd be willing to do that?"

"I'd like to help."

Marley looked at Jack. "Want to leave Hunter with me for the rest of the day?"

He shrugged. "It's up to Hunter."

"Please, Grandpa," she pleaded.

"Looks like you girls got yourself a date." He stepped back toward the door. "And I better get back to the gallery. Town is hopping today." He glanced at a painting of a lighthouse leaning against the wall. Marley had just finished it yesterday. "Anything you'd like me to take back with me?" he asked her. "Or are these for Santa Barbara?"

Caught off guard, she didn't know what to say. On the one hand, she liked the idea of getting an optimum price for her work, on the other hand, this was Jack — the man who'd believed in her work enough to hang it in his gallery. "Why don't you go ahead and take that one?" she told him.

"Really?" He brightened. "How about the price?"

"I'll trust you to figure that out." She smiled at him — a genuine smile this time.

"Okay." He nodded as he picked it up and studied it. "It's really nice. I'll price it accordingly."

"Thanks, Jack."

"See you later," he called as he headed out.

Marley, aided by Hunter, went to work setting her bungalow to order. "The trouble with a small house," Marley told Hunter as they worked on the kitchen together, "is that if you don't keep everything in its place, it gets messy fast."

"I love your house."

"Thanks, Hunter. I do too."

"And I like that you don't have a TV."

"Really?" Marley peered curiously at her. "You used to complain about that."

"TV is boring." Hunter scrubbed hard on the stovetop. "Leah watches TV all day long. She doesn't even know how to draw or paint or color or anything."

Marley chuckled. "Well, maybe you should teach her."

"I don't think she wants to learn."

After the house was looking pretty good, Marley handed Hunter the leftover paints still in her palette as well as small canvas. "Why don't you see what you can do with this while I take a shower?"

"Really?" Hunter stared at the blank canvas. "A real painting?"

"Sure. You're a good artist."

"What should I paint?"

"What do you want to paint?"

Hunter looked over at Marley's unfinished piece. "A boat."

"Then paint a boat." Marley pulled out several other photos, laying them around on the nearby table. "But make it your own boat — however you want it to look. Not just like the photos."

Hunter nodded eagerly. "Okay!"

Marley took her time in the long-overdue shower — one of the many benefits of an on-demand water heater. When she got out, she checked on Hunter, who was still intently working on her canvas. "Don't look yet," Hunter warned her.

"Okay. I guess I'll do my hair then."

"Good idea," Hunter called back.

Marley took her time doing her hair. Mindful of what she'd been telling Abby about French women, Marley decided to put some extra effort into the rest of her appearance as well. She told herself she wasn't primping for Jack's sake, although she knew she was looking forward to seeing him again when she took Hunter back to him. She was embarrassed to have been caught looking so frowsy, especially considering how Sylvia usually looked — coiffed and perfect.

"You look pretty," Hunter told Marley when she finally emerged.

"Thanks."

"Is that because today is New Year's Eve?" Hunter asked.

Marley slapped her forehead. "It's New Year's Eve today?"

"Uh-huh." Hunter's attention turned back to her painting.

"How the time flies." She looked around her tidied bungalow. "I think you must've gotten here just in the nick of time."

"Huh?"

"To help me start the New Year right. It would've been such a shame to welcome the New Year like a pig in a pig pen."

Hunter laughed. "Okay, you can come look at my picture now. I'm almost done."

Marley came over to see that Hunter had nearly filled the canvas with a lopsided sailboat, which was painted blue and green and red. All around the boat was blue with a small yellow sun, complete with sunrays, in the corner. "That's beautiful," Marley told her.

"Is it okay if I give it to Grandpa?"

"Of course. It's yours to do with as you like. Do you want Grandpa to hang it in the gallery to sell?"

"No, I want him to hang it in his house.

I'll give it to him for his birthday."

"When's his birthday?"

"January fourth."

"Wow, that's coming right up."

"I know." Hunter nodded eagerly. "Sylvia is planning a surprise party for him. You're coming, right?"

Marley didn't know what to say — this was all news to her. "Uh, sure, I think so."

Hunter turned and peered curiously at her. "Did you and Grandpa have a fight?"

"No, of course not."

"Oh."

"After the paint dries, you'll have to sign your name on the bottom," Marley told Hunter as she finished. "I have a special brush for that. Now let's get these brushes and your hands cleaned up. Have you had lunch yet?"

Discovering they both were hungry and that her cupboards were bare, Marley asked Hunter if she wanted to go grocery shopping with her. Fortunately, Hunter was game. As they made their way through the grocery store, Marley learned through tidbits of conversation that Sylvia and Leah were becoming a big part of Jack's and Hunter's lives. Marley wasn't particularly surprised by this, but she was dismayed and confused.

Marley rewarded Hunter for her help, which was truly helpful, by letting her buy a New Year's Eve party pack, which was conveniently displayed right next to the check stand. Of course, the glittery hats and blowers and confetti seemed cheesy to Marley, but to Hunter they shouted of party and fun times.

"Can we have a New Year's Eve party?" Hunter asked as Marley was driving back to the bungalow.

"Well, it is New Year's Eve," Marley conceded. She remembered the invitation to the party at Paul and Abby's tonight. She'd planned on going, and Abby had told her that Jack was invited too. But thanks to her painting frenzy, she'd lost track of time. "We could have a New Year's Eve lunch party," Marley suggested.

"No, I mean a real party," Hunter urged. "Where we stay up until midnight."

"Oh?"

"Grandpa and Sylvia got invited to a *real* New Year's Eve party tonight. And Leah is supposed to babysit me, but I heard her saying she doesn't think that's fair. Why don't you and me have a party, Marley?"

Marley was torn in several directions — partly mad, partly hurt, and mostly indignant that Hunter was being treated as a castoff again. "Okay," Marley declared. "You and me *will* have a party."

"Yay!" Hunter clapped her hands. "What will we do?"

"Uh, I'm not sure. Make popcorn?"

"Yeah. And how about brownies?" Hunter had encouraged Marley to buy a brownie mix.

"Yes. Definitely brownies."

And just like that, she and Hunter were planning their New Year's Eve party — a party of two. And, hey, Marley consoled herself, it was a step up from the Christmas Eve pity party for one. Marley didn't call Jack until nearly six.

"I was wondering when I'd hear from you," Jack told her. "How's it going?"

"Great." Marley kept the upbeat tone in her voice. "Hunter and I are having a wonderful time. So great, in fact, that she'd like to spend the night here. Would that be okay?"

"Spend the night?" He sounded caught off guard.

"You don't mind, do you? I promise to take good care of her."

"Oh, I'm not worried about that, Marley." He cleared his throat. "But you do know that it's New Year's Eve, don't you?"

"Oh, sure. In fact, we're having our own

little New Year's Eve party."

"Really?"

"Hunter explained that everyone else has plans, and I love the idea of a quiet little celebration at home." She grinned at Hunter. "And there's no one I'd rather ring in the New Year with than my little buddy here. Right, Hunter?"

"Right on!" Hunter shouted into the phone.

"So, unless you have any objections, I'll keep Hunter until tomorrow."

"No, no objections."

"And you and Sylvia have a delightful evening, Jack. Happy New Year!" Unable to carry out her charade a second longer, she hung up. After that, she called Abby, explaining why she'd have to decline on her invitation.

"But we're having fireworks," Abby protested.

"Fireworks?"

Hunter, who'd been listening, started getting excited. *"Fireworks?"* she repeated hopefully.

"Paul's going to shoot them out over the ocean, and Lucy's going to be here too. Why don't you bring Hunter over?"

"I guess we could do that if Hunter wants to."

"And if you do come, maybe you won't mind giving Mom a ride home? Nicole picked her up and brought her over to help, but she doesn't have her own wheels."

So it was that around ten o'clock, after Hunter and Marley did their own little celebration, complete with brownies and popcorn, blowers and hats, Hunter bagged up her party goodies (for her and Lucy to use again) and they bundled up and headed on over to Paul and Abby's, where Lucy was thrilled to see that someone closer to her size had finally arrived.

Marley was only mildly surprised to see Jack and Sylvia at the party. But Jack looked shocked to see Marley, coming right over to her. "Is something wrong?" he asked with concern.

"Not at all," she said lightly. "Abby enticed us to come over for the fireworks. As soon as that's over, we'll head back home." And then she waved at Caroline, who was alone, excusing herself from Jack as if she had something urgent to discuss with Caroline. But when Caroline got a phone call that sounded like it was from Mitch, Marley moved on. She felt like she was spending all her time and energy trying to avoid Jack. Just as she joined Janie and Victor, asking about Lisa's welfare, she wondered why she was going to so much trouble.

"She hasn't bolted yet," Janie told Marley. "And although she said she didn't want to at first, she changed her mind and came with me tonight."

"She didn't know I was going to be here," Victor said a bit sadly.

"She's still keeping you at arm's length?" Marley asked.

He nodded. "I'm sure she sees me as threat."

"At least she likes Ben," Janie said. "She and Nicole and Ben and some of the other young people just left for a walk on the beach."

"That's great." Marley focused on Janie, still trying not to catch Jack's eye, although she felt certain he was staring at her.

"Tomorrow, I'm driving Lisa down to Northern California," Janie said. "To the same rehab place that Ben's friend raved about. I'm feeling hopeful."

"That's fantastic."

"Don't look now," Janie said quietly, "but I think Jack is coming for you."

"Hey, Jack." Victor smiled. "How's it going?"

"Okay." Jack made some polite small talk then turned to Marley. "Do you think I could have a private word with you, Marley?"

She blinked. "A private word?"

He made an uneasy smile toward Janie and Victor. "Would you excuse us?" Then he took Marley by the arm. "Maybe we should go outside."

"Okay." She nodded, glancing over to where Sylvia was watching from a distance. Marley was curious as to how Sylvia would react to this, but perhaps she'd assume this was some kind of impromptu business meeting regarding Marley's paintings. For all Marley knew, it was. But Marley stayed with Jack as he led her toward the front door and then out.

Once they were outside, Jack continued to walk. "I've left a number of messages for you, Marley . . . did you get them?" His voice sounded slightly strained.

Marley nodded nervously.

"I wanted to thank you in person for the chess set. It's fabulous. And I'd actually been hoping I could entice you over for a game. But everything's been so crazy and busy lately — and you've been so —"

"You're welcome, Jack. I saw the set and thought of you."

"I wanted to give you your Christmas

present too, but you've been a little hard to reach."

"Yes, I got your message, Jack." Of course, when she heard that particular message on Christmas Day, she assumed that he'd run out and bought her something just to recompense her for his gift, and she was uninterested in a payback gift. If they were parting ways, they should do it quietly and without playing games.

"I'd actually been hoping to spend this evening with you, Marley."

"Really?" She turned and looked curiously at him.

"You didn't get that message?"

She shrugged. "I'm not sure, unless I mistakenly deleted it." She had gotten a bit careless in deleting messages from him. It seemed easier that way. There was a long pause as they continued walking down the darkened street, with only the sound of the nearby surf pounding and an occasional car to break the silence.

Jack stopped walking and placed a hand on her shoulder. "I just want to know one thing, Marley. Are you intentionally pushing me away?"

"Pushing you away?"

"Yes. You've been so distant. I told myself you were consumed with your art. And I can understand that. I mean, having the kind of attention you've recently received, well, naturally you'd be distracted by your career. But seeing you this morning, then talking to you on the phone this evening . . . I got worried."

"Why would you be worried?" Marley hated playing coy, and yet she was in unfamiliar territory.

"I'm worried because I think I'm losing you, Marley." Jack sighed. "And I can accept that, even if I don't want to. Mostly I just want to know. Living on Limbo Lane is for the birds. And, really, I always felt you were too good for me, Marley. Too smart and talented, too young, too pretty, too —"

"What?" Marley leaned forward, peering into Jack's eyes in the shadowy light of the street lamp. "Are you nuts?"

He looked surprised. "Not completely. I mean I've been accused of being a little crazy — aren't all artists a bit unbalanced?"

She just shook her head. "Okay, Jack, now I have a question for *you*."

"Shoot."

"Well, I was under the impression that you and Sylvia were, uh, dating."

"Dating?" Jack sounded horrified. "Are you serious?"

"Absolutely."

"We are *not* dating."

"You're here together tonight."

"Because you wouldn't come with me. And Paul invited Sylvia and Leah and everyone who was at the Christmas party. When Sylvia heard you weren't coming, she asked if it would be all right for us to ride over here together."

"And you don't think of that as a *date?*"

Jack got a look like the lightbulb had just been turned on. "Oh, Marley, you don't think . . . ?"

She nodded.

"You honestly think that Sylvia thinks that she . . . that I . . . that she and I . . . ?"

"Like they used to say in the old days, Jack, and maybe even when you were younger" — she chuckled — "I think Sylvia has set her cap for you."

"Oh, Marley, I don't think so. She's just new in town, and she and Leah have been so helpful with Hunter. I thought that was helping you, too, giving you time to paint and get your life back. But, really, I don't think that Sylvia has the slightest interest in an old coot like me."

Marley narrowed her eyes. "First of all, you're not an old coot — you're more like an old fox."

His brows arched.

"But that's beside the point, Jack. The point is, it's not unreasonable that someone like Sylvia would be attracted to you."

"But I'm not attracted to her."

"Does she know that?"

He looked honestly flummoxed. "I have no idea. I mean, naturally, I'm polite to her. She's my employee and a friend."

"Has she spent time at your house?" Marley already knew the answer to this. Hunter had mentioned it while they were grocery shopping.

"Well, yes. But that's because she drops off and picks up Leah. And sometimes the two of them have planned a meal there. But that's because my kitchen is all set up, and they aren't really settled in yet. And Sylvia likes to cook."

"Right." Marley nodded with a skeptical look.

Jack just shook his head. "I never thought of it like that, Marley, I swear I *never* . . ."

Marley put both her hands on his cheeks. "I believe you, Jack. But call it women's intuition or whatever, I'm sure that Sylvia thought of it like that. I've seen her look at you. And, trust me, I'm not the only one."

"Oh dear." He looked truly puzzled. "So what do I do? Fire her?"

"No, of course not. She's a good employee. And she needs the work as badly as you need a worker."

"Then what?"

Marley thought hard. "Well, Jack, I think you just need to draw the line, and then you don't let your relationship cross over it. If Sylvia offers to fix you dinner, no matter how nicely she puts it, you say, 'No, thank you, Sylvia.' If she asks to accompany you to a party, you suggest she find another ride."

"Okay. I can do that."

Marley started walking again, shoving her hands into her pockets.

"But back to *us*, Marley." Jack hurried to catch up, his slightly offbeat gait reminding her of the prosthesis that had replaced his missing leg. Sometimes she completely forgot about his accident. Not that it mattered, but it took her by surprise.

"*Us*, Jack?" She slowed down.

"We're still an *us*, aren't we?" he asked hopefully.

She turned and smiled at him. "Are we?"

He reached over and took her hand. "We are as far as I'm concerned. Not a thing has changed with me."

She studied him closely, and she believed him. "Nothing has changed with me either, Jack. But just for the record, I might be a little gun-shy. I mean, I've had some experience with a man who was unfaithful to me. I don't ever want to go through that again. So I suppose if it I see it coming — or even think I see it coming, well, I just run the other way."

"I can understand that, Marley. But I promise you, that is not who I am. I would never be unfaithful to you."

"I believe you, Jack."

He leaned in and kissed her with such sweet and tender passion that she felt slightly breathless. And then — *ka-boom* — the sky lit up with fireworks.

"Wow!" Marley laughed. "That was quite a kiss!"

CHAPTER 23
ABBY

The week prior to the cruise passed in a crazy and frantic rush. There were many moments when Abby wondered if her cruise tickets were really a prize or a curse. For starters, it just figured that two different parties would want to book a room at her inn the same week of the cruise. Thanks to Caroline's suggestion, Abby came up with a gracious way to let them down. She apologized profusely, promising a discount coupon for the next time they booked a room with her. Of course, that meant she would lose a bit of money on down the line, but perhaps she would gain a loyal customer or two as well.

The next problem came with Janie. They'd all been so relieved to know that Lisa was safely tucked into her rehab facility in California. But when Abby heard, via Caroline, that the place had an open-door policy, meaning the rehab patients signed them-

selves in and could sign themselves out —
there was no lockdown — she felt concerned. Naturally, that made it very easy for
Lisa to walk out on the second day of her
stay. Janie was frantic and didn't know
whether to go down there and try to look
for Lisa or just wait and see. She confided
to Caroline, who told Abby, that if Lisa was
out wandering the streets again, Janie might
be forced to forgo the cruise! How could
she possibly enjoy a luxurious vacation
knowing her daughter was starving on the
streets? Abby understood that (she was a
mother, after all), but it still made her mad.

Janie sat tight, however, and Lisa called
the next evening to say she was sorry, that
she'd gotten scared, and that she really did
want rehab after all. The rehab facility had
a one-time-only return policy (kind of like a
get-back-in-jail free card), so Lisa was allowed to reenlist. However, if she bolted
again, she would be locked out for good.
Abby wondered if this kind of reverse
psychology really worked. But Janie seemed
hugely relieved. And so far so good. Lisa
was still in the treatment facility.

Then there was Marley. It seemed that she
and Jack were rekindling their romance,
and, as a result, Marley had lost interest in
the long-awaited cruise. She even suggested

that Abby invite Doris to go in her place.

"But we are the *Four* Lindas," Abby had protested. "Not the Three Lindas and one mom." So Marley promised, rather half-heartedly, that she would still go. But then she confessed that, despite Jack's claim in having no interest in Sylvia, Marley was still deeply insecure. She worried that Sylvia would work her feminine charms on unsuspecting Jack and steal him away. Of course, Abby had no response to this. To admit to her own insecurity would only reinforce Marley's doubts, but it was Abby's experience that men were sometimes jerks.

Then there was Caroline, who'd been privy to all of these wet blankets. Abby suspected that Caroline was simply playing Miss Congeniality, which she did so well, by pretending that nothing was wrong between her and Mitch. But Abby knew better. Mitch had suddenly decided to go home, and on New Year's Eve no less. Abby wasn't saying anything, but a man in love doesn't suddenly dump his date on New Year's Eve, does he? Not if he's truly in love. So was Caroline suffering a broken heart in silence? If so, perhaps a warm, sunny cruise with good friends would be just the right medicine.

Then, last and possibly least, there was

316

Abby and Paul. Throughout the holidays, they'd both been on their best behavior, which was nothing to brag about. But with the holidays behind them and real life ahead, Abby felt them starting to unravel again. When Paul missed their scheduled counseling appointment the first week of January, Abby was more than a little miffed.

Still, she was determined not to rock the marriage boat. She was imagining the much bigger boat she'd soon be boarding, as well as the distance she would be putting between her and Paul. Seriously, if Abby didn't have children and friends, she would be tempted to get off on one of those sunny Mexican ports and refuse to get back on. Who knew? Maybe she would do it anyway. Perhaps she was destined to run a sweet little adobe B and B south of the border.

Finally, the day of the trip arrived, and somehow — to Abby's utter amazement — all Four Lindas and their bags, which were considerable, were on the flight to San Diego. Once they got settled in, everyone seemed to be in fairly good spirits. They were in even better spirits as they boarded the cruise ship. Best of all, after they'd seen their cabins and changed into more comfortable clothes, they sat on deck in the sun with margaritas in hand.

"To the Four Lindas," Marley started the toast.

"And to Abby for sharing her dream trip with us," added Caroline.

"And to our loved ones at home," Janie said a bit quietly.

"To Mexico!" Abby proclaimed.

"Did you guys know that Paul sent Abby a big bouquet of flowers?" Caroline announced. She and Abby were sharing a cabin. "They were already in the cabin when we got here. Just like in a movie."

"Oh, that's so sweet of him," Janie told her.

"And so unlike him," Abby said wryly. Of course, the flowers made Abby suspicious. What was Paul feeling guilty about, or trying to make up for, or camouflage? What exactly did he plan to do while she was gone? Had she been a fool to leave him home alone?

As she leaned back in the deck chair and sipped her drink, she decided not to go there. No, she refused to let her frets over Paul spoil this week for her. She was going to have fun, and that was all there was to it! Seven days of sun, fun, and friends — what could be better?

It had been Abby's idea to dress up for dinner on their first night of the cruise, but now she was regretting it. "This dress looked a lot better on me in the shop," she told Caroline as she scowled at her image in the full-length mirror.

"It's lovely, Abby. And the blue is perfect with your eyes." Caroline tucked Abby's bra strap under the dress's shoulder. "Just stand up straight. Let's do something with your hair, and then I'll help you with your makeup."

"Good luck." Abby turned away from her own reflection. "I don't know what made me think I could look pretty. Honestly, that ship sailed a long time ago."

"Oh Abby."

"It's true." Abby sighed. "I used to be considered pretty."

"You still are pretty."

Abby laughed. "And you still are sweet. But be honest, Caroline, do you remember how I used to look?"

"Of course. You were the prettiest girl in high school. We all remember."

Abby stood a bit straighter. "Well, some thought you were prettier, Caroline."

Caroline smiled as she tucked and pinned another strand of Abby's hair. "I didn't really come into my looks until my twenties."

"And when I think of poor Janie back in

high school" — Abby chuckled — "skinny as a stick, braces, zits, and that hair."

"Well, time has certainly been good to her because she's gorgeous now."

"I guess it's only fair," Abby said. "But I still can't help but wish to turn back the clock sometimes. It's not easy getting old."

"Really?" Caroline peered into Abby's eyes. "You'd want to do it again?"

"Oh well. Probably not. Not really. I guess I just wish I wasn't getting old so fast. Honestly, it feels like my aging clock is running a lot faster than some. Like yours and Janie's. At least I have Marley. She and I can relate."

Caroline laughed. "Well, Marley is feeling pretty good these days."

Abby tried not to feel jealous. "Yes, she's in love."

"And love can make you feel younger."

"I suppose." Abby realized she needed to stop this gloomy attitude before it spoiled the whole evening. "And I suppose that's why you look so young and radiant too."

Caroline's smile faded. "Don't be so sure."

Abby regretted her thoughtless comment. She'd forgotten about Mitch's hasty departure and Caroline's silence on the subject. "But you do still love Mitch, don't you?"

"I'll get some makeup for you. I've got a

new mineral powder I want you to try. It's amazing." Caroline hurried into the bathroom. Maybe it was wrong of Abby to press her. But if they were going to be roommates for a week, wasn't it better to just get things out in the open?

"First we apply some moisturizer. Give me your hand."

Abby stuck her hand out, palm up. "But back to you and —"

"The *top* of your hand." Caroline turned Abby's hand over and squirted something creamy onto it.

"Why?"

"Your hands get wrinkled too. Didn't you know that?" Caroline started rambling about beauty secrets, which Abby was sure was simply a smoke screen, but just in case, she decided to listen. Finally, after a lot of brushing and fluffing and who knew what else, Caroline proclaimed Abby done. "Check it out."

Abby turned to look at herself in the mirror and actually did a double take. "Not bad, Caroline. I guess I should take your beauty tips more seriously."

"Maybe so. Don't be fooled into thinking that women just naturally hold back the years. There are some tricks to aging more gracefully — and I didn't spend thirty-some years in Hollywood for nothing." She laughed. "Not that it got me anywhere."

"I wouldn't say that. From where I'm standing, your life looks pretty promising. You're still beautiful, and you managed to catch the interest of a very wealthy man." Abby made an apologetic shrug. "But if you really don't want to talk about Mitch, well, I can respect that."

Caroline's smile faded. "It's not that I don't want to talk about him, it's just that I'm not really sure how I feel about everything. I think this week will be a good time for me to figure things out."

"Absolutely. And if you need to talk, I'm here for you."

Caroline smiled. "For now, I just want to be lighthearted and happy. Okay?"

"You've got it."

To Abby's delight, it seemed that all Four Lindas wanted to be lighthearted and happy tonight. The four of them were not only the life of the party at their table, where they were seated with two couples — an older couple celebrating their fiftieth wedding anniversary and a pair of fortysomething newlyweds — but they continued to be the life of the party wherever they went. Before the evening was over, it seemed that most of the people on the ship were aware of the

Four Lindas and how Abby had won her trip on the TV show. It almost felt like they were celebrities, and Abby really was having fun! So much so she could almost put her worries behind her. Almost.

The next morning, Abby lingered over breakfast, enjoying an extra cup of coffee after her friends left to do some exploring on the ship. Irene (one half of the anniversary couple) had stayed behind while her husband returned to their room to get her sweater. Although Irene was probably closer to Abby's mother's age, as they chatted together it seemed as if she was a peer.

"Bernard and I have certainly had our ups and downs over the years," Irene was saying. "I'd never try to convince anyone otherwise."

Abby had already disclosed that although she and Paul had been married a good long time, it was still a little bumpy. "Sometimes I wonder if we can possibly make it to fifty," Abby confessed.

Irene nodded with a knowing expression. "Yes, I remember feeling that way too. But, looking back, I can say that it was well worth the effort. So many experiences and history and family are shared. How do you replace those things?"

"That's true." Abby took a sip of coffee.

"But sometimes I worry that no matter what I do, our marriage is doomed to fail." She confessed to Irene that she was worried about Paul's interest in another woman.

Irene sadly shook her head. "Well, a marriage can survive that, too. As long as both parties want it to survive and are willing to forgive. I'm not suggesting it's easy, just that it's a worthy investment."

"I suppose." Abby felt guilty for having unloaded so much on poor Irene. "Anyway, you are an inspiration to me," she told her. "I hope Paul and I will be where you and Bernard are too someday."

Bernard returned with Irene's sweater. "Care to take a stroll, my dear?"

She smiled up at him and told Abby goodbye, leaving Abby at the table by herself to mull over Irene's sage advice. On many levels it made perfect sense. But at the same time it sounded impossible. Paul was not Bernard, and Abby was not Irene. She finished the last of her coffee and set out to find her friends.

As she exited the dining room, she reminded herself of her resolve not to obsess over Paul and her marriage. This was her chance to escape all that and just have fun. And what a beautiful place to do it. The blue ocean and blue sky seemed to stretch into eternity. She breathed deeply the fresh sea air as she walked back to her cabin, where she planned to change into some sunning clothes and soak in all the goodness.

In her cabin, she saw the bouquet of flowers — such a pretty selection of festive colors just perfect for a Mexican cruise — and they made her feel guilty. Here Paul had gone to all this trouble, and all she could think were negative thoughts. For that reason, she decided to call and thank him.

When he answered, even after she cheerfully greeted him and profusely thanked him, he sounded glum. "Are you okay?" she asked. His recent heart attack came to mind. Surely he wasn't having health problems again.

"As okay as I can be."

"Oh, Paul, are you feeling bad because I'm gone?" She found that hard to believe, but touching.

"Well, yeah. I guess so."

"Oh, but that's obviously not what's troubling you. Is it your health? Do you need to make a doctor's appoint—"

"No, I'm fine," he snapped.

"Well, I was just concerned, Paul. No need to get all grumpy about it."

"I'm sorry, Abby." He actually did sound contrite.

"What is it, Paul?" She softened her tone. "You really do sound down in the dumps. Is something else wrong?"

"I . . . uh . . . I didn't want to say anything."

Abby reached for the chair behind her, easing herself down into it, preparing herself for terrible news. "What is it, Paul?"

"Oh Abby, I don't want to spoil your trip. Just forget about it, okay? Forget I said anything."

"Paul!" she exclaimed. "Tell me what's wrong — right now. Just tell me quickly, please. Get it over with." She took in a deep breath, bracing herself. She knew what it was — Paul was about to tell her the marriage was over, that he'd been seeing Bonnie, and that Abby should start talking to Janie about getting a divorce.

"Oh Abby." He let out a groan.

"I know it's going to be bad, Paul. But I swear if you don't just tell me, I'm going to have a heart attack myself. Honestly, I feel like I can barely breathe. Please, just get this over with." She really did feel like she should call for the ship's physician.

"It's just that, well, business has been slow."

"I know it's been slow," she shot back at him. But she didn't want to talk about business. "Tell me what's going on!"

"Well, it's worse than you know, Abby. It's bad."

"What's worse?" she demanded.

"Business. Aren't you listening to me?"

"Of course I'm listening. Just spit it out."

"I'm going bankrupt, Abby."

"What?" Abby shook her head, took in a deep breath. "This is about your construction business?"

"Yes, that's what I said, wasn't it?"

"Well, yes."

"I didn't want to tell you. Didn't want to spoil your trip. I knew it was coming. I've been sitting on those lots for too long. But the building just hasn't picked up, and property prices are still down. I've held on as long as I could. But it's winter again, and it's just not working. I'm going down . . . fast."

"Oh Paul. Are you sure?"

"I just met with the accountant today, honey. He said filing bankruptcy is the only way out. We'll lose the land, the unfinished houses . . . even our home."

"Really?" Her voice sounded hoarse.

There was a long silence. "See, I knew you'd be upset, Abby. That's why I didn't want to tell you."

"And that's everything, Paul?" She waited.

"You mean you want more? How much bad news do you need, Abby? I just told you my whole world is caving in. Isn't that bad enough?"

"Of course it's bad, Paul. But we still have each other. Don't we?"

He let out a long sigh. "Yeah. I guess so."

His less-than-enthusiastic response hurt.

"Anyway, I hope it doesn't spoil your trip, Abby. You should get off the phone. I've heard these international phone calls cost a fortune."

"Okay."

"I'm serious, Abby. Don't be using the credit cards. The trip is free, right? You shouldn't be spending at all. We're going to need every penny we've got to survive this."

"But what about —"

"I mean it, Abby. We're stretched way too thin. What with my failed business, and your inn, which has been nothing but another expense, we're losing everything."

"You mean I'll lose my bed-and-breakfast too?"

"We were partners in the construction business, Abby. We go down, we go down together."

"Oh, Paul!" She felt tears coming.

"We can talk about it when you get home, Abby. Sorry to spoil your trip with it. But remember, you forced it out of me. And you're the one who called. Hang up now, Abby. Save a few bucks."

They said good-bye and Abby shut off her phone, then sat down and cried. She was relieved that Caroline didn't return. She went into the tiny bathroom, threw cold water on her face, donned a pair of big sunglasses, and went back out to pretend that nothing whatsoever was wrong.

Chapter 24
Janie

Janie told Marley and Caroline she wanted to explore the ship's library and, to her relief, neither of them cared to join her among the dusty books. Apparently none of the ship's other passengers were interested in the library this morning either. She was the only one in the room, so she pulled out her cell phone and called Victor. He had promised to keep tabs on Lisa and the rehab place for her.

"Hey, Victor," she said lightly. "How's it going?"

"Okay."

Something about the way he said *okay* suggested that perhaps it wasn't so okay. "Really?" she pressed. "Everything is just fine?"

"I can't lie to you, Janie. I wish I could. But I can't."

"What's going on?"

"Lisa checked herself out of rehab."

Janie let out a groan.

"But it's not all bad, let me tell —"

"Not all bad?"

"Listen to the whole story."

"I'm listening."

"Well, you know Ben's school doesn't start up until tomorrow. Anyway Lisa called him on her cell phone, telling him she just couldn't take it in the rehab place. It might've worked for his buddy, but it wasn't working for her."

"Right, after less than one week, she knows it won't work."

"So anyway, Ben drove down there to get her."

"You're kidding? Ben did that?"

"He's a good kid."

"I'll say."

"And he's bringing her back up here."

"But what's she going to do up there?" Janie ran her fingers through her curls and wondered if there was some easy way to get off this boat and catch a flight back home.

"Well, I told Ben to tell her she can stay here with me."

"But she doesn't like you, Victor. And like you said, Ben's got to get back to school."

"She doesn't like me when you're around, Janie. But with you gone, maybe she'll be

331

forced to like me. Or at least put up with me."

"And what if she doesn't?"

"I don't know. I haven't exactly had time to come up with a plan B."

"I'm sorry," she said quickly. "I'm so thankful for what you and Ben are doing, Victor. I'm just frustrated. I think I'll grab a flight out at the next port. Unfortunately, we won't be in Los Cabos until tomorrow."

"No, don't do that, Janie. I can handle this."

"Really?"

He chuckled. "Well, I'm not sure I can. But, to be fair, you weren't doing that great on your own either. Like I've told you, Lisa is going to do what Lisa is going to do. You can't force her."

"I know. I just want to help her." Janie sighed. "I don't want her back on the streets. Especially in the winter."

"I know."

Janie thought hard. "I have an idea."

"What?"

"If you don't mind helping me —"

"Of course I'll help you, Janie. I'll do anything. Just tell me what to do."

"Well, you still have a key for my house, right?"

"Yes."

"Tell Ben to take Lisa there. Get her enough groceries for week, but don't give her any money. Tell her she can have the place to herself until I get back, and if she needs anything, she can call you. Right?"

"Are you serious? You want her to stay by herself at your house?"

"Absolutely."

"But aren't you worried? I mean what if she . . . uh, well, you know."

"It's just a house, Victor."

"True."

"Lisa means a lot more to me than a silly old house."

"I know."

"Will you do that?"

"Of course."

"I'll keep my phone on. Call me if you need to. Honestly, I'd have no problem catching a flight back home if I need —"

"You won't need to, Janie. I'll do everything I can to hold this thing together until you get back."

"Thank you, Victor. I owe you big time."

He chuckled. "Hmm. Well, I might try to collect when you get back."

"Honestly, I am so grateful for you."

"Hey, you'd do the same for me for one of my boys, right?"

"Absolutely."

"I love that we both agree our kids are a huge priority."

"I love that too, Victor." She sighed. "And I love you."

"I love you, too, Janie. I'm trying not to be jealous."

"Jealous?"

"Someday I hope you and I can do a cruise together . . . in my boat."

"I hope so too."

"You do?"

"You know I do."

"Okay. I'm holding on to that thought, Janie. I better get busy getting your house ready for Lisa. They should be here in a couple of hours."

Janie felt a mixture of emotions as she shut down her phone. Oh, she wasn't terribly surprised that Lisa had bolted again, just disappointed. Why did Lisa have to do everything the hard way? And yet Janie was extremely grateful to Ben and Victor. What would she have done if they hadn't stepped up? But more than anything else, she felt fearful — fearful for Lisa. What if she didn't like being cooped up in Janie's house? What if she went out looking for drug connections? Certainly they were around. Janie had heard how coastal towns were the worst when it came to drug trafficking. And what if Lisa invited her drug-addicted friends to stay at Janie's house?

Janie felt slightly sickened at that thought. What if her lovely renovated home was overrun with a bunch of creepy dopers and thugs and who knew what else? She'd have to check in with Victor again, ask him to keep tabs on things. Poor Victor, he hadn't known what he'd gotten into when he'd gotten involved with Janie. Sure, she might've looked like a neat little package at first glance, but there was a lot of baggage that came with her.

"You're still here," said Caroline as she poked her head into the library. "Find any good books?"

"No." Janie made a forced smile. "Guess I'll stick with the ones I loaded on my Kindle."

"We found Abby. She and Marley want to do a craft class." Caroline wrinkled her nose. "You won't find me cooped up in any library or craft room. I'm here for the sunshine and fresh ocean air. I'm going to go hang by the pool."

"I'll join you," Janie told her. As they walked back to their cabins to change into sun wear, Janie considered telling Caroline about Lisa. But remembering how they'd all agreed that this trip was about fun and sun, she just didn't want to put a damper on the day. Besides, she told herself, Victor was handling it. Okay, how that was even possible was a mystery, but she could hope for the best. And she could pray. If worse came to worst, and she really did need to make a fast exit from the cruise, she would explain the situation. Until then, she would keep on her happy face — or at least her all-is-well attorney face. She'd had years to perfect that one.

Before long, she and Caroline secured a couple of lounge chairs on the sunny side of the pool, and the air temperature, which was only in the high seventies, was just about perfect. "Isn't this delightful?" Janie said. "Can you believe it's January?"

"I know. I was just thinking about how it's summertime where Mitch is."

"That's right. He's down under, isn't he?"

"Yeah. He's in Auckland to start with. Then after a week, he heads over to Sydney. What a life, eh?"

Janie nodded. "But it could be your life too, Caroline."

She shrugged. "I guess."

"What do you mean, you guess? Mitch is always asking you to go with him."

"Yeah." Caroline leaned over to rub sunscreen on her legs. "I'm just not sure. I need time to think things over."

"Really?" Janie tipped up her sunglasses and peered curiously at Caroline. "What's there to think over?"

"Oh, I don't know."

"I mean, he's in love with you and you're in love with him, right?"

Caroline snapped the cap back on the sunscreen and handed it to Janie. "You better use some too. Despite our fake spray-on tans, we could still burn."

Janie took the bottle and began slathering it on herself. "Mitch has the life you say you've always wanted," she continued. "And he's independently wealthy. Victor said he could retire anytime he wants."

"Really?" Caroline looked surprised by this.

"Well, you know he and his business partner sold their software company for millions."

Caroline looked like maybe she didn't know this. "I know he's well-off. But I thought Mitch had to keep traveling because of the contract — I mean the terms of the way they sold the corporation."

"I don't know about that. But I do know he told Victor he could retire if he wanted to."

"If he wanted to?"

"I think he's enjoying all this international travel on someone else's dime." Janie laughed. "Don't you think so?"

Caroline nodded with a creased brow. "Maybe so."

"But you always wanted to travel," Janie rubbed lotion on an arm. "Seems like you've got it all now, Caroline."

"Seems that way."

But something about Caroline's expression suggested something else.

"Everything's okay with you and Mitch, isn't it?"

Caroline shrugged then leaned back. "I'm not really sure, Janie."

"Sorry, I didn't mean to sound so nosy."

Caroline smiled. "It's not like I have any secrets, really. I'm just not as sure as I thought I was. I think when Mom was taking so much of my time, Mitch looked like a knight on a white horse. I'm not so sure now."

Janie had always loved Caroline — her sunny disposition and can-do attitude, but right now she respected her more than ever before. Janie had assumed that Caroline would've jumped at the chance to land a guy like Mitch — wealthy, attractive, available. What more could Caroline possibly want? Apparently there was something. And that was something!

"Have you noticed we're the young ones on this boat?" Caroline said quietly as they were sunning themselves.

Janie chuckled. "Yes. I guess we really are cruising with the oldies after all."

"Don't look now, but at the moment there are a couple of oldies looking in our direction."

"What do we do?"

"Let's just have fun with it," Caroline said lightly. "Let them think they're having fun too."

A deeply tanned white-haired man walked over and smiled down at them. "Mind if we join you lovely ladies?"

"Not at all." Caroline waved to the empty lounge chairs. "I can't believe more people aren't out enjoying this scrumptious weather."

"I think a lot of passengers are afraid of the sun," the second man said. His hair was a more steely gray and his tan not quite so dark.

"What a delightful first day at sea," the white-haired man said as he sat in the lounge next to Janie. "It's not always this nice."

"Have you done a lot of cruises?" Caroline asked.

"Oh, yes. I think I spend about half my life on a boat."

They all introduced themselves. The one beside Janie was Stan, a retired dentist and Bill was a retired optometrist. They were from Alberta. Both were single, and it sounded as if they'd been friends for years and traveled together a lot. Janie suspected they might be a couple, but that simply made her more comfortable with their company. She remembered Victor's goodbye to her the night before they left. "Don't let some handsome guy try to steal you away from me," he'd told her. However, she didn't think Victor would be too concerned about these old boys.

They inquired as to what Janie and Caroline did. "I don't do much of anything," Caroline admitted.

"Ah, you must be married to a wealthy man," Bill teased.

"No." Caroline shook her head. "I'm single."

"But she's got a very wealthy boyfriend." Janie told them a bit about Mitch.

Bill looked disappointed. "So, I suppose I haven't a chance, eh?"

Caroline giggled. "Don't be too sure about that."

Bill brightened. He turned to Janie. "How

about you?"

"Oh, Janie's a successful attorney," Caroline said proudly. "She used to live and work in Manhattan."

"Manhattan, eh?" Stan nodded. "Impressive. Where do you live and work now?"

So they told them a bit about growing up in Clifden, and about how their Four Lindas reunited, and a number of other silly, inconsequential things. But the more they talked, the more Janie began to suspect these guys weren't actually a couple after all. In fact, as they got better acquainted, it surfaced that they were widowers whose wives had been sisters. The four had vacationed together for years, but after losing their wives within three years of each other, the two brothers-in-law decided to continue the tradition anyway. "We're vacation buddies," Bill said.

"Works out nicely," Stan told them. "We save a few bucks, and we know when to give each other space."

"Say, do you girls play cards, eh?" Bill asked hopefully.

Soon they relocated to a patio table. Stan ordered drinks for everyone, and they began playing a game of rummy called Three-Thirteen that was surprisingly fun. "I wonder if Abby and Marley are enjoying their craft class," Janie mused.

Caroline laughed as she won the hand. "I know I wouldn't be having nearly as much fun there as I'm having right now."

"Stick with us," Bill told her. "We're full of fun."

Janie exchanged glances with Caroline. But Caroline simply winked like this was all just a silly game. Maybe it was. Still, it was hard for Janie to enjoy it completely, especially knowing that dear Victor was probably hard at work stocking Janie's house with groceries for Lisa. And then the poor man would probably feel he needed to play babysitter or security guard until Janie came back. Maybe she would cut this trip short after all. Abby would have to understand.

CHAPTER 25
CAROLINE

By the end of the third day at sea, Caroline realized that she'd fallen into the phony-baloney trap. It was just the game that everyone played, so why not play along? Questions like, "Where are you from?" or "What do you do?" came consistently on a ship full of strangers. Again and again, she'd hear Janie say she was an attorney and Marley that she was an artist, and even Abby sounded larger than life when she'd tell people she ran a bed-and-breakfast in a quaint seaside town.

Eventually Caroline tired of telling people she was a nobody who did nothing. She began talking up her life and pretending she'd really had a dramatic career that went beyond bit parts and commercials. She even acted as if she really did plan to marry her millionaire boyfriend. Who knew? Maybe she would. It all made for a good story. And, really, what did it matter? Besides, people seemed to enjoy the fantasy. Having spent many years in Hollywood, she was well acquainted with illusion.

But in the still of the night, after everyone else was asleep, Caroline felt like a fraud. Worse than that, she felt like a failure. Really, what had she done with her life? Not much. The more she thought about it, the more she thought perhaps she should call Mitch and apologize and tell him she had changed her mind about traveling with him. Maybe it didn't matter whether or not they were married. Maybe she should just be thankful that someone with the kind of resources Mitch had was interested in her. Really, did she want to grow old alone?

"You seem quiet this morning," Abby said as they were getting ready for breakfast. "Are you feeling okay?"

Caroline paused from applying her moisturizer and looked at Abby. "I'm not sure."

Abby looked concerned. "You're not sure?"

Caroline forced a shaky smile. "No, I'm fine. I think I just need a cup of coffee."

"You're probably worn out from last night." Abby shook her head. "Who would've thought two old guys like Bill and Stan could dance like that?"

"And take turns with all four of us." Caroline fluffed her hair. "I'll bet they're tired this morning."

"I don't think Paul could've kept up with them." Abby looked slightly sad.

"Are you missing Paul?"

"I . . . I . . . yes, I suppose I am." Abby turned away, hurrying to the bathroom. But Caroline could've sworn she saw tears in Abby's eyes. Was it possible that something had happened with Bonnie again? Caroline had been paying close attention to those two and had been spending a lot of time at her house — partly because it was exciting to see it coming together, and partly because she felt a responsibility to Abby. But now that they'd departed on the cruise, and with no one was around to keep an eye on Paul, was Abby worried? Caroline considered asking her, then realized talking about it would probably just make things worse. Really, what could Abby do besides feel bad? Besides, Abby wanted this trip to be fun.

Caroline slipped her feet into her sandals and wondered why she felt so tired. Was it always this much work to have fun? Was she just getting old, or perhaps simply regretting her inability to make up her mind about Mitch? Whatever it was, as Caroline walked with her friends up to the dining room, she felt slightly off. And when she smelled the food, even the coffee, which she'd thought she wanted, she realized she had no appetite whatsoever. Not only that, she felt slightly queasy.

"I wonder if I'm getting seasick," she mused out loud as they were sitting down at their table.

"But the ocean is perfectly calm," Marley pointed out.

"You know, Irene wasn't feeling well this morning," Bernard told them. "She's still in bed."

Caroline took in a deep breath, telling herself she was imagining things, but as she reached for the napkin, she realized this was for real. "I, uh, I don't think I'm feeling too well." She stood quickly. "Excuse me."

"Do you want me to come with you?" Abby offered.

"No." Caroline shook her head. "I think I just need some air."

She hurried past waiters and out of the dining room. Outside she leaned into the railing and took in some deep breaths, but that only seemed to make her feel worse. Her head was throbbing too. Finally, she decided that the only thing that sounded good was the comfort of a bed and a nearby toilet. That's right where she headed — fast. She got there in the nick of time. Thankful to see the tiny bathroom, she put it to use, emptying the contents of her stomach. Finally, feeling exhausted and empty, she put a cold washcloth to her head and tumbled into bed.

"Are you okay?" Abby asked as she let herself into the room. "Everyone is worried."

"I'm sick," Caroline said weakly.

"Seasick?"

"I don't know." She sighed. "I think I just need . . . sleep."

"Janie's not feeling too good either," Abby told her. "At first I thought it was just the power of suggestion, but then she really started to look a little green around the gills. Marley just helped her back to their cabin, and I think she's hurling."

"Oh." Caroline couldn't think of a response to that.

"I'll go find you some Sprite," Abby said. "And maybe some medicine."

"Yeah. Sprite might be good." Caroline closed her eyes, which felt like lead weights were attached. "Just . . . need . . . sleep."

And she did sleep for a while, but when she woke up she was shivering and cold, and, to her surprise, Janie was lying next to her. "What are you doing here?" Caroline asked in a hoarse voice.

"Sick," Janie answered, barely opening her eyes.

"Marley and I are playing nurse," Abby said from where she was seated in the chair with a magazine in her hands. "How about some Sprite?"

"No." Janie groaned and rolled over.

"Not yet," Caroline told her. "But are there more blankets? I'm freezing."

"I'm burning up," Janie said as she pushed the covers off. "Is the AC broken?"

Abby came over and tended to them, although with her eyes closed, Caroline couldn't be sure what she was doing besides bumping the bed, which made Caroline's skin crawl. She wanted to tell Abby to go away but couldn't find the words.

The day continued to pass in a haze of misery, restless sleep, and occasional news flashes from their "nurses."

"It sounds like about a hundred or so people are sick, and not just the passengers. Some of the crew got it too," Marley reported. "They call it a norovirus, whatever that is. I heard the ship's doctor is running his legs off because some of the older passengers have health problems that complicate matters. It's possible we won't be allowed into port until it's over."

"When will it be over?" Janie asked in a

pitiful voice.

"I heard it usually runs two to three days."

"How long has it been so far?" Caroline asked.

"Just a day."

Janie jumped up, making another dash to the bathroom. Caroline was relieved she didn't need to throw up again. She tried to imagine she was feeling better, but her body ached like she'd been run over by a truck.

"Stan and Bill are just fine," Marley told her.

"Uh-huh." Caroline tried to sound interested, but she really wished Marley would stop talking.

"They say they're immune to ship sicknesses. You know, because they travel so much. But they did have some advice. Bill suggested aspirin, and Stan said a shot of whiskey would help."

Caroline pulled the blankets closer around her neck and up to her ears, hoping it would block the sound of Marley's voice. But Marley continued to prattle until Janie emerged from the bathroom and said, "Please! Be quiet."

Marley didn't say much after that. Caroline vaguely wondered if her feelings were hurt. Not that she cared so much at the moment. But later they'd have to apologize.

She also marveled that Marley and Abby weren't sick. Of course, if they were sick, who would take care of them?

Thankfully, Caroline started to feel better by the following afternoon. Although she was weak, she was able to sit up in bed and sip on some chicken broth. And by the end of the day, Janie started returning to normal as well.

"You guys are lucky," Abby told Janie and Caroline as the four of them sat in the cabin together. Marley had brought a plateful of food down from the buffet, which the two "patients" were picking at. "The other ones who got sick are still pretty bad off."

"Yeah, the ship's not a whole lot of fun tonight," Marley said. "Most of the people who got sick are still in bed, and the ones who aren't sick are all afraid they'll get sick. Well, except for the ones like Stan and Bill. They still seem to be enjoying themselves. They send their best wishes, by the way."

"I feel so bad," Caroline told Abby, "for ruining your trip like this."

"It's not your fault," Abby said. "I feel bad that I brought you girls on a cruise where so many people got sick. Bill told me that we'll probably get some cruise vouchers to make up for it. Not that I'm planning any more cruises anytime soon." She looked tired.

"I'm just thankful I didn't get sick," Marley told them. "You girls should be thankful too, because I absolutely hate being sick. I'm the worst patient ever. I'd be whining and complaining like you wouldn't believe."

"And did you notice anything different?" Abby asked. "I mean about Marley or me?"

"Different?" Caroline studied them. "Well, now that you mention it, you both look rather lovely. Is that because you didn't get sick?"

"While you girls were sleeping it off, we took turns getting some spa treatments today," Abby told her. "I had those free coupons that came with the cruise tickets, and since there were so many spa cancellations due to the sickness, we made the most of it."

"I had a hot stone massage this morning." Marley sighed. "It was amazing."

"I was just happy to finally cool off," Janie told her.

"And I had a seaweed wrap," Abby said, "followed by pedicure and manicure." She held out her hands.

"Very nice." Caroline nodded.

"And I had a facial." Marley patted her cheek.

"Well, I'm glad we didn't spoil everything for you," Caroline told them. "I was feeling guilty about you girls being stuck playing nursemaids to us."

"I'm sorry I grumped at you for talking," Janie told Marley. "Honestly, it felt like my head was going to explode or implode or just melt down."

"It's a bad habit," Marley admitted. "When I don't know what to do, like if someone's sick, I tend to talk too much. Sorry about that."

"I'm sorry too," Caroline said. "I think I was unappreciative too."

"All is forgiven," Abby told them. "We're the Four Lindas, remember? We have to forgive each other. Forgive and forget."

Caroline took a whole-wheat roll and broke it in half. "You know, while I was feeling really, really horrible, like so sick that I almost wanted to die, I thought maybe God was punishing me."

"Punishing *you?*" Abby asked. "Whatever for?"

So Caroline confessed how she'd felt guilty for exaggerating about herself and her so-called life. "I'm not usually like that. It's just that I was starting to feel embarrassed," she explained. "You girls are so impressive — an attorney, an artist, the owner of a bed-and-breakfast — and I'm just a nobody." Caroline's eyes were tearing up. "A failure."

"You're not a nobody," Abby told her. "You are the sweetest person, Caroline. Everyone loves you. And you were an actress. We saw you in those commercials."

"And you gave up a lot to take care of your mother," Marley reminded her. "That is not a failure. Really, don't you think that being a kind and generous person is better than being famous?"

"Besides that, what you said about possibly marrying a millionaire is true," Abby injected. "And then your life will be as glamorous as you've been saying. Think about it, Caroline — you'll be able to do whatever you like and travel all over the world."

"But I don't think I'm going to marry him." Caroline sniffed loudly.

"Why not?" Marley handed her a tissue.

"I don't think Mitch truly wants to be married." She blew her nose. "And even if he did want to, now I'm not so sure that I want to get married." Now she started crying even harder. "I . . . I just don't think I'm the marrying kind."

"Then why are you so sad about it?" Janie asked.

"Because . . . because I don't want to grow old *all alone.*"

"But you have us," Abby reminded her.

"Yes. But I guess I don't want to grow old all alone . . . and . . . and *be poor too.*" Caroline felt silly and shallow for admitting this, but it was the truth — the plain, ugly truth. "I mean it'll be bad enough to be old and alone, but what if I end up like my mother? What if I get sick and I'm poor and I don't have anyone or anything and —"

"Don't be silly," Marley said. "Like Abby said, you have us."

"Yes, but you all have men in your lives — real men. Not like Mitch. He's here today and gone tomorrow. Maybe gone forever now that I turned him away." She was crying even harder. "And — and — *you're not poor!*"

Abby sat down on the bed, putting her hand over Caroline's. "Well, Caroline, as a matter of fact, I *am* poor." The room got quiet, and Abby told them how Paul was going bankrupt and losing his construction business and their investment property and everything. "And not only will we lose the new house, which I never thought I'd feel too badly about — but I do — I'm going to lose the inn as well." Abby was crying too.

"Oh my!" Marley handed her a couple of tissues.

"So, see, Caroline, you are not alone in your poverty." Abby looked at her with watery eyes.

Caroline hugged Abby. "I'm so sorry, sweetie. I had no idea."

"But we still have each other. If I have to be poor, at least I'll have friends." Abby wiped her wet cheeks. "I didn't want to tell you guys about this. I wanted to keep the cruise all happy and lighthearted. But it seems pointless now. I just hope I didn't bring everyone down with my bad news."

Janie sighed as she leaned her head against the headboard. "Since misery loves company, I might as well share my bad news too."

"*You* have bad news?" Caroline peered curiously at her.

"Lisa walked out of the rehab facility. And she's already used up her second chance." Janie's chin quivered. "After all our hard work, the intervention, I just don't know why she couldn't try harder. Why did she give up so easily?"

"Who knows?" Marley shook her head.

Caroline reached over and patted Janie's knee. "I'm so sorry, Janie."

"You know, while I was so sick, I was thinking about Lisa, wondering why . . ." Janie reached for the tissue box, which was in the center of the bed. "I just felt so helpless, you know? Not just because I was sick and felt so lousy. But I just feel so helpless when it comes to Lisa. I realize there's really nothing I can do. Not a thing. Well, besides praying. Even that's been hard."

"We can pray for her too," Marley told Janie. "I've been praying for her a lot. In fact, I've been praying for all of us."

"Good for you, Marley." Caroline smiled at her. "It's nice to know one of the Lindas still has her act together."

Marley laughed. "My act together? Are you kidding?"

"At least your life isn't falling apart," Abby told her.

"Don't be so sure."

"Come on," Abby said. "Not only are you a famous artist now, selling your work at —"

"I sold some paintings," Marley said offhandedly, "and for all I know I'll probably never sell another one. I haven't heard a word back from Thomas in Santa Barbara. He was so excited, I thought I'd hear from him by now. My paintings might be gathering dust in a back room somewhere even as we speak. Who knows? Maybe he'll try to return them to Jack."

"You're just being an insecure artist," Caroline told her. "Give it some time."

"That's not all." Marley confessed how she was still quite worried about Sylvia going after Jack. "I'm trying to act like everything's fine, but underneath it all, I'm worried."

"But you know Jack loves you," Janie pointed out.

"I hope you're right," Marley told her. "But from what I've seen, Sylvia is a determined woman. And as Abby can attest to, men can be fickle creatures."

Abby just shook her head. "You know, when Paul told me he had bad news, I immediately thought he meant about him and Bonnie. I was absolutely certain that my marriage was over." She made a weak smile. "Instead, we're just going to lose everything."

"Everything but your marriage," Caroline reminded her.

"So it seems." Abby shrugged. "But I suppose that could still go by the wayside too."

"Don't go looking for more trouble," Janie warned her.

"That's right," Marley said.

"Wow, you know what's funny?" Caroline

said suddenly. "Not laugh-out-loud funny. Maybe just ironic. But there we all were, going around this pretty ship with our happy faces on, talking about our wonderful, successful, blissful lives, and the truth is we've all got problems. Real problems."

"Are you suggesting we should go around talking about all our problems?" Abby scowled. "Good grief, that would depress everyone on the boat."

"Just the ones who aren't already sick in bed," Marley said wryly.

Caroline laughed. "No, I'm not suggesting we go around dumping on everyone. That would be seriously twisted, and it wouldn't take long before people started running when they saw us coming."

"We could rename our group the Whining Lindas." Janie reached for a piece of pineapple.

"We don't have to pour out our troubles on everyone," Caroline said quietly, "but I do think we should always be truthful with each other."

And so they all agreed, promising that come what may, they would be honest with each other. No pretenses.

CHAPTER 26
MARLEY

Marley knew it was unnecessary, not to mention expensive, but with only two days left on the cruise, she decided to call Jack. Mostly she wanted to tell him about the amazing sunset she'd seen tonight, and how she'd taken all kinds of photos, and how the moon was hanging over the ocean . . . and how she wished he was here . . . or she was there. When his cell phone went directly to voice mail, she decided to try the house. Hunter would be in bed by now, and Jack would probably be sitting by his fireplace, reading a book. She could just imagine him there. But when a female voice answered the phone, Marley was so caught off guard, she didn't know what to say. "Is Jack there?" she stammered, wondering if she'd called the wrong number.

"He's busy. Can I take a message?"

"Sylvia?" Marley ventured.

"Yes?"

"Oh, this is Marley." She tried to sound natural. "I didn't recognize your voice. I'm in Mexico, and I was just calling to say hi."

"Yes, Jack told me you were cruising with your friends. How lovely. Is the weather delightful?"

"Yes, it's been great." Then, for lack of anything else to say, Marley told Sylvia about the sickness on the ship. "But Janie and Caroline are much better."

"Oh, that's good to hear."

"Well, would you tell Jack I called?" Marley didn't know what else to say. She wanted to ask where Jack was and why he was busy — and more than that, why Sylvia was at Jack's house at this hour. Instead, she said good-bye. Then she went back inside, joining her friends in a booth in the ship's lounge as they listened to a comedienne talking about some childhood humiliations. But Marley had a hard time focusing on the jokes as she continued to ponder why Sylvia was at Jack's and why she didn't let Marley speak to Jack.

Finally the act ended and the women started chatting among themselves, but Marley was still stewing. "What's troubling you?" Caroline asked her.

Marley started to say "nothing" but then remembered their promise. She told them about the phone call.

"Why didn't you just tell her to put Jack on the phone?" Abby asked.

"It's like I couldn't think. I was so surprised. My mind was running around in circles."

"So what do you think she was doing there?" Janie asked.

"I have no idea." Marley shook her head. "At this hour it just seems odd. Why couldn't Jack come to the phone?"

"Because he was in the bathroom?" Caroline suggested.

"Maybe he was doing something with Hunter."

"Maybe Sylvia was babysitting Hunter," Abby tossed out, "and maybe Jack wasn't even there."

"Then why would Sylvia say he was busy?" Marley asked.

"Because she wants you to think he's busy?" Janie offered. "To create the illusion that something's going on between them?"

"So that you'll act jealous," Caroline declared. "And then you'll get mad at Jack and say something stupid and that will increase Sylvia's chances with him."

"Or maybe Sylvia sneaked into Jack's house," Abby teased, "and she gave him a cup of drugged tea and then sat by his phone just hoping you'd call so she could get your goat and possibly ruin your romance with Jack."

Marley couldn't help but laugh. "Well, I suppose it could be any of those scenarios. And probably none of them. But I feel better just getting it out in the open. You girls are good medicine."

They started tossing out even more preposterous explanations for why Sylvia was answering Jack's phone. "She's really an alien from Uranus." Caroline giggled. "And she's kidnapping Jack to the mother ship so they can examine his prosthetic leg." Soon they were all laughing so hard that other passengers were watching and whispering.

"I guess we should start our own comic act," Abby said.

While Marley could see the humor in the situation, and she suspected she'd overblown it in her mind, she still felt worried as she got ready for bed. It wasn't so much that she didn't trust Jack. It was more that she didn't trust Sylvia. But, as was becoming her habit, she decided to pray about it rather than obsess. However, it wasn't easy to push her worries away. Perhaps the reason was that Marley felt more acutely aware than ever of how much she really loved Jack. How much she didn't want to lose him. If it wasn't past midnight, she would be tempted to call him and find out exactly what was going on — and to set him straight in regard to her feelings. She knew that he knew that she loved him. They'd both stated it clearly. But perhaps she'd failed to express adequately just how much she loved him!

The next morning Marley got up early. Tiptoeing through the cabin, she pulled on her cargo shorts, T-shirt, and sandals. Then, silently getting her camera and cell phone, she let herself out. She hoped Janie would catch some more sleep. She strolled the nearly deserted decks, snapping sunrise photos while the dawn light glowed and until her camera's battery grew weak and the smell of coffee tempted her to take a break.

She desperately wanted to call Jack, but she knew that mornings were a busy time for him. He needed to get Hunter's break-fast into her, go over what she needed for school, make her lunch, tame her curly hair, assure her after she'd tried sixteen outfits that she looked absolutely perfect, and finally get her loaded onto the bus for school. He'd told Marley before how ex-hausting it was and how he admired moth-ers who did it with more than one child.

"I wouldn't know about that," she'd admitted to him. "But I have heard that it gets easier with each additional child."

He had laughed. "Thankfully, I don't need to be concerned about that."

Then Marley knew that he took a little time to straighten his house a bit. She'd suggested he hire someone to help. Leah was good at watching Hunter after school, but her ability to tidy up was questionable. It would be close to ten when Jack would head over to the gallery. Sometimes he picked up a newspaper and a cup of coffee before he unlocked his doors. And although his sign said the shop opened at ten, no one in town took these things too seriously. It was unusual to have customers first thing in the morning.

Marley planned to call him around ten thirty, after he'd had a chance to drink his cup of coffee and settle in some. Fortunately, Sylvia never came to work until noon, so Marley felt relatively sure she wouldn't have to deal with her again. Just the thought of that was unsettling. What had she been doing at Jack's last night? As Marley dialed the shop phone number, she told herself that if by chance Sylvia did pick up, Marley would hang up. Even if Sylvia checked the caller ID, Marley could always claim it was a pocket dial or disconnect. Such things were common with cell phones.

To her relief Jack answered. "Marley!" he exclaimed. "How is my lady of the high seas?"

She laughed. "I'm fine, Jack." Then she described the amazing morning and the photos she'd taken.

"It's raining here," he said glumly.

She told him how she'd called last night. "The moon over the ocean was so amazing. I just wanted to share it with you."

"You called last night?"

"Yes." She kept her voice even. "Sylvia answered."

"Sylvia was there?"

"Yes. She said you were busy."

"What time was it?"

"Around ten." Marley held her breath, waiting.

"I must've still been at the chamber meeting."

Realization sunk in. It would've been a chamber night. "Oh. Was Sylvia watching Hunter for you?"

"No. She was picking up Leah. They're sharing a car again. Sylvia's is in the shop."

"Oh." Marley felt ridiculous.

"Did you think . . . ? I mean, were you worried about why Sylvia was at my house at such a late hour?"

"A little." She bit her lip.

"Oh, Marley, I'm sorry. But I don't understand why Sylvia said I was busy. Was that what she actually said? She didn't mention the chamber meeting?"

Marley thought hard. "I'm pretty sure she just said you were busy and that she'd give you a message. Then we chatted for a bit."

"She never mentioned that you'd called."

Marley sighed. "The truth is, I was pretty upset about it last night, Jack. I feel really silly admitting it now. But I was."

"I'm sorry, Marley."

"Oh, it wasn't your fault. It's just that I got so worried. I thought Sylvia might be stepping in. You know." She feigned a laugh. "Trying to steal you from me."

"No one can steal me from you, Marley. My heart is yours — yours alone."

"Thanks." She was so relieved that he hadn't laughed at her. She remembered times when she'd expressed something like fear or insecurity to her ex-husband and he'd made fun of her.

"If you don't mind, I think I'll mention it to Sylvia."

"Oh, I don't want to create a problem, Jack."

"No, I won't make it a problem. I just

think I need to lay my cards on the table, so to speak. Sometimes it's those unsaid things that get people into trouble."

"That's true. And speaking of unsaid things, last night, when I was still stewing over this, I realized just how much I love you, Jack."

"Really?" He sounded pleased. "Tell me more."

"I do love you, Jack. Maybe I needed to get on this big silly boat just to see how much I could miss you. But I'm afraid I love you a whole lot more than I ever expected to love anyone again."

"Why would you be afraid of that?"

"Oh Jack. You know why."

"Because you're afraid you'll get hurt."

"Right. And last night I thought maybe that's what was happening, you know, with Sylvia. Like history repeating itself."

"I will never do that to you, Marley. I am a one-woman man. And you, Marley, are my one woman."

They talked a while longer, and Marley not only felt completely reassured, she felt slightly lightheaded. People were milling around her, waiting to meet friends for breakfast. Her friends were coming her way.

"I wish I were home," she whispered into the phone. "I miss you, Jack."

"Only two more days," he told her. "And if you're not busy, I'd like to make a date with you on your first night back. You interested?"

"You bet."

They said their good-byes, and, feeling on top of the world, Marley grinned at her friends.

"Was that Jack?" Caroline asked.

Marley nodded, slipping her phone back in her shorts pocket.

"Everything okay back on the home front?" Abby asked.

Marley filled them in as they walked to breakfast. She didn't give all the details, but she did mention how he planned to say something about the phone call to Sylvia. "I just hope she doesn't quit on him. Jack really needs the help, and Sylvia's good in the gallery."

"Just as long as she keeps it in the gallery," Caroline said.

"I can trust Jack." Marley nodded. "He told me he's a one-woman man, and I believe him."

"What a guy," Janie said as they sat down.

"Sounds like a keeper to me," Caroline told her.

"Yeah." Abby nodded. "Better hold on to that boy."

"Don't worry," Marley assured them. "I plan to."

CHAPTER 27
ABBY

Although Abby had done a fairly good job of putting her impending financial disaster out of mind, now that it was the final day of the cruise, she felt that in the same way this ship was sailing to its final port, she could be sailing into what would surely be a hurricane.

"Are you okay?" Janie asked her as they sat beside the pool, sipping their happy-hour drinks. Marley and Caroline had surprised everyone by signing up for skeet shooting. Really, who knew?

"What?" Abby gazed blankly at Janie. "I'm sorry, did I miss something?"

"Yes, but it was unimportant." Janie peered curiously at her. "Really, are you okay? You're not getting a late batch of that norovirus, are you?"

"No, I'm healthy as a horse." Abby patted her solid midsection. "And it's plain to see I've been eating like one too."

"Everyone overeats on cruises." Janie set her drink down. "I've been thinking a lot about your financial situation. And I've wanted to say something, except I hated to drag you back into it. Especially since we were trying to make our last days of the cruise the best."

"Yes." Abby nodded. "I was actually just sitting here thinking I should be crowned the Queen of Denial. Because that's what I'm trying to do — deny that it's really happening. I'm wishing I didn't have to go home. Maybe I should jump ship."

"Do you want to talk?"

Abby shrugged. "Yes . . . and no."

"Okay, I'm going with the yes." Janie took in a deep breath. "And the reason I'm going with the yes is because I think I have a right to know what's going on."

Abby blinked as realization set in. "Oh, my!" She put her hand over her mouth. "I nearly forgot. You're a partner with me in the bed-and-breakfast."

Janie nodded. "And for that reason, I think you need to hear my thoughts on the subject."

Abby nodded. "Yes, of course."

"Well, I don't know exactly what Paul's decided to do, whether he's already filed bankruptcy or chapter seven or eleven or what. But I have a feeling we can keep the inn."

"Really?" Abby leaned forward. "I mean I understand that you can't possibly lose your half, although I'm not even sure how to sort that all out. But you think I can keep my part too?" Of course, even as Abby said this, she realized it was kind of ridiculous. Janie was the one who'd made most of the financial investment.

Janie started talking, but most of what she said went right over Abby's head. "You know," Abby said, "you need to talk to Paul about this. I mean before it's too late."

"Do you want me to call him?" Janie offered.

"Oh, would you?"

"Sure." Janie pulled out her phone and handed it to Abby.

"I think you'll have the most luck on his cell phone." Abby dialed his number then waited for him to answer. "No, this isn't Janie," she quickly explained when he recognized the caller ID. "I'm on her phone, and I asked her to speak to you. She might have some legal advice."

"Legal advice?"

"For our, uh, our financial situation."

"Oh, Abby, I've got it under control. You just need to —"

"Look, Paul, I am half of our marriage, and it's my financial boat that you're floating, or sinking, and I am appointing Janie to represent my legal rights. So you better listen to her. Okay?"

"Well, okay."

"Okay then." She handed the phone back to Janie. "Give him what for," she said quietly.

Janie glanced around. Others were nearby enjoying their drinks. "Mind if I go somewhere more private?" she asked Abby.

Abby waved her hand. "Not at all." In truth, Abby was relieved. It wasn't that she wanted to stick her head in the sand — well, maybe she did — but it was also very frustrating to hear about all this money business. It was one thing to lose everything she had, everything she'd worked for, but to keep rehashing it over and over . . . well, that just seemed like cruel and unusual punishment.

Janie didn't return for quite a while, and Abby started to feel guilty. First of all, how was she going to pay Janie for her time? Plus she was forcing Janie to work when she should be on vacation — and the last day of the cruise, too. Not only that, Janie was using her own phone, and Paul had said that international calls were very expensive. The ship was nearly to the California border, though, so maybe that wouldn't be an issue. Weren't phone calls tax deductible anyway?

Finally, and to Abby's relief, Janie came back. But it was impossible to read her expression. "Well?" Abby demanded. "Did he listen to you?"

Janie smiled. "I'm not sure that he did at first, but after a while, I think he realized I was making some sense. Obviously, I can't help him too much with the loss of his construction business or even your new house, but I feel fairly certain we can keep the inn out of it."

"Are you sure that Paul understood this? He seems to think the inn is considered communal property and that we'll lose it too. At least my half."

"I told Paul what he should do to keep the inn separate, and he promised to do it."

Abby was afraid to get her hopes up. "If your idea works, Janie, do you think that it would be okay if Paul and I lived at the inn?"

Janie shrugged. "I don't see why not. The key here is that you and I own the inn, Abby. Paul's name isn't on any of the papers. At the time I wasn't so sure that was a good idea. Now, I'm very, very thankful. You should be too."

Clasping her hands, Abby closed her eyes

and let out a deep breath. She wasn't sure if it was a silent prayer or a desperate plea or what, but she meant it. She really meant it. She looked at Janie. "Thank you, Janie."

"It's too soon to know for sure that my plan will help, but I feel confident."

"Well, it helped me."

Marley and Caroline came back. "Man, you should see that girl shoot." Marley pointed at Caroline. "If you're ever in a dangerous situation, you better hope she's packing heat."

Caroline laughed. "Yes, you'll see me toting a shotgun around Clifden any day."

"You could take up hunting," Abby said. "Paul and his buddies might let you join them." She grimaced. "At the rate we're going, Paul might have to take to hunting again just to bring us home something to eat. And fishing too." She smiled. "Maybe I'll have to start gardening again. You know I actually have missed it. But it's impossible to get much to grow at the beach. Too windy."

"You could grow things at the inn," Caroline suggested. "Chuck and I will be out of your hair before long. And I've been very careful about cleaning up his messes. It looks like things really grow well back there."

Abby nodded. "I used to have a lovely garden back when the girls were growing up. I'd love to have one again."

"So maybe it's true that every cloud has a silver lining," Caroline told her. "For all of us."

Abby told them about how Janie had just spoken to Paul. "So keep your fingers crossed," she said. "Or pray, whichever comes most naturally."

That night, when Abby was in bed, she did pray. Not that it came naturally, but she did believe in prayer, and she did believe that it would take someone as mighty as God to turn things around for her and Paul. She wasn't thinking of only material things either. She was thinking about their marriage, their values, their futures. She remembered when they'd been younger — how they'd gone to church regularly, taken the girls to Sunday school, taken their faith seriously. Then the girls got older and went their own ways, and time and busyness had distracted them. But lately — what with Paul's heart attack, their marriage troubles, and now this financial situation — well, Abby wondered if God hadn't just been trying to get their attention all along. Maybe it was about time they sat up and listened.

Maybe it was time to go back to church, too.

CHAPTER 28
JANIE

Janie's first conversation with Victor following her bout of ship flu had been hard to decipher. Initially, she thought he was trying to comfort her by padding things a bit. Reassuring her that he was doing everything possible to keep things under control, he told her not to worry and that he'd let her know if there was a problem. As if there were no problems! Janie might've still been slightly impaired from her illness, but she wasn't stupid.

She had a strong suspicion Victor was in over his head. She knew that both his sons had been more like her Matthew — conscientious, hardworking, basically easy. Nothing whatsoever like Lisa. Whether Victor would admit it or not, she knew it couldn't be going as smoothly as he'd made it seem. The next time she called him, pressing him for more details, he confirmed this.

"Lisa accused me of spying on her," he

confessed sheepishly.

"She said that?"

"Well, she caught me lurking around the neighborhood the second day she was staying alone in your house."

"Lurking?"

"Uh-huh."

"Seriously?"

"You see, I got this brilliant idea." He let out a sarcastic laugh. "I'd driven slowly by a couple of times, and I was starting to feel a little conspicuous, like my car was going to be recognized if I kept it up. To be honest, I felt like a stalker. So I thought I'd park my car a few blocks away and then I'd casually stroll by, you know, like I was out taking a walk. I figured this would give me a better chance to have a good look and see how it was going, make sure she was home, and that she wasn't partying or whatever."

"And?"

"All I can say is that girl of yours must have radar or ESP. It's like I'm still a block away, and out she pops and catches me."

"Really? She caught you spying on her?"

"Oh, yeah. And your daughter has no problem with confrontation either."

"I can only imagine." Janie cringed to think of Lisa out on the street, yelling at Victor.

"So I was honest. I told her I was concerned about her."

"How did she respond?"

"She told me to mind my own business." He chuckled. "I wanted to tell her that she is my business, but I figured that wasn't too smart."

"No, that wouldn't be wise."

"I'm doing this for you, Janie. And I promised you I'd keep an eye on her, so I figure she's my business too. Anyway, I'm not giving up."

"I appreciate that."

"Maybe someday she will too."

"So when you walked by, could you tell . . . was she doing anything, uh, questionable?" Janie wasn't even sure she wanted to know the answer.

"Nothing that I could tell, but naturally she didn't invite me in."

"Naturally." Janie felt a tinge of guilt for putting Victor through all this. Yet, at the same time, she was thinking, *Welcome to my world.* He might as well enjoy this sneak peek into the life of Janie Sorenson.

"So the next day, I thought I'd wear a disguise."

"A *disguise?* Are you kidding?"

"Just a hat and a raincoat. And it *was* raining."

"But she caught you again?"

"Uh-huh. Then yesterday, I waited until dusk, thinking she wouldn't be able to see me."

"And she did?"

"I think she must be sitting by the front window, just watching for me."

"At least it gives her something to do."

"Maybe she's enjoying our little cat-and-mouse game." He chuckled.

"I'm just relieved to know she's still there."

"That's what I keep telling myself, too."

"I'll be so glad to get home."

"Just enjoy the last of your trip, Janie. You needed this break. Losing those two days being sick was such a shame. You are feeling better, right?"

"Yes. Today was delightful. I sat in the sun and ate real food and everything." She had to smile at how sweet the simple pleasures had felt after being sick.

"Well, I hope you come home refreshed."

"So that I'll be ready to pick up where you left off? In your little cat-and-mouse game?" she teased.

"I hope Lisa won't pull that with you."

"Don't be too sure."

"So do you have any plans? I mean to find Lisa help?"

"My only plan is to start over." Janie cringed to think of the momentum they'd lost. She hoped "starting over" wouldn't require another intervention. "I've heard that it's important to find a rehab situation that fits the addict's personality. I might've rushed things too much in getting her into that other one. Besides, I know that Lisa has to own it — treatment is useless if the addict doesn't genuinely want it."

"That's true."

"There's another thing I'm coming to accept too."

"What's that?"

"Well, most of my life — my adult life anyway — I've felt fairly much in control of most things. In fact, I work really hard to maintain that kind of control. It's just the way I like it. I guess I'm basically a control freak."

"We all have our faults." She could hear the smile in his voice.

"And in my control-freak life, there have been a couple of situations that completely unraveled me." She looked out over the ocean, the endless miles of sparkling blue.

"When Phil died."

"Yes." Janie sighed. "And then with Lisa. I lost control with both of them."

"You do understand that you can't control

other people, Janie."

"Believe me, I know this."

"Sometimes you just have to love them and trust God with the rest."

"That doesn't come easily to me. But I think I might finally be learning to accept it. I thought about my control issues while I was sick. You know, being sick is a painful reminder of how little control we actually have over life. Not just over other people, but little things, too. The more I think about it, the more I realize that the only thing I can control — and not even always — is my own mind."

"But isn't there some freedom in that too?"

"Freedom?" Janie was trying to grasp this.

"Because when you give up the idea of controlling people and situations, you are forced to step back and relax. It frees you to just let things happen."

"Even to step back and watch someone you love having a train wreck?" Janie was thinking of Lisa again.

"If someone is bound and determined to have a train wreck, there's not much you can do anyway. In fact, you'd be wise to step out of the way."

"And watch them get killed?" A rush of fear ran through her.

"Hopefully not. But at least if they're injured, you won't be on the casualty list, and you'll be in better shape to help them pick up the pieces."

Janie thought about this. "You're right, Victor."

"Really? You think so?"

"I also think you're just what I need in my life."

"I like the sound of that."

"I really appreciate your help with Lisa." She chuckled. "Now you need to take your own advice."

"How so?"

"If you see a train wreck coming, just get out of the way. Okay?"

"You got it."

Janie told him a bit about the situation with Paul and Abby. "I know you won't say anything to anyone," she said. "But I think maybe Paul could use a friend. And I know he respects you."

"Maybe I'll give him a call. I'd actually been thinking of asking him about doing a small building project for me."

"A building project?"

"Yeah. I was thinking of adding a guest-house to my property."

"A guesthouse?"

"Yeah. I was looking at my lot, and I think

384

there's room. It gets a little crowded when both boys come to visit, and they're both talking about spending more time here next summer. With Marcus getting married, that adds another person to the mix. Having more room just seems like a good move. My place is a great little bachelor pad, but who knows? Maybe someday it'll need to be more. Doesn't hurt to look to the future. In fact, I might even ask Paul about doing a full-blown addition as well."

"Well, you certainly have the location for it, Victor." Janie suspected that Victor's thoughts "to the future" might have something to do with her. And while that wasn't an unpleasant idea, it was more than she could deal with. She felt she had her hands full with Lisa. "Paul can use some work. Abby said that other than Caroline's remodel, which is nearly completed, he doesn't have any work lined up."

"Then I'll consider myself lucky to get him while he's available."

Janie felt a rush of gratitude and affection toward Victor. "Paul should feel lucky too," she said quietly, "for your friendship. I know that I do, Victor."

"Try not to worry about Lisa," he assured her. "I promise that if any train derails, you'll be the first to know. Okay?"

"I appreciate that."

They finished up their call. As Janie slipped her phone into her bag, she realized once again how much she cared for Victor. Even so, she hoped he wasn't considering enlarging his house for her benefit. His little beach house was so perfect as is. Maybe she should call him back and tell him not to talk to Paul. She reached for her phone — then stopped herself.

"Let go," she quietly told herself. It was time to stop being a control freak. It was Victor's choice to change his house or not. Janie was simply a bystander. A very fond bystander, but a bystander nonetheless. She thought of Lisa again, about how Victor had told Janie to back away from the train wreck. How could one do that with a beloved child? What if Lisa's bad choices really did lead to her death? Just the idea of planning Lisa's funeral (something Janie hated to admit she'd done in her mind more than once) was so disturbing that Janie didn't even know if she could survive it, or if she'd want to.

Janie looked out over the ocean again, noticing a string of seabirds soaring over the waves. Were they pelicans? They looked so free and happy. They obviously had no troubles. Nor did they have control. Not over the ocean, the winds, or the weather. They didn't even have control over the fish they were probably looking to catch for lunch. All they could control were their own sweet movements as they flew in what seemed a lovely choreographed dance over the water.

Those birds were in the moment — perfectly and completely in the moment! With natural abandon, they freely enjoyed the sun on their backs, the wind under their wings, and the beautiful world surrounding them. Nothing more, nothing less.

Suddenly Janie wanted that too. She longed to spread her wings and fly with that kind of abandon and freedom. But when she looked down at her hands, they were tightly clutched around the ship's railing as if she thought the ship was going down and she had to hang on for dear life. But she knew that her firm grasp had more to do with her concerns for Lisa than anything else. It felt like her worries and fears were gnawing and clawing at her insides, which wasn't healthy. But wasn't that just part of being a mother? Weren't moms supposed to hurt when their children hurt? Weren't they supposed to wake up in the wee hours of the morning, having panic attacks over their children's welfare? Especially when said children were mindlessly speeding a hundred miles an hour down the dead-end path of self-destruction? And yet, really, what could she do to stop the train wreck?

As badly as Janie wanted to relinquish control (of which she was fully aware she had none), it was so difficult to release her own child. Was she supposed to just toss Lisa out to the nether-sphere and wait for calamity to catch up with her? How did a mother do that?

Even so, Janie knew it was pointless to attempt to continue holding on to Lisa. In fact, it was worse than pointless. It was caustic and toxic. She had to release her daughter, to let her go. *Just let go.*

Janie took a slow, deep breath of fresh air and imagined herself letting go of Lisa. Then she took her thoughts to a new level. She let go of Lisa and placed her in God's hands. Oh, Janie had prayed for her daughter before countless times, but her prayers, like so many other things, had always been about control. *Help Lisa to get well. Help Lisa to realize her choices are lethal. Help Lisa to conform to my expectations of what my daughter should be.* This time she just handed it all over to God. *Your will be done,* she prayed. Then she let go of the railing, and, lifting her hands and her head, she spread her arms. Feeling a sea breeze embracing her, she imagined herself sailing over the waves, free and with abandon, repeating her new mantra: *Let go . . . let go . . . let God.*

Chapter 29
Caroline

Caroline felt certain that she was the happiest of the Four Lindas to get back home to Clifden. Poor Abby had not only Paul but their financial challenges as well. Janie had Lisa, and Caroline was hoping that no news was good news. Even Marley, although she seemed glad about getting to see Jack again, still had the Sylvia factor to contend with. Apparently Jack had offered to give Sylvia notice on her job, but when Marley heard about that she felt guilty about leaving someone jobless.

But Caroline felt no particular pressures on her homecoming. All she really had to do was free Chuck from the kennel. She was glad to make it there just before closing time, and she had never felt so loved in her life as when Chuck bounded out and nearly toppled her over as he planted his paws on her chest and licked her face. Talk about true love! Then, with Chuck loaded in the back of her mini SUV, she drove directly to her house to check on the progress.

She unlocked the front door and turned on the lights, and with Chuck following right at her heels as if worried she might leave again, she walked around and just looked and looked — oohing and ahhing and almost afraid to believe her eyes. Everything was finished! Not only that, it had been completely cleaned. The wood floors, unveiled from their brown paper covering, gleamed with warmth and life.

Caroline had planned to do the final cleanup herself, but she didn't mind so much as she ran her hand over the smooth soapstone countertop. Even the new stainless appliances were in place, and the refrigerator was running — with water and ice! The backsplash tiles, a sunny selection of yellows and oranges, were up and grouted and sparkling. Even the laundry room was finished, with tile floors and the new bright-orange washer and dryer set in place. She couldn't believe it. It was like Christmas in January!

She went down the hall, seeing that the tile was laid in the bathroom and all the plumbing fixtures were in place and the water source was turned on.

"Let's check out the bedroom," she told

Chuck as she continued on to what had once been the worst part of the house. She flicked on the light. "Oh, my!" Caroline stared at the room. The walls were a creamy yellow, and the freshly installed carpet was clean and white — a highly cleanable product, Bonnie had said when Caroline questioned whether it was dog-friendly. The whole effect was warm and cheerful and bright. Caroline couldn't wait to start unloading her storage unit and moving in.

She went to the master bathroom and turned on the overhead light, which was a brushed-nickel chandelier that Caroline had questioned, thinking it was more appropriate in a dining room, but Bonnie had insisted belonged in here. And Bonnie was absolutely right! It gave the bath an elegant feel. The dimmer switch was like magic. This bathroom was beyond anything Caroline could've dreamed up. The walls were a very pale green with pale green glass tiles. Clean and fresh and spalike. Delightful.

The jet tub was in place as well as the rest of the plumbing, and it took all of Caroline's self-control not to fill the bath and climb in. "You must wait for the fluffy white towels and some scented bath oil," she told herself. "Do this thing right." She ran her hand over the glass blocks enclosing the shower and even turned on faucets and tried the toilet. Everything worked perfectly. And everything looked absolutely wonderful. She felt like singing and dancing — in fact, that's what she did.

"Oh, Chuck!" she exclaimed as she sat down on the edge of the tub. "I feel just like Dorothy when she clicked her heels together and ended up back in Kansas with Toto." She leaned over and hugged her dog. "Isn't it good to be home, boy?" He wagged his tail and licked her face as if he understood.

She walked around the house a few more times, taking in every little detail again and again. Finally, she realized she was tired. Although it was hard to leave, she went around and turned off the lights, promising herself to get up early tomorrow and start unloading the storage unit. Caroline couldn't remember the last time she'd felt so perfectly happy — or so hopeful.

Back at the B and B, Caroline's delight was replaced with restlessness. No one else was staying at the inn, so she decided to put her energy to work by packing up her things. Not that she had much to pack. The bedroom furnishings all belonged to the inn. But she packed her personal belongings, and then she cleaned her room as well as the bathroom she'd been using. Then she told herself to go to bed, get some rest. Tomorrow would be a busy day.

In the morning, Caroline called Mario and asked if he knew anyone who'd like to make a few bucks helping her to empty and move the contents of her storage unit. Mario sounded happy to have the work for himself and his brother. By ten thirty, almost everything in the unit had been moved to her house. She had them place most of the larger pieces of furniture in the house, but the smaller things and boxes were spread all throughout the garage in a mess of confusion and disarray.

It was weird seeing the garage filling up like this again, and it reminded her of how bad things had been when Caroline first moved back home. Thanks to her mom's pack-rat ways, it had been impossible to walk through the garage, as well as much of the house. It hadn't been only unsafe, but unhealthy, too. She didn't even like being reminded of it. She was determined never to allow that to happen again.

For that reason, she was ruthless in deciding what to keep and what to give away, and she'd already scheduled Mario to come back at the end of the week to pick up her castoffs. Even though it was hard to let go of a few things, she realized that she wanted to avoid any temptation to hoard. She did not want to fall in that trap. And she believed that her mother, at least where she was now, would be relieved to know that Caroline was avoiding it.

Caroline worked as quickly as she could, but it felt like slow going. Sometimes she got stuck and didn't even know what to do next. So many of her old things didn't seem to fit in this beautiful space. Consequently her cast-off pile was growing, and her house was looking not only sparse but uncoordinated as well. Her plan had been to get everything in place — or mostly — so that she could have her friends over for lunch tomorrow. She'd spoken to Marley and left messages for Janie and Abby. She wanted to hold everyone at bay today so she could give them the grand tour together. But she wanted the house to be polished, too.

"Hello in the house?" called a female voice.

Caroline poked her head out from where she was carrying a box into the laundry room. "Bonnie?"

"I thought I'd find you here," Bonnie said as she met Caroline in the kitchen, handing her a basket with a loaf of artisan bread and bottle of wine. "Welcome to your house!"

"Thank you." Caroline beamed at her.

"So tell me, what do you think?"

Caroline threw her arms around Bonnie. "I love it! Thank you for all your work!"

"I didn't mean to crash in on you. But I was so excited to see your reaction." Bonnie frowned slightly, as if noticing partially unloaded boxes cluttering the sleek kitchen counter. "So you're moving in?"

"Sure." Caroline set the basket on the one free space on the counter, then removed something from a packing box. Pulling the tissue paper away, she revealed a lime green Fiestaware dinner plate and set it in an upper cabinet. "Is that a problem?"

"No. Of course not. The inspections are all complete. It's your house." Bonnie glanced around. "I guess I was just hoping I could talk you into letting me help you with the furnishings, too. It would be fun to see the whole place pulled together."

Caroline laughed. "Well, I'm sure I could use the help. But the truth is I can't afford to buy much in the way of new furnishings just now. My insurance money is nearly tapped out, Bonnie." She held up a cereal bowl, a bright shade of tangerine, and shrugged. "And even if my stuff isn't terribly stylish, I kinda like it anyway."

Bonnie nodded. "And it is your house, to enjoy as you please."

Caroline could tell that Bonnie still wanted to have a hand in the décor. "I'll tell you what, Bonnie, if my financial situation improves and I decide to take this place up a notch or two, you will be the first one I call. Okay?"

"Okay." Bonnie smiled. "I'm really glad you like it."

"I don't like it. I *love* it!"

Bonnie glanced around the kitchen again. "You know, Caroline, if you want I could give you a few tips. I mean for free. Like how to arrange items or hang pictures or place furniture — if you like, that is."

"Are you kidding?" Caroline controlled herself from hugging Bonnie again. "Would you? Could you?"

"Absolutely." Bonnie grinned happily. "And I just happen to be free today. So how about you keep unpacking things and I'll figure out where they should go. Will that work for you — I mean, do you mind if I boss you around a little?"

Caroline laughed. "Boss away!"

For the rest of the day, Caroline unpacked, and Bonnie arranged and rearranged. Not only that, Bonnie went through Caroline's reject pile in the garage and rescued several things. She even made suggestions for recycling some old pieces. "If you paint this rocker a soft green and recover this cushion with a pastel plaid, it would be nice in your bedroom." She set some paint and fabric samples on the rocker. Then she suggested painting the coffee table white, and putting marble tops on Caroline's old bed stands, and freshening up a hutch with glass knobs and robin's-egg blue paint.

Later in the day, Bonnie approached Caroline with some hesitation. "You know, Caroline, if you could afford a couple hundred dollars, I could bring in some accessories that would really make this place sparkle."

"Two hundred dollars?" Caroline considered her bank account. Her plan was to find employment, but that might take a while. In the meantime, she wanted enough to get by for the next couple of months or until her condo sold. She looked around the living room. "Okay," she said. "Let's go for it. And hopefully I'll get a job soon."

With that green light, Bonnie took off, coming back later with bags and boxes. While Caroline filled her linen closet, Bonnie put the finishing touches on the place. When Caroline saw it, she knew that the money spent had been well worth it. "This looks amazing," she told Bonnie as she admired artful touches of candles and vases and things. "I don't care if I have to live on beans and rice for a week just to enjoy this."

"And if you repurpose those other pieces I showed you," Bonnie told her, "your house really will look like a designer's original showplace."

"And without costing the big bucks," Caroline said happily.

Bonnie held up a finger. "Just don't tell everyone how frugally we did all this. I still need to make a living, you know."

Caroline laughed, and then she offered to take Bonnie to dinner as a thank-you.

"I'll take a rain check if you don't mind." Bonnie gave her a mysterious smile.

"Sure. That's fine." Caroline studied her. "Do you have some big plans?"

"I have a date with a guy I met last week." Bonnie's eyes twinkled.

"Anyone I know?"

Bonnie told her a name, but Caroline didn't recognize it. Mostly she was relieved that it wasn't Paul — and she couldn't wait to tell Abby this good news. "Thanks again!" She gave Bonnie a last hug. "I couldn't have done this without you."

Caroline didn't want to leave her house, not even to get some much-needed groceries, so she decided to order pizza to be delivered. She fed Chuck and continued puttering and admiring, finally sweeping and cleaning up the mess from all the unpacking that had gone on. Then, just before the pizza was due to arrive, she plugged in her stereo and put in several of her favorite CDs.

Caroline laid out a gold place mat, linen napkin, and one place setting from her best dishes, a classic white pattern with gold trim, as well as a crystal goblet. Next she decided to really celebrate by uncorking the wine that Bonnie had brought. Feeling a bit indulgent but happy, she set the bottle on the dining room table right next to the candles that Bonnie had artistically arranged. Then she lit the candles. Okay, it was a little over the top for pizza — and dinner for one. But it was so fun, not to mention picture-perfect. Like the old L'Oréal commercial used to say, she was worth it!

With Chuck sleeping at her feet under the dining table, and with candles glowing and music playing, Caroline dined on her very first meal in her newly renovated home. She felt completely and incredibly happy.

Later, as she washed her dishes, she decided it wasn't so bad being alone. Not really. In fact, she knew she would rather be alone and happy than stressed out in a relationship that wasn't just right. At the moment, she felt fairly certain that a relationship with Mitch wouldn't be even close to right. Maybe it was just a case of bad timing, or maybe it was simply a bad match. But Caroline knew that when in doubt, it was best not to take the leap. So she wouldn't.

In the bathroom, as Caroline lit the white candles that Bonnie had arranged with some seashells alongside the jet tub, she felt hopeful. And as she slipped into the steamy water, she experienced a surprising sense of victory. Leaning back into the citrus-scented bubbles, the last dregs squeezed out of an old bottle of shower gel, Caroline realized she'd reached a new milestone. She knew that not only could she be perfectly content without a man in her life, she could take a pass on a handsome millionaire as well. Some might think it silly or shallow for a person to get such delight from something like this, Caroline thought, but she felt thrilled. Victorious. And that felt seriously good.

The next morning, Caroline felt even happier. After a great night's sleep — her first night in her new house, back in her old bed — she felt on top of the world. And when she went to the grocery store, getting what she needed to stock her new cabinets and fix a good lunch for her friends, she felt like a brand-new woman embarking on a brand-new life. She had a sense of excitement or adventure, like she was finally doing something or going somewhere, although she wasn't even sure where exactly. She no longer felt stuck.

As she stood in line at the check stand, she wondered how long she'd lived in a holding pattern. She assumed it had started with her move to Clifden, with feeling slightly trapped as she had cared for her mother. But as she wheeled the grocery cart through the parking lot and unloaded the bags into the car, she realized this had been going on long before that. On the way home, Caroline realized she'd been in a holding pattern for most of her adult life, as if she'd been waiting and waiting and waiting. Waiting for someone or something to happen — someone or something to rescue her. Rescue her from what? Her life? Her expectations? Herself?

But as she drove into the driveway of her new house, which still looked a lot like the old house from the outside (Mitch had been right about that) she realized that she no longer needed rescuing. With that knowledge came an astounding sense of peace.

It took three trips to carry her bags into the house. She lined them on the sleek kitchen counter and finally went back for the last one. But on her way in this time, she paused at the front door and looked up to the sky.

"Thank you, God," she whispered, "for being the only rescuer I needed." She sighed and almost started to go inside, but stopped. "And thank you, Mom, for knowing how badly I needed this place. Thank you — and I dedicate it to you."

Then she went inside, turned on some music, and started fixing lunch for her friends. Like last night, she set the dining room table beautifully, this time with four places.

"Oh Caroline," Janie gushed as she arrived a little before noon. "This place is so amazing — it's so you!" She handed Caroline an elegant bag of French bath products. "I thought you might enjoy these in your new bathroom."

"Thank you! I had just enough shower gel for one bath last night. This will be perfect."

Abby came next, and she had a basketful of kitchen goodies. "In case you feel like doing some baking," she told her. She glanced around. "Wow, everything looks fantastic, Caroline. So stylish. Did you do this all yourself?"

So Caroline confessed to Bonnie's assistance. "But she refused to let me take her to dinner last night," Caroline said quickly, "because she had a date! And she looked pretty pumped about it too."

Abby brightened considerably. "Oh, well, isn't that nice?"

Next came Marley, and to Caroline's delight, she'd brought a painting with her. "I thought this might look good in your new house."

"Oh Marley!" Caroline held up the bright-colored painting. "It's absolutely gorgeous. How about this bare wall in the dining room?"

"Perfect," Janie proclaimed.

"Let's hang it now," Marley said with enthusiasm.

Before long, the colorful painting was hung and all four friends were seated at the dining table, each with a glass lifted to toast Caroline's new digs. And then Caroline bowed her head and said grace. "Dear Father God, thank you for all my wonderful blessings. Thank you for my dear friends — *my sisters.* Thank you for this amazing home, thank you for being more than enough, and thank you for this meal." Then she said amen and smiled at her friends.

"I'm so happy," she said as they began to pass the food around. "I don't know when I've ever been so thoroughly happy." She told them of her latest revelation about feeling victorious and about not needing to be rescued. "I know not everyone can relate," she said apologetically. "But the truth is I've spent most of my life waiting, just wishing and dreaming that my prince would come." She laughed. "I was like one of those pathetic princesses waiting for a man to walk up, you know, so her life could begin. Sometimes I'd try to believe I'd moved beyond it, but when push came to shove, I was still hoping my white knight would rescue me. And it just feels so good to not to need or want that anymore."

"Does that mean that you and Mitch really are history?" Janie asked.

Caroline shrugged. "Maybe so. Although I guess it's presumptuous to act like I can predict the future. Let's just say that if Mitch and I are history, I'm okay. Because I feel completely content just as I am. Besides that, I'm determined not to compromise my own values for someone else's. If Mitch is the right man for me, I expect him to act like it. If he's not, I can be perfectly happy on my own."

Her friends let out a little cheer and

another toast.

After a few minutes of congenial visiting, there was a lull in conversation, and Marley tinkled her fork against her glass. "And now I have a different sort of announcement to make. That is, if no one minds." She glanced nervously at Caroline. "I don't want to rain on your parade or steal your thunder or any other kind of bad-weather metaphor that may or may not apply."

Caroline laughed. "There's no way you can do that, Marley. Go for it. What's your announcement? And I'd like to be the first one to wager you've sold some more paintings." She pointed to the one on her wall. "And thank you again for that one. I refuse to part with it, ever!"

Marley giggled in a way that sounded totally unlike her. "No, no more painting sales, not yet anyway. But, trust me, girls, this is even more exciting." She paused, looking around the table. "Besides Ashton, who already knows my news, I wanted to tell my three best friends." She held her left hand in front of them, fluttering her fingers as if to show off an interesting-looking ring — on her wedding finger.

"What?" Janie demanded.

"Jack proposed!" Marley was beaming.

Congratulations were shared all around.

"Jack had planned to ask me at Christmas," Marley explained. "But all the craziness with Hunter was a distraction. And then there was Sylvia, and, of course, like a big chicken, I ran off to avoid everything. Jack thought maybe I wasn't as in love with him as he'd hoped. Anyway, he decided to hold his horses. Then we had some good talks, and he simply waited for the right moment. So last night he took me to dinner, and just before dessert, he got down on his one good knee —"

"What about his bad leg?" Caroline asked with concern.

Marley laughed. "He told me he'd been practicing." She let them have a closer look at the ring. "Jack had it made for me. See the wavy lines of the platinum setting? They represent the sea, and the pale blue stone is aquamarine, which is my birthstone, and the blue zircon is Jack's birthstone, and the diamond, well, that's for both of us."

"That's exquisite," Caroline told her. "So artistic and perfect for you."

"When's the date?" Janie asked.

"I know it'll sound awfully soon," Marley told them. "But Jack and I, well, we're not getting any younger. To be honest, the date was Hunter's idea. She's over the moon with excitement. It's something she's been hinting at for ages. Naturally, she'll be in the wedding and —"

"When is the date?" Abby demanded. Then she looked embarrassed. "It's just that I might want to help with it, Marley, I mean if you don't mind. I just love weddings!"

"Actually, I was going to ask about having the wedding at your B and B," Marley told her. "Do you think —"

"Tell us — when is the big day?" Janie commanded.

"Valentine's Day!" Marley giggled again. "Is that corny or what?"

"That's absolutely perfect," Caroline said with enthusiasm. "Your anniversary will always be special and memorable."

"I'm going to have all my bridesmaids wear red." Marley grinned at the three of them. "You all look good in red, don't you?"

"Meaning?" Janie tipped her head to an angle.

"Meaning, I want you all in my wedding. I figure if I'm going for corny, why not just do it up right and force my best friends to join me? My first wedding was a bit of a disaster. For that matter, so was my marriage." She sighed. "I'd like to do things differently this time."

"I'd be proud to wear red for you," Caroline proclaimed.

"That's easy for you to say." Abby made a face. "You look good in everything."

"Maybe we could wear various shades of red," Janie suggested. "With my auburn hair, there are only a few reds that don't look frightening on me."

"That's a great idea," Marley told her. "And don't worry, I won't make you wear ruffles or anything too bizarre. Although I like the idea of something a bit offbeat or slightly Bohemian."

Caroline lifted her glass. "Here's to Marley and Jack," she declared.

They all toasted the newly engaged couple, and soon they were vying for who was going to do what. Janie said that she and Victor would host an engagement party, Caroline offered do a shower, and Abby wanted to cater the wedding. "I figure if the B and B doesn't take off right away, I can always do some catering on the side. Maybe I could host events there too." She grinned at Marley. "Like weddings!"

"Are you sure you'll still have the inn by mid-February?" Marley looked concerned. "I mean, I'll understand if you don't."

Abby glanced at Janie.

"It's looking more and more like a possibility," Janie informed them. "I had some phone conversations with the accountant and lawyer yesterday. We're going to try really hard to keep the old house."

"And here's an amazing little news flash," Abby announced. "Paul actually hopes we can keep the old house too. I just about fell over when he said that. Last night he told me he'd missed the old place nearly as much as I had, but he'd been too proud to admit it, since the new house had been his idea from the get-go. He even confessed that he sometimes feels isolated living out there on the beach all by our little lonesome. He said it was even worse when I was gone on the cruise for a week." She chuckled. "I think he might've actually missed me."

Caroline lifted her glass again. "Well, here's to you and Paul surviving your latest challenges." After they'd all toasted to this, Caroline turned to Janie. "Now, you don't have to go into all the details, but I've really been praying for Lisa, so just give me a little update, okay? Like, is she still home?"

Janie set her glass down. "Thanks to Victor, she *is* still here in Clifden."

"Thanks to Victor?"

"Believe it or not, Victor had been keeping tabs on Lisa while I was gone — from a safe distance, since you know how she feels about him. Then, on the morning we were coming home, Victor got worried after he went by and wasn't accosted by Lisa out on the sidewalk." She explained how Lisa had this uncanny sense of knowing every time he was in the vicinity. "Anyway, Victor decided to check on her. He went up to the house and knocked on the door, and when no one answered, he thought she'd probably taken off. So he used the key I'd given him and let himself inside." Janie sighed and shook her head. "Unfortunately, he was a bit shocked with what he found."

"What?" Caroline gasped. "Hurry, tell us."

"Lisa was out cold. And she'd left a . . . a note."

"But don't worry, she's okay now," Abby quickly assured them as if she'd been in the loop.

"Was it a suicide attempt?" Marley asked quietly.

Janie just nodded, but her eyes were filled with tears.

"Why didn't you call me?" Caroline demanded. She was trying not to feel hurt for being left out.

"I — I told Abby," Janie admitted.

"But only because I called her," Abby clarified. "We were expecting her to come out to the house to discuss business. Otherwise, I would've been in the dark too."

"I honestly thought Abby would fill you

girls in," Janie said contritely. "I'm so sorry. But there was so much to deal with that first day — I was overwhelmed with details. Victor was so involved already, I had to let him continue helping. He'd gotten Lisa to the hospital, and stood by while they pumped her stomach, and waited until she came to. We were already on our flight by then. He didn't call until after we landed. Anyway, by the time I got there, she was stabilized, and most of the next day I just tried to be available to her and the doctors and everything."

"It's so great that Victor was there to help," Caroline told her.

Janie nodded. "I have to give it to him . . . he was a rock. And when I thought about calling in my girlfriends for backup support yesterday, well, I knew it would make him feel replaced or unnecessary. Besides, I knew you girls were busy getting back to your own lives. And Victor seemed so happy to be helping out. I couldn't take that away from him, you know?"

They all nodded, agreeing that was wise.

"The really amazing thing is how Lisa has changed her attitude toward Victor. But even more amazing is that she's willing to try rehab again." Janie let out a weary sigh. "Actually, the psychiatrist working with her refused to release her from the hospital unless she agreed to rehab."

"Well, that's a relief," Marley told her.

"Yes," Janie agreed. "It seems like a good thing came out of a bad thing. I spent hours trying to locate a good rehab facility. I wanted a place that Lisa could relate to and respond to."

"And in the midst of all that, she was still helping Paul and me," Abby reminded them. "So don't feel bad for being out of the loop. Our little Janie has had her hands full."

"Anyway, the good news is I decided on a place up in Washington, near Seattle. And Lisa really likes the sound of it. They have an outdoor program with hiking and rock climbing and everything. They said they can take her two weeks from now."

"Two weeks?" Caroline frowned. "How are you going to deal with everything for two long weeks?"

"One day at a time," Janie told her. "Because, really, it's up to Lisa. She has to choose it and want it and participate in her own recovery." She explained about her recent decision to give up trying to control everything. "I think having Lisa around will be part of my training."

"Well, don't forget you have friends,"

Caroline reminded her. "We're here to help too." As Caroline said this, she realized how often her friends had helped her when she felt helpless. It would be good to be on the other end of things for a change.

CHAPTER 30
MARLEY

If anyone had told Marley, just one year ago, that she would be where she was today, she would've told them they were nuts. Marley remembered exactly how she'd felt on the previous Valentine's Day. Nearly suicidal. Okay, maybe that was an exaggeration. But she'd felt depressed and lonely and completely hopeless regarding her future. Giving up hadn't sounded half bad.

But here she was, just one year later, up in the master suite of Abby's inn, wearing a vintage lace wedding dress in a sophisticated shade of ecru along with her favorite red cowgirl boots. The retro boots has started out as a joke. Marley happened to have been wearing them when she modeled her delightful gown for the Lindas. She and Caroline had found the dress on a quick shopping trip to Portland. The boots and the gown made for an interesting ensemble, which her friends insisted looked quite stylish. "And you wanted Bohemian," Caroline had reminded her. Then Marley remembered how much Jack loved her red cowgirl boots and decided, *Why not?* Even now, she thought they looked perfect — in a quirky Clifden sort of way.

Caroline, already wearing a coral-red silk dress, had arrived early to help Marley with her hair today. Not that there was much to do with hair as short as Marley's, but as usual, Caroline was working her magic. Right now, she was using some kind of goo to make Marley's bangs do things Marley thought her hair was incapable of doing.

"You are a magician," Marley told her as she watched Caroline working.

Caroline laughed. "It's the hair product that's magic, Marley."

"Well, I do appreciate your expertise."

"I used to consider going to some sort of beauty school." Caroline was starting to work on Marley's makeup. "I thought I could learn to do hair or maybe cosmetology," she continued absently. "Even now, I sometimes wonder if I could do something like that or if I'm too old."

"Never too old," Marley declared. Of course, she selfishly hoped that Caroline wasn't really considering such a thing. She had been such a lifesaver at the art gallery, stepping in to work after Sylvia quit. Caroline turned out to be such a natural with the customers, warm and friendly, making everyone feel comfortable whether they knew a thing about art or not. Sylvia had given Jack no notice and simply didn't show up for work one day. Later, she claimed to have found another job, although her timing was right on the heels of the announcement of Jack and Marley's engagement.

"I feel guilty," Marley had confessed to Jack.

"Don't," Jack told her. Then he told her a bit more. It seemed obvious that Sylvia really had set her sights on him. He'd felt blindsided by this, thinking her helpfulness had been just that — helpfulness. But after that phone conversation with Marley, when she'd confessed her concerns, he had managed to put two and two together. Unfortunately, or perhaps not, Leah seemed to have been part of the mother-daughter package deal. Consequently, Marley had returned to grandmother mode (and more) and helped with caring for Hunter.

"Jasmine isn't coming to the wedding," Jack had informed Marley last week.

"You heard from her?" Marley was surprised.

"I emailed her shortly after we got engaged," he told her. "For some reason I thought she might be interested." He let out a sad laugh. "Right now the only thing that interests Jasmine is Jasmine."

"Maybe it's for the best," Marley assured him. "For Hunter. And us."

He had smiled then, kissing her. "See, this is why you are so perfect."

"Okay," Caroline announced, bringing Marley back to the moment. "How about that?"

"Oh Caroline." Marley smiled at her image in the mirror. "I feel pretty."

"You are pretty!"

"That's for sure," Janie said as she came in carrying a garment bag. She leaned over and gently kissed Marley's cheek. "A beautiful bride!"

Marley laughed. "Who'd've thunk? At my age?"

"And your usher is downstairs," Janie informed her, "looking quite handsome in his retro tux."

"Ashton is here?" Marley stood.

"Do you want him to come up?"

Marley looked at Janie, who had partially disrobed as she prepared to put on her dress. "No, I can wait. I'm just happy he's here."

"He looks well, Marley." Janie smiled. "He

and Jack are visiting, and I can tell Ashton is happy for you."

Marley sighed, then looked around. "So where are Abby and Hunter?"

"Abby is taking care of some last-minute things in the kitchen. And Hunter is already all dressed and adorable. She's working on a surprise for you. She told me not to tell you anything more."

Marley just nodded.

Janie slipped her dress, a rusty shade of red, over her head. "The reason I'm running late is because Lisa called right before I left."

"How is she?" Caroline asked eagerly.

"Oh, she sounds so good," Janie told them. "I know you can't tell much from a phone call. But her voice, the tone of it, it's just so alive. It reminds me of when she was a girl. She used to have so much energy and enthusiasm." She turned around to have Caroline help with the zipper. "Am I a fool to believe that she could become that girl again?"

"No, of course not," Marley told her. "We have to believe in our children no matter what, Janie. That's just part of being a mom, right?"

Janie nodded. "Yes, I think so."

Abby burst into the room. "Sorry to be

late, Marley. I'll hurry and dress."

Marley sat on the bed, just watching as Caroline and Janie helped Abby to get ready. Abby's dress was a faded rose red. She was surprised to see that those three shades of red together, in three different dress styles, looked so perfect together. Now she wouldn't say this to them, because she knew they'd just laugh, but she really did think they could wear those dresses again.

Abby was talking about the food she'd been working on in the kitchen — the seafood feast that Jack had requested. "I've got clam chowder and crab cakes and shrimp skewers and baked salmon. The works." She also told them about how things were starting to pick up for the B and B. "Those great reviews I got from my mystery guests might've helped." She chuckled.

"Hey, I wrote nothing but the truth," Caroline told her.

"Me, too," Marley chimed in.

"I frequent the inn quite a bit too," Janie admitted.

"Well, anyway, summer is getting fairly booked up." Abby sighed. "I told Paul that he and I might need to consider living somewhere else in order to rent out this room."

"Where would you live?" Caroline asked.

"Paul thinks he might be able to turn the garage into a guesthouse that we could use as our private space."

"That's a great idea." Marley had to marvel at how much Paul seemed to have evolved in the past couple of weeks. Not only was he helping Abby with the inn, he seemed to be enjoying socializing with her friends more. He seemed happier. More relaxed.

Marley continued watching her friends as they did their final primping, joking and chatting and just being themselves. She knew they were all in their fifties — which in all reality was beyond middle age — and yet it felt as if they were still girls or young women. The lilting sounds of their voices, their enthusiasm, their love and loyalty to one another — it all seemed timeless and wonderful.

Finally they were done, and Marley knew that the wedding would be starting any minute. "I have something for each of you." Marley went over to her purse, which was on the bed, and removed four small boxes. She'd gone to the same jeweler that Jack had commissioned to make her ring and asked him to make silver necklaces for the Four Lindas. She'd drawn the pendant design — a curly L set in a heart with their four birthstones set into it. "Something to remind us that we are, and will always be, the Four Lindas," she explained as they opened the boxes. One by one, they expressed their delight and exchanged hugs. Then Caroline popped open a bottle of chilled champagne and handed out glasses.

"Here's to you, Marley," she said. "May your marriage be as blessed and beautiful as you are!"

The others made similar toasts. And finally Marley lifted her glass. "And here's to us," she told them. "Here's to friends!"

"To the bright future of our friendship," Janie said.

"To the Four Lindas!" Caroline shouted.

"Friends forever," Abby declared.

Marley grinned at them. As much as she was looking forward to this big event — her wedding and her honeymoon and her marriage — she was also looking forward to the continued friendship of these women . . . her dear friends!

AFTERWORDS

. . . a little more . . .

When a delightful concert comes to an end, the orchestra might offer an encore. When a fine meal comes to an end, it's always nice to savor a bit of dessert. When a great story comes to an end, we think you may want to linger. And so, we offer . . .

AfterWords — just a little something more after you have finished a David C Cook novel. We invite you to stay awhile in the story. Thanks for reading!

Turn the page for . . .

• **Discussion Questions**

DISCUSSION QUESTIONS

1. Marley feels insecure in Jack's love because of the hurtful experiences in her first marriage. Is it possible for a person to fully shed the worries attached to painful life events? Why or why not?

2. Is Marley's avoidance of Jack between Christmas and the New Year mostly understandable or mostly selfish? Explain.

3. Have you ever spent a holiday alone? What was the experience like for you? Did any good come out of it?

4. Janie questions the best way to handle Lisa's drug-addiction issues. What does she do well or poorly? What do you wish she had done differently? How might the outcome have been different without the involvement of Janie's friends?

5. Why is it so difficult for Janie to surrender Lisa to God? What does "surrender" mean to you when you think about children, spouses, careers, crises, and so on?

6. How does Caroline arrive at a place of such contentment even though she has no career and her romance with Mitch seems to be a thing of the past? How is her house a symbol of the transformation taking place in her own life? What is required for a person to be truly content?

7. What does Abby believe about Paul, her marriage, and herself that informs her behavior? Which of Abby's beliefs might be rooted in untrue perceptions? Is it possible for a married person to correct false perceptions of his or her spouse? How?

8. If you were Paul and Abby's marriage counselor, what would you have advised them to do to work on their relationship? When can a separation be healthy for a couple? In what circumstances might it be damaging or unwise?

9. What did each of the Lindas gain during their separation from Clifden and from loved ones on the cruise? How does "get-

ting away" inform one's perspectives of a situation? How does it foster an ability to "let go"?

10. What qualities and experiences do the Four Lindas share that allow their friendship to endure? What is most important for friends to have in common (such as shared experiences, shared values)? What is most inspiring or hopeful to you about the way these women interact with each other?

ABOUT THE AUTHOR

Melody Carlson is the best-selling and award-winning author of more than 150 books for adults, children, and teens including the previous Four Lindas titles: *As Young as We Feel, Hometown Ties,* and *All for One.* She and her husband, Chris, live in the Pacific Northwest near their two grown sons and granddaughter.